WHIPPING TRIANGLE

'Bend over your desk,' Rhonda repeated menacingly. 'If I don't see your bottom in the air before I can count to three, I'll call your staff in here to see you. One . . . two . . .'

Reluctantly Muriel bent over her desk.

'Further,' Rhonda commanded. 'Grasp the front of the desk with your hands and hold on tight. Don't let go until I tell you. All right. Now spread your legs apart.' Rhonda lifted her own skirt to reveal her tights and pants – and to emphasise Muriel's nakedness. Slowly she removed her pants while her victim flushed with fear and embarrassment. Rhonda knew that Muriel dared not disobey or cry out for help.

'Open your mouth,' she told her victim.

When she did, Rhonda stuffed her pants deeply into Muriel's mouth, gagging her. Then she picked up a metal ruler from the desktop.

'I imagine you can guess what this is for.'

WHIPPING TRIANGLE

G C Scott

This book is a work of fiction.
In real life, make sure you practise safe, sane and
consensual sex.

First published in 2007 by
Nexus
Thames Wharf Studios
Rainville Rd
London W6 9HA

www.nexus-books.co.uk

A catalogue record for this book is available from the British
Library.

Typeset by TW Typesetting, Plymouth, Devon

ISBN 9780352340863

Printed and bound in Great Britain by Clays Ltd, Elcograf S.p.A.

Contents

1

Dinner

The chime of the doorbell broke Paul's concentration. He was listening to Beethoven's Sixth, a particular favourite, and he was annoyed at the interruption. Like most people, he was nevertheless conditioned to answer the summons of the bell. Through the spy-hole of the front door he saw a uniformed delivery-man. He opened the door. The messenger presented him with a small packet that was heavy for its size. He set it on the hall table by the telephone in order to have a free hand to sign the receipt. Only after he had closed the door did he notice that the package was from Rhonda Stuart, with whom he had a dinner date that evening.

The arrival of the package reminded him that he needed to order some flowers. She liked that acknowledgement of her beauty. Paul preferred dark-haired women, and Rhonda was a striking brunette who wore her hair long. She always dressed so as to show off her fine figure and long legs, the latter being one of his fixations – of which she was well aware. Rhonda always wore panty-hose or stockings because she knew it pleased him (and most of her other clients), and Paul appreciated her making the effort. He postponed opening her package to call the florist, arranging to have the flowers delivered to her apartment in the late afternoon.

That done, he returned to the study to resume listening, deliberately delaying opening the package to heighten the pleasure of anticipation. Rhonda always had some surprise for him when they were going out for the evening. Usually it had some bearing on their subsequent activities, a hint of things to come. The first time it had been a riding crop. Paul had wondered if she intended to use it on him, or whether he was to use it on her. On that occasion it had been the former, and Paul had come away with some sore places and a new appreciation of the finer nuances of the sexual act. On another occasion the roles had been reversed. That time, Paul had been an awed witness to the spectacle of a mature woman in full arousal, screaming in pain and pleasure as he lashed her. He had emerged from that encounter with a new appreciation of the uses of pain, and of his capacity to inflict it. Watching Rhonda in a frenzy of pleasure, he had found it hard to stop lashing her. That had shaken him, but he had overcome the experience as she taught him the uses of pain. She was an altogether remarkable woman.

The shepherds were performing their hymn of thanksgiving, but he could not concentrate. Images of Rhonda Stuart and the things they had done together were stronger than those conjured up by the Pastoral Symphony. He had learned gradually that Rhonda enjoyed inflicting pain more than receiving it, and that her real forte was domination. He had learned, too, that being dominated occasionally, giving up all responsibility to another, was a refreshing novelty. As a rule he always came away from one of those evenings with a feeling of relaxation – despite the sore bits.

2

For a time Paul had thought of asking her to move in with him – or vice versa, which was much the more likely outcome, but he had postponed asking. There was always the possibility she would refuse, and the embarrassment would drive them apart. Then there was the matter of her other men – and women. Gradually he had come to see that Rhonda preferred to choose her companions from a varied group, and was not really a one-man woman. Nor was he, as he came to realise, a one-woman man. He congratulated himself on not being jealous of her other companions.

The closing bars of the shepherds' hymn came and went unheeded save as a background to his reminiscences. Paul returned to the hall to fetch the package. Back in the study, he unwrapped it to discover a stiff cardboard box. Inside the box there was an oddly shaped contrivance of welded stainless steel resembling an oversized locket. There were three small brass padlocks as well. They were open, with a strip of packing tape across the hole where the end of the staple would go. And there were no keys. Puzzled, Paul removed the thing from its box, to find a folded sheet of paper beneath it. 'Readde mee' was written on it in Rhonda's hand.

The paper turned out to be a set of directions for the use of what she quaintly referred to as a 'Cockke Cayge'. 'Thys Devyse,' she had written, 'is desynnede to curbb the base Desyres of the rampant and thoughtlesfe Mayle.' The instructions continued in the same mock-Elizabethan language to tell him what was expected of him. In short, he was to wear the 'Cockke Cayge' when he came to pick her up. The locks would ensure that he could not escape from it, for she had the only keys. From all this, Paul concluded that she was going to assume the dominant role during the coming encounter. He felt

3

his 'Cockke' stir with excitement as he read her instructions.

The 'Cayge' was designed to fit over his balls and to enclose his cock in an intricate mesh of bars. It hinged at the top so that it could slip over the wearer's penis and scrotum. When closed, the small padlocks held the device in place. There was a circular bar designed to encircle the base of the scrotum. One of the locks held it closed behind the balls at that point. The other lock dangled beneath the balls and held the cage closed from the bottom. Yet another bar went between the balls, dividing them vertically all the way around from front to back. The long piece enclosed the cock and was held closed beneath it with the third lock. At the end of the penis there was a ring obviously intended for the attachment of a lead. Paul had no doubt that Rhonda had the lead to hand.

The prospect of having his cock and balls locked up while Rhonda led him about by the chain was an exciting one. They had never done this before. Paul was impressed by Rhonda's ingenuity and enterprise in locating the cage. He could imagine her going into the town's adult shop without embarrassment and asking for what she desired. More likely, though, she had asked Ted Collins, resident blacksmith and purveyor of custom bondage equipment, to make it to her design. Her straightforward approach to what would embarrass most people – even those who were seriously into B & D – was unusual. Especially in a woman. It was one of the many things he liked about her.

Paul set the device on his desk and tried to think of something other than the coming evening's activities. He was only partially successful. His eyes – and his imagination – kept straying back to the intricate

4

cage that lay open before him. He chose what he would wear (a pair of casual slacks and a dark-blue blazer with light-blue shirt and tie). There were still too many hours between then and the time to leave. And his cock kept erecting and subsiding as he imagined what they would do later that evening and night. Finally, when he could bear the restless urge no longer, Paul decided to try the cage on for size.

In the study he took off his trousers and under-pants and picked up the device. It was awkward at first, but finally he managed to close it around his sexual organs. It was snug, not too tight, but his cock would certainly be out of action when locked inside. He toyed with the idea of locking it, but remembered that he would not be able to remove it if he did. Later, he decided, removing the cage then laying it once more on his desk.

The rest of the afternoon dragged. He could not concentrate on anything. It was a relief when the time came to dress for the date. This time it was easier to fit the cage into place, though there was a small moment of panic after he had closed the padlocks. There was no escape. His cock swelled, pressing against the bars of its cage. It was uncomfortable, exactly the kind of reminder Rhonda liked giving her consorts. She wanted them to know who was in charge. Under his trousers, when he dressed himself, he could see a slight bulge in the area of his cock. It would be almost unnoticeable unless one knew what to look for. Rhonda would certainly notice.

Paul was conscious of the device whenever he moved around the apartment. When he sat he had to reach down with one hand and pull his cock and balls from between his legs. Otherwise the steel cage got in the way and felt uncomfortable. It would probably need the same attention when he went to pick up

5

Rhonda. In any case, it would be impossible to forget that his cock was locked up.

Rhonda thanked him for the flowers with a smile. She looked her usual stunning self in a tight red velvet dress that reached to her ankles. It was slit boldly to mid-thigh on each side, allowing her legs to show through in tantalising flashes of sheer black nylon. Her long dark hair was brushed carefully and fell around her shoulders. She wore a cameo brooch as a choker on a black velvet ribbon around her throat. Ravishing, Paul thought, as he kissed her. Her perfume filled his nostrils like an aphrodisiac. Rhonda stepped back from his embrace so that she could inspect him. As she did so, she did a quick Crocodile Dundee test to ensure he was wearing the cock-cage as she had instructed. She smiled archly when she felt the metal beneath his trousers.

She said nothing about keys. Nor did Paul ask. Those were the rules they observed. She would unlock him when she was ready. It was solely her decision.

'Ready to eat?' she asked him.

Paul had expected her to offer a drink before they went out. She usually did. This time there was an unwonted air of hurry, as if she were anxious to leave the apartment. Paul would have liked a hint of her plans for later. In particular he would have liked to know how long she intended to keep him locked up, but Rhonda usually preferred to keep her consorts in suspense. He nodded. She was in charge. Rhonda picked up her purse and they left.

In the car Rhonda smiled at him and raised her skirt so that he had a good view of her legs. She was wearing stockings and garter belt that evening. Paul felt his cock becoming erect within its steel cage. It was not a comfortable sensation. Rhonda smiled at his obvious discomfiture. She enjoyed the role of the teasing dominatrix. On one previous occasion she had bound him helplessly and then paraded before him in her underwear. When his cock got erect, she had lashed him – and it – for his temerity. His major hope on this evening was that as on most former occasions she would eventually allow him – and herself – a great deal of pleasure after demonstrating her authority. But he could not be sure. He remembered yet another occasion on which she had bound him and had teased and lashed him for hours before going to bed, leaving him helpless all night in her bedroom while she slept. In the morning she had masturbated herself with a long dildo, forcing him to watch passively while she climaxed repeatedly. She had got dressed and was ready to leave before she set him free and sent him home with a bad case of blue balls. 'Be sure to lock the door when you leave,' she had admonished as she left.

There were many restaurants in New Orleans to choose from, yet even at this relatively down-scale establishment Paul had made a reservation. The familiar waiter was on duty. Paul felt self-conscious as he made small talk with him while he led them to a table by the window overlooking the Bucktown Canal. He felt as if the cock-cage would be obvious to everyone. Rhonda enjoyed his discomfort.

They ate a seafood dinner, the speciality here as it was of so many of the small family-run restaurants in the West End area of the city. Beer was the beverage of choice. Wine would have been out of character in these surroundings. Near the end of the meal Paul found himself needing to go to the toilet. He told Rhonda, who seemed oblivious to the difficulties presented by the cock-cage.

'I need the keys,' he said sotto voce. 'I'll put the damned thing on again afterwards.'

'How do I know you will?' Rhonda asked with a smile. 'I'm not sure I can trust you with your cock on the loose. The keys are at home anyway, so you'll have to work out a way to do what you have to do.'

Paul couldn't tell if she spoke the truth or not, but short of taking her purse with him to the men's room there was no way he could find out. He stood up and made his way to the toilets. As luck would have it, there was another man already there. Paul couldn't use the urinal in any case, so he had to wait until the man was finished with the cubicle, hoping that he would not have a messy accident in the meantime. Eventually the other man came out and with a muttered apology left the place to Paul. Hurriedly he closed the door and lowered his trousers and underwear. He sat on the toilet and let the floodgates open. The cock-cage diverted some of the stream, but most of it went into the pan. He mopped up the overspray with paper and got dressed again. In a curious way, the inconvenience excited him too. It was one more way for Rhonda to remind him that she was in control of his body even when she was not present.

Rhonda smiled sweetly at him when he got back to the table. 'I knew you'd manage something,' she said, conveying an impression of gloating at her power over men in general and him in particular. 'Don't sulk,' she continued, 'you know you love it.'

Which was true enough. Paul smiled and held her chair while she stood. In her red velvet dress Rhonda was a flamingo among pigeons. Paul was conscious of many admiring or envious glances from the men, and of the sour glances of their wives. Though he was *her* captive, he strove to give the impression that she was *his* possession.

Rhonda was perfectly aware of the tensions, but

was secure enough in her mastery to let them pass over her. Anyway, she was not going to reveal the true situation to the others. She let him preen. He would pay it all back later.

The restaurant parking lot was dark and relatively uncrowded. A quick look around revealed no one in sight. Rhonda stopped Paul with a hand on his arm. They were in a pool of shadow, invisible from the street. He thought she was going to kiss him. She had done so many times in public, turning the ceremony into an erotic occasion as she rubbed against him and moaned theatrically. On his side, Paul usually emerged from the embrace with an erection that was hard to hide. This time, however, she had a different idea.

'Unzip your pants and get your poor cock out. It must need fresh air by now.'

Ah-ha! he thought. She has the keys after all. Images of a fuck in the parking lot came unbidden. His cock tried to stiffen in its steel prison. It was not a pleasant sensation. It wanted out. He wanted it out, and into Rhonda. He unzipped with alacrity, exposing his imprisoned cock to the night air.

And to the dog leash which Rhonda took from her purse and quickly snapped to the ring at the end of the cage. She tugged the chain sharply.

'Arrgghh!' he said, pain and surprise fighting for mastery. But he could do nothing except follow that compelling lead. He hoped there was no one around to witness this striking woman leading him along by his cock. He gripped the chain and tried to take it away from her.

Rhonda slipped the leather loop over her wrist and gave the leash a real tug.

Paul emitted another muffled scream as his cock took the strain. He released the chain. 'All right! All right!' he gasped. 'Let up.'

'No more tricks?' Rhonda asked, maintaining a hard pull.

'No . . . no more tricks,' he gasped.

'Sure?' Rhonda asked, the tension not slackening. 'Going to do whatever I say?'

Paul felt as if he was on the verge of parting company with the family jewels. 'Yes! Whatever you say. Let up!'

Rhonda reluctantly relented.

The cessation of pain made him gasp. Paul rubbed his abused cock.

'Come along, then,' she commanded, leading him towards the car. 'Give me the keys,' she ordered, tugging him around to the passenger's door.

Paul fished them from his pocket and handed them over. Rhonda held the leash short and tight, a reminder of the consequences of disobedience. She opened the door and tilted the seat forwards. She got into the rear seat, maintaining the tension on his cock. Tilting the seat back into position, she ordered him to get in. Then she told him to place his hands behind the back of the seat.

Paul resisted. 'What are you doing?'

Another tug on the chain silenced his protests. He put his hands behind the seat. And jumped in surprise when he felt Rhonda lock his wrists together with a pair of handcuffs. But there was nothing he could do.

'Now,' she said brightly, 'isn't that better?' She reached over his shoulder and dropped the leash into his lap. 'It's always wise to do what women say. It saves a great deal of pain.' Rhonda scooted across the rear seat and opened the opposite door. She climbed out and got into the driver's seat, then reached over and buckled Paul's seat belt, effectively trapping him in the seat. She reached further across to lock his door from the inside. 'Comfy?' she asked.

Paul did not reply

'Sulking is petty,' Rhonda told him. 'But I know how to deal with bad habits.' She opened the driver's door and got out.

Paul looked at her in alarm. 'Get in and close the door! Someone will see what we're doing with the light on.' He struggled against the seat belt and the handcuffs.

'Tsk, tsk,' Rhonda said with a shake of her head. Her long hair swished back and forth over her shoulders with the motion. 'You still don't realise who's in charge here. But you will. Now hold still while I kiss you good-night.'

Paul recoiled. 'You're not going to . . .?'

'Yes, I am,' Rhonda replied. 'I'll get a taxi. There's someone I need to see tonight.' She got out and closed the door.

The sound of the lock turning was loud in the sudden silence. Then Paul broke it. 'Rhonda! Please! You can't leave me like this!'

She turned back to him. 'I can't hear you. You'll have to speak louder.'

'Please don't leave me like this!' he shouted. 'I'll do whatever you want. Just let me go!'

Rhonda appeared to consider his words. Paul looked desperate. After long moments she relented. She unlocked the door and got into the driver's seat. She was smiling smugly – the smile of a woman who has won her point and is enjoying the defeat of her opponent. She settled herself comfortably and glanced at her captive. 'Right then. My rules. Here we go.' She put the key into the ignition switch. 'No more demands. Understood?'

Paul nodded silently.

Rhonda lifted her bottom off the seat in order to work her skirt up to her hips. Her garter belt was red,

11

the taut straps lying on her full thighs and curving intriguingly under her rounded buttocks. In the light of a street lamp Paul saw that she wore no pants. Her thick bush of pubic hair was slightly darker than her more public hair. The sight sent disturbing signals to his imprisoned cock. He tugged at the handcuffs but subsided at her warning look.

'Look as much as you like,' she invited. 'The show is for your benefit.'

Paul doubted that there would be much benefit. He had never encountered Rhonda in this mood. His cock, seemingly with a mind of its own, continued to strain against the cage. It was most uncomfortable and unsettling. Rhonda was uncompromising.

She started the engine and drove off with her captive, back towards the city. Paul hoped that she didn't intend to let people see him like this: hand-cuffed, his cock in a steel cage and hanging out of his pants, the dog leash with which Rhonda led him trailing to the floor. But as they continued to drive it looked as if that was what she was going to do. She seemed oblivious to her own exposed bits, but then she could twitch her skirt down whenever she wanted to.

Rhonda drove through well-lighted areas, along Canal Boulevard rather than the darker West End Boulevard where he would have felt more comfort-able. In the lighted streets he felt as if he were on a stage for all to see, though no one seemed to even notice the car, let alone its captive passenger. He reflected that it would be relatively easy to kidnap someone and drive them away. No one would notice.

He relaxed somewhat when she turned into the darkness of City Park. There was less traffic, though several cars were parked there. Some had steam on their windows. Some rocked rhythmically on their springs. From his boyhood Paul knew this as a lovers' lane, but he had not been back for many years. Apparently it was still used by houseless lovers. Rhonda was letting him see how lucky they were not to have to join them. There was her place – or his – when sex was in the air. He was surprised, therefore, when Rhonda parked in a vacant spot and turned to him with a grin.

She made him uneasy. She had been acting strangely ever since he had picked her up. Rhonda's next move disturbed him even more. She reached over him and reclined his seat until the handcuffs were nearly touching the floor in the back of the car. Then she reached into his open fly and pulled his imprisoned cock and balls fully out. She wasn't going to leave him here, like this, was she?

Apparently not. Rhonda hiked her skirt up to her waist and turned in the confined space to mount him in the sixty-nine position. They had done this before, to their mutual satisfaction, but never in a public place. And never in handcuffs. Rhonda settled herself with her nylon-sheathed thighs on either side of his head, holding him in position while she lowered her cunt over his mouth.

'You know the drill by now,' she said. 'Get busy.'

'What about me?' Paul asked.

'I shall breathe warmly on your cock as you bring me off,' she replied with a grin in her voice. Rhonda lowered her cunt to his mouth.

Paul's protests were cut off, leaving him only one thing to do. It was not as if he disliked performing cunnilingus on Rhonda, or on any other woman. It was just that he liked some reciprocal action. Rhonda's proposal promised not much in the way of reciprocity. Nevertheless, he opened his mouth and used his tongue and teeth on Rhonda's labia and clitoris. She responded nearly at once. This was her favourite position, he knew. He licked her cunt, tasting her clean salty tang as she grew wet between the legs. Paul felt a warm draught on his cock as Rhonda's breath grew rapid. She took his imprisoned organ into her mouth and closed her lips around the steel cage. Her tongue touched his cock between the steel bars of the cage, fleetingly, partially, tantalisingly. His cock responded by swelling within its prison. He groaned as the cage pressed against it.

Rhonda was oblivious to his discomfort. She was enjoying the effects of his mouth on her cunt, moaning softly as he licked and bit her clit. She pressed herself down on his face as she shuddered with her first climax. It was only a small one, compared with what he knew she was capable of, but it was enough to make him feel deprived as well as painfully uncomfortable, cock-wise. Rhonda's attentions to his imprisoned cock tantalised rather than satisfied. But she expected him to do much better than that for her, and Paul knew he would have to make her come as often as possible or suffer her displeasure. A displeasure that he was in no position to avoid. A displeasure that, he knew from experience, he would wish to avoid at all costs. Rhonda's displeasure expressed itself in both a positive way (a severe lashing being the mildest form) and in a negative way (usually prolonged sexual deprivation coupled with extreme provocation). The former he had experienced, and the latter was now in progress. He applied himself more resolutely to the job in hand.

His renewed zeal resulted in yet another moan from Rhonda, accompanied by yet more agitated motion. The second climax was obviously more earth-moving for her. Paul guessed, from past experience, that later ones would be even more satisfying.

And he was right. Rhonda moaned and shuddered, her nylon-sheathed thighs clamping his head ever more tightly as the successive waves of her orgasms swept through her. In a fleeting moment of clarity when she lifted herself slightly from his face Paul saw that the windows of the car were as steamy as those of the other vehicles parked near by. Rhonda's hips moved frenziedly as she came. Paul tasted the salty wetness in his mouth, and lost himself in the task of giving his captor the best ride he was capable of. Had his hands been free, he would have used them as well to service Rhonda, knowing what she liked best: one finger inside her cunt and another inside her arse-hole would have driven her wild.

Rhonda did not seem to miss his fingers very much. Her orgasms were now almost continuous, as were her moans and shudders. Her tongue licked at his imprisoned cock, but not effectively enough to make him come as well. And the cage constricted him painfully as his cock strained to erect within its confines. Rhonda suddenly stiffened above him, grinding her cunt against his face. She screamed in ecstasy, a long loud signal of release and pleasure. Then she slumped atop him. Paul turned his face aside to avoid suffocation, and smelled the odour of her sex with each breath he drew. He relaxed in the knowledge of a job well done, and in relief as he reflected that his demanding mistress was unlikely to punish him further for failing to satisfy her.

Finally Rhonda raised herself from his face. Paul had a good view of her thrilling legs in their sheer nylon stockings as she rose. Her crotch was in full view as well, the wet curls of her pubic hair plastered to her skin by the combination of his saliva and the juice of her own sex. She sighed – a good sign, Paul knew – as she disentangled herself from him and worked her way back into the driver's seat. The process allowed him a good view of various other bits of her anatomy not usually on public view, though that did not do him much good.

Once back in her seat, Rhonda's skirt was still up around her waist. Her long full legs were in full view, the sheer nylon of her stockings lending a sheen to her flesh. Despite himself, Paul could not look away. She knows me too well, he thought. She knows how much I enjoy the sight of a woman's legs in stockings.

Rhonda, seeing the direction of his glance, slid a finger under one of the garters and snapped the elastic against her thigh. 'Pretty nice legs, even though I'm not an Irish barmaid.'

'Raise the seat, please,' he asked. 'I feel too exposed lying like this. Someone is sure to notice.'

Rhonda shook her head. 'I like you like that. It will remind you who's in charge. You can see my legs nearly as well from there as you would if you were sitting up. And I can reach over and squeeze your little cock whenever I want to.' She squeezed him as she spoke. 'Be a good boy and maybe I'll let you out of prison later. No promises, though.'

She started the car and drove away without saying anything else. In his enforced reclining position, Paul could not see where they were going – only a shifting view of street lights and the occasional traffic light. At one intersection a couple looked right into the car and, Paul sensed, directly at him. He felt as if he were on public display. 'Move,' he hissed at Rhonda. 'They're looking right at me.'

'How do you know they're not looking at my legs?' Rhonda asked with a glance at the couple. 'Anyway, I can't go until the light changes. You wouldn't like it if I got stopped by a cop, would you?'

The light took several hours to change to green. Rhonda waved cheerfully at the couple standing on the corner as she drove away. In the rear-view mirror she could see them looking after the car. 'Do you think they'll call the cops? They might be memorising your licence plate number. We might have the law on our trail soon.'

'It's all right for you,' Paul retorted bitterly. 'All you have to do is pull your skirt down. But what about me?'

'Always thinking about yourself,' Rhonda said. 'What about me? How would I explain you to them?' She did not seem overly concerned. Nevertheless, she drove carefully. 'I don't want us to be stopped tonight. I have a nice surprise planned for later. I think you'll like it.'

'What is it, a new whip?' he asked bitterly.

'Maybe. But you'll just have to wait and see.'

Rhonda parked outside her apartment building. 'Wait here,' she told Paul, 'while I distract the doorman.'

'No, don't leave me like . . .'

But she was already out of the car and crossing the sidewalk to the front door of the building. She probably hadn't even heard his plea. Paul tugged futilely at the handcuffs. The street lighting seemed to illuminate his imprisoned cock as if a spotlight were trained on it. There were few people about at that time of night, but to him it seemed as if the entire city were strolling past the car and looking in at the funny man with his cock in a cage.

After a sweaty eternity Rhonda came back and opened the passenger door. She raised the seat to the upright position and unlocked the handcuffs. Grasping the leash, she tugged sharply to get him out of the car.

17

Paul was horrified. 'I'm not going to cross the sidewalk and walk through the lobby like this,' he protested.

Rhonda simply pulled harder. Willy-nilly he followed, protesting the whole way. 'Be quiet,' Rhonda told him calmly. 'Otherwise you'll get us noticed.'

'Oh, and you think no one will notice you pulling me along by the cock?'

'Be quiet,' she hissed. She paused to lock the car while he shifted nervously from foot to foot in the street.

Pulling him along by the chain, Rhonda pushed open the door of her building. Despite the sensitivity of the parts by which she led him, Rhonda thought she would have to dig in her heels and pull with both hands to get him inside. But the pull proved irresistible. Eventually he had to move. He also saw the sense in making the least fuss possible. Grasping the chain with one hand to take the strain off his cock and balls, he allowed Rhonda to lead him into the building.

There was no one in the lobby, not even the doorman who normally stood at the desk. Rhonda calmly walked up to the desk and dropped the car keys on to it. Paul felt as if there were eyes everywhere, staring at him as Rhonda led him across the lobby and over to the bank of elevators. The doors took forever to open, and Paul was terrified that there might be someone inside. The elevator was empty. She led him in and pushed the button for her floor. The doors took forever to close, and the upward ride seemed endless. And what if someone was waiting to board the elevator when it stopped at Rhonda's floor? He was almost a nervous wreck when they finally reached her apartment door.

Rhonda began to search her purse for the door key.

'Hurry up!' he hissed, trying to look inconspicuous.

'Oh, damn!' Rhonda swore. 'I can't find the key! We'll have to go back and search the car. Or maybe I lost it at the restaurant?' The question hung in the air. She looked worried.

Not half as worried as Paul felt at the prospect of retracing that terrifying journey back to the car. 'Shit! Couldn't you be more careful?'

Rhonda looked contrite. 'Well, there's nothing else for it. Come along.' She turned back to the elevators with a strong pull on the chain.

'No! I'm not coming.' Paul sounded desperate. 'Unlock this damned cage and let me go!'

'I can't,' Rhonda replied with a sheepish grin. 'The keys are in my apartment, and we're locked out.' She pulled the chain sharply.

Paul shuffled forwards, close to panic.

She relented. 'Only kidding,' Rhonda said as she took the key ring from her purse. When she saw the look on his face she retreated a step and tugged on the chain.

He looked murderously at her but became more amenable to the suggestion conveyed through his cock. Rhonda opened the door and led him inside. Paul sagged against the wall in the foyer, feeling weak with relief. Rhonda briskly hung up her purse and walked into the sitting room. Paul followed perforce. She released the chain from his cock-cage and told him to make them both a drink.

2

Muriel

Rhonda entered the spare bedroom and closed the door. Paul heard her moving around as he took ice from the fridge and poured the drinks. They were ready when Rhonda emerged, smiling. She had put on something more comfortable, simply by taking off the red dress (and everything else) and reappearing in her stockings and garter belt.

'I'm glad to see someone's enjoying all this,' he said sourly.

'You mean you're not having fun?' Rhonda asked, grinning openly.

He had to admit that he had enjoyed the evening whenever he was not frightened out of his wits. Rhonda was a better judge of what to do with him than he was himself. It was hard to be angry with someone who knew his likes and dislikes so well. He smiled wryly at her. 'Touché.'

'Come sit beside me.' Rhonda seated herself on the sofa and crossed her legs with a whisper of nylon on nylon. 'But wouldn't you be more comfortable without your clothes? And anyway it's impolite to stay dressed when your hostess is naked.'

Paul took off his clothes and stood before Rhonda in nothing but the locked cock-cage. 'Now we match better!' He sat down beside her with his arm on the back of the sofa.

She moved into the circle of his arm and snuggled against him. She placed his hand on her breast with a contented sigh. With her own hand Rhonda reached to caress his cock and balls within their cage of steel. 'Poor thing,' she said softly. 'He looks rather pathetic in there. Should we let him out?' Her fingers encircled his imprisoned cock.

Paul knew enough about her to recognise a rhetorical question when he heard one. Rhonda was not going to unlock him until she was ready, and only she knew when that might be. He concentrated on her firm breast beneath his hand, while trying to ignore the uncomfortable swelling of his cock beneath hers. If the ordeals she had inflicted on him in the past were any indication, this painful and frustrating state of affairs could go on for hours. Or even days. There was the whole of the weekend before them, and Rhonda was a consummate mistress of the fine art of sexual torture. Nor was there any assurance that she would remove the cage on Sunday evening. She might force him to wear it all week. That thought was both disturbing and exciting. He had never been cut off from his cock.

'You may stroke my legs if you like,' she told him. Even this near to her, he was far from reaching the release her closeness usually promised.

Rhonda allowed Paul to fondle her breasts and stroke her legs for a long time, while she manipulated his cock and balls within their steel cage. He was developing a severe case of blue balls before she finally signalled an end to that part of the evening's entertainment. It was she who appeared to be benefiting most from the activity. Her nipples were erect, and Paul could see her breasts rising and falling agitatedly as she drew in great lungfuls of air. He also imagined he could smell her cunt, even though he had

21

not touched her there. He knew enough about her likes and dislikes to refrain from any intimacy she had not specifically asked for. On the other hand, she usually rewarded him for respecting her wishes. Just at that time he was hoping she would produce the keys to his cock-cage, unlock him and invite him to enter her.

But she did not. She released his cock and sat up. 'I think that's enough for now. We aren't getting anywhere this way.'

Paul refrained from observing that this state of affairs was hardly his fault. It would have been, he knew, counter-productive.

'We need to move on,' Rhonda continued. 'I have a surprise for you this evening, and now might be a good time to let you see it. However, I will have to replace the handcuffs before I show you my special treat.'

Paul knew then that the 'surprise' she alluded to was going to be another of her many look-but-don't-touch exhibitions. She was fond of that form of sexual torture – the thing to be seen but not touched – but this evening she apparently had something else in mind. Nevertheless, he nodded assent and waited while she stood up and crossed the room to get the handcuffs. He stood as she returned and brought his hands behind his back. Rhonda locked the cuffs around his wrists. Paul stood still, waiting for her to make the next move. He was not very surprised when she snapped the leash to the ring on the end of his cock-cage and tugged him towards her bedroom door. By now Paul had become used to being led by his cock. In fact he now quite liked the idea – so long as Rhonda did not tug too hard. The pull excited him as he followed her into her bedroom. They had spent many pleasant if sometimes painful nights there, and he hoped that this would be one more.

There was a strange woman in Rhonda's room. She was lying on the bed, nude. And she was bound hand and foot. Her back was to the door, but she struggled to roll over when she heard them enter the room. Paul saw then that she was also gagged. She looked to be about twenty-five, certainly no older than thirty. She was a brunette, her hair short but stylishly arranged. Her eyes were a deep dark blue, and she stared at the two of them in some alarm. With a shock Paul realised that she must have been lying in the empty apartment all the while they were eating dinner – and while he had been eating Rhonda in the car. She was very attractive. Like Rhonda, she had long full legs, a narrow waist and full breasts. Just now her nipples were erect, whether from excitement or alarm Paul could not tell. Her face was long, with a slightly pointed chin, her mouth wide and generous, her lips red and full. The gag pulled her cheeks into a grimace, but Paul was struck, nonetheless, by her great beauty.

Rhonda led Paul to the bed by the chain. The bound woman on the mattress watched in dismay. Was she thinking I'd come to rescue her from the evil duchess, he wondered. His helpless shrug said, *I'm a prisoner too*. The brunette struggled against the ropes that bound her and made muffled noises behind her gag. When she subsided, Rhonda bent to check the ropes, though Paul knew that anyone bound by her had little chance of escape. Satisfied, Rhonda stood erect and gestured to Paul. 'Muriel, meet Paul. Paul, Muriel.'

Paul nodded at the introduction. He was accustomed to Rhonda's habit of treating the bizarre as an everyday occurrence. Muriel was obviously less so. She struggled once again, moaning behind the gag. Paul could not tell if she was genuinely in distress, or if she was simply embarrassed to be seen by a stranger in this state. He knew that she must have consented earlier to let Rhonda bind and gag her, but perhaps she had not bargained on being left helpless while Rhonda went out, or on meeting a strange man when she returned. She appeared agitated at his presence.

Seeking to reassure her, Paul said, 'Don't worry. Rhonda does this all the time. Relax and let her do whatever you've asked her to do. I won't tell anyone about you if you don't speak about me.'

Muriel reddened at the mention of her having asked Rhonda to 'do something to her', but her protest was choked back by the gag. Paul knew that she must have sought Rhonda of her own volition. His quondam mistress did not need to solicit business. People came to her because of her skills in ministering to their special needs. Their perversions, perhaps, if you wanted to be censorious, but he was very much aware that he too lived in a glass house. Happily so, in the main. Looking at Muriel as she struggled against her bonds, he thought that he would like to get her into the glass house as well. They could always draw the blinds.

He strove not to let his interest become apparent to Rhonda. He was not in a good position to resist in case she became jealous. Normally she was not, but she might at least regard his interest in Muriel as a breach of good manners. After all, he was nominally her escort for that evening, even though the handcuffs and leading chain made the term ludicrous. His cock, however, was not so circumspect. It swelled within its steel cage. Nor was Rhonda as unobservant as he had hoped. However, she chose not to react – just then. She smiled tightly at him and tugged him away from the bed by his tell-tale cock.

Rhonda tethered him to the door-knob before returning to Muriel's side. She rolled her captive over to inspect her bonds. Muriel's hands were tied tightly together in front of her, her wrists pulled down against her mons veneris by a rope that went between her legs. It emerged from between her arse-cheeks and went up around her narrow waist. Paul recognised a crotch-rope when he saw one, and he guessed that Muriel had been teetering on the verge of an orgasm the whole time he and Rhonda were eating. She might well have fallen over the edge, he decided, as he saw the dampness at the roots of her dark hair and on the bedspread around her body. Another rope encircled Muriel's upper arms and chest, below her breasts. It pulled her arms close together, forcing her full breasts together between them. Her shapely legs were tied at ankles and knees.

'Muriel likes to be whipped,' Rhonda said conversationally to him as she checked over the knots she had tied hours before. 'She also likes to be left tied and gagged in an empty house. I met her at a bondage weekend in the country. She was tied up all weekend, pretty much as you see her now, with only some brief periods when she was being whipped or fucked. She said later that she had enjoyed it all.'

Muriel blushed to the roots of her hair as Rhonda casually dissected her personality to a stranger. However, Rhonda was nothing if not even-handed. To Muriel she went on, 'Paul likes to be dominated from time to time. He and I met at a dinner dance two years ago. I was with another man who happened to be handcuffed that evening. Paul made discreet enquiries. I made some not-so-discreet replies. We went home together and have got on like the proverbial house afire since then. He comes around now whenever he feels the need of some sexual torture.' She paused. 'But this time he's found something he didn't expect.' She indicated his cock-cage. 'I think I'll let him keep it for a week or two, to remind him of the dangers of trifling with other women.'

Paul wondered if she had decided to keep him locked up after seeing his reaction to Muriel. At the same time he felt a mixture of excitement and dismay at the idea of having his cock held incommunicado, as it were, for an indefinite time. For one thing, that would keep him from making a date with the attractive dark-haired woman, as he had intended to do. Or at any rate, it would keep him from anything more than heavy petting if they did get together.

The ceiling of Rhonda's bedroom was dominated by a stout hook with a pulley fastened to it. A rope ran from the pulley down to a strong cleat on the floor. The purpose of the arrangement would have been obvious to anyone who saw it, even if they had not known whose room it was. Rhonda was not one to hide her proclivities from her intimates. Her in-your-face approach was refreshing. Paul had spent a fair amount of time strung up beneath it. Now it was clear that Muriel was about to experience the direct approach.

She looked frightened, now that the time had obviously come. Rhonda untied her legs and helped her to stand beside the bed. When it was clear that Muriel was not going to fall, Rhonda led her beneath the hook. There, she untied the rope around Muriel's waist and pulled it out from between her arse-cheeks and legs. Paul could see that the rope, where it had pressed into Muriel's cunt, was appreciably darker than the rest of it. So she had obviously enjoyed her solitary bondage session. Rhonda untied the rope binding Muriel's upper arms and attached the rope binding her wrists to the hook on the pulley rope. She gave a lusty pull, and Muriel's arms rose above her head. Rhonda kept on pulling until the dark-haired woman was standing nearly on tiptoe, her shapely body stretched tautly. With her arms stretched high over her head Muriel was exposed from every angle and could do nothing to protect herself from whatever Rhonda – or anyone – cared to do to her. Rhonda tied the rope off and stepped back to admire the effect.

Paul admired it as well. His cock noticed in the usual (but now painful) way. Rhonda noticed his notice and gave him another smile that promised nothing very good in the near future. It was a difficult situation for everyone.

Rhonda proceeded to make it more difficult for Muriel by choosing a light, whippy cane from the umbrella stand that in more normal homes held nothing more threatening than ... umbrellas. She showed it to the helpless woman before stepping behind her. Muriel twisted her head to keep Rhonda in sight, as if knowing when the blow was coming would make it less painful. Rhonda moved further behind her victim. Muriel twisted her entire body this time. Rhonda made tsk-tsking noises and laid the cane on the bed. She gathered some of the rope that had bound Muriel's legs and used it to tie her ankles together.

'There,' she declared to no one in particular, 'that will hold you in position. Be careful about your balance, Muriel.' Rhonda picked up the cane and once more moved behind her dark-haired captive. This time Muriel could only twist her head, so that the area behind her was entirely out of her view. From that position Rhonda struck her across the top slopes of her bottom. Muriel made a muffled noise from behind her gag, an expression of pain and surprise that emerged as a nasal grunt. A red stripe appeared on her flesh, and Muriel shivered. All her muscles tensed as she waited for the next blow.

Paul, from his vantage point across the room, admired both Rhonda's technique and her appearance. She presented a striking spectacle as she raised her arm to strike Muriel again: her full breasts bobbing, her legs superb in the sheer nylon stockings. The garter straps, red against her white flesh, made an erotic contrast that he had appreciated more than once, but never got tired of.

Muriel was less well placed to admire her tormentor. She looked fearfully over her shoulder. The next blow landed on her buttocks. It was the first of a veritable rain of blows that descended, marking her from buttocks to mid-thigh with fiery red stripes. Muriel's grunts rose in pitch, becoming nasal squeals. She shook with every lash, her moans choked back by the gag. Rhonda laid into her unprotected rear elevation with a single-mindedness and energy that anyone – except perhaps Muriel – would have found remarkable.

Paul was excited by the beating. He knew from personal experience what it felt like, and he also knew how arousing it could be – after one let oneself go. His gaze shifted from victim to torturer, finding the sight of both immensely arousing. Just how arousing it could be was measured by the painful swelling of his cock within its steel prison. He couldn't help his arousal, or its consequences. No doubt that was exactly what Rhonda had intended when she chose the cock-cage for him to wear that particular evening.

She was using his own body, his own reactions, as an instrument of torture. He admired her genius in the subtle infliction of pain, even as he suffered it.

Muriel's pain was considerably less subtle. If she had not been gagged, she would have been screaming under the cane. The neighbours would have noticed straight away that something unusual was going on. Doubtless it would be more aesthetically satisfying to allow Muriel to scream, but the tormentor had to forgo that pleasure. Rhonda had practised the subtle art of the gag for a long time, as Paul himself knew. In her clothes closet there were many other types, from full leather helmets covering the entire head to pony-girl bits. She even had one steel head-cage that locked on to the victim, rendering them effectively blind. One evening he had worn only that, and been amazed at how helpless he had been. Paul was glad that Rhonda had not chosen it for Muriel, for her face was most attractive.

Tears overflowing her cheeks and travelling down to her gag showed how severe the beating was. But Rhonda was not intent only on inflicting pain. When she saw Muriel's tears, she laid the cane aside and reached around from behind her trembling, moaning victim to cup both her breasts. Rhonda's fingers teased and pinched Muriel's nipples, causing them to become erect – and their owner to groan with something that sounded curiously like pleasure.

Paul guessed that Muriel was going to derive considerably more pleasure – as well as pain – before the evening was much older. That was Rhonda's way. She was so skilful at mixing pain with pleasure that her victims – including Paul – could not separate the two in their own minds. Muriel would no doubt feel the same before too long – else why had she chosen to submit to Rhonda?

Muriel's groans were definitely sounds of pleasure now. Rhonda's attention to her breasts and nipples continued. Paul thought he saw her shudder – an orgasm? If so, it had taken remarkably little time for her body to shift gears. The next time she shuddered it was immediately noticeable. Definitely an orgasm. He continued to watch Rhonda arouse the other woman.

The next stage came when Rhonda slid one of her hands to Muriel's belly and began to rub her mons veneris and to push her fingers between Muriel's legs. Muriel moaned loudly. Her back arched and her hips jerked forwards as if to push herself against Rhonda's fingers. The violent jerking of her hips continued for several minutes, as if she were embracing an invisible lover, and then with a loud groan Muriel's knees buckled, leaving her hanging by her wrists from the ceiling hook. It looked as if she had passed out, but if so it was only momentary. Her knees straightened suddenly and she struggled to regain her balance. Then once more she stood, suspended tautly, her bound feet taking part of her weight. Her head hung down between her arms and her eyes were closed.

Rhonda stood back as if to gauge her next move. After a moment's thought she slackened the rope that held Muriel on tiptoe. When she was standing firmly on her feet, Rhonda tied it off once more, leaving Muriel still suspended. From the closet she selected a double dildo with a harness. Rhonda impaled herself on one end and strapped the harness around her hips with the ease of long practice.

To Paul, perforce standing aside from the action, the sight of his mistress striding about in nothing except garter belt and stockings, and with the long dildo protruding from between her thighs, nearly produced a spontaneous orgasm despite his imprisoned cock. If this went on for much longer, he would be begging for relief himself, though he knew that he was unlikely to get it. Rhonda enjoyed men begging her to let them come. She would relieve them only when she wanted to.

She picked up the cane and moved around in front of her captive. Once again she showed Muriel the instrument of her torture. This time there was little mystery about the next targets. Muriel shook her head violently, no. Her dark-blue eyes were open wide, pleading silently with her tormentor. Her eyes fell on Rhonda's dildo and she went pale.

Rhonda paid no attention. She took aim and struck Muriel directly on her breasts. There was a nasal howl, and Muriel shuddered from the pain. A red line sprang out on her abused breasts. Others followed. Muriel moaned loudly at each blow. Paul thought he could guess what was going to happen next. Rhonda confirmed his guess when she paused to untie Muriel's ankles before once again taking position in front of her. His imprisoned cock swelled painfully as he imagined the effect of a blow between Muriel's thighs.

And that is where the next blow landed, eliciting a muffled howl from the tortured woman. Muriel had spread her legs when her ankles were freed. Now she clamped her thighs tightly together to protect her cunt from further assault. Rhonda lashed her belly and breasts until she howled in pain. Her thighs loosened, and the next cut went up between them. Paul thought Muriel would levitate. She stood on tiptoe, shuddering and moaning. Rhonda lashed her again, the long dildo bobbing as she moved.

The beating went on, the front of Muriel's body turning red as her back had done. The cries were more strident because of the increased sensitivity of the targets. Paul wondered how she could endure it – or if she could derive pleasure from *this* punishment as well. Muriel's protests, if that is what her muffled howls were, did not cause Rhonda to stop. Paul hoped that she had known what would happen before she allowed Rhonda to tie her up. Neither he nor Muriel was in any position now to put a stop to the proceedings.

After what seemed like an eternity, Rhonda stopped hitting her captive. She laid the cane aside and regarded Muriel's tear-streaked face with apparent satisfaction. The dark head was bowed and she shuddered in the aftermath of the beating. She stood in front of her victim and guided the protruding dildo into Muriel's cunt. The ease with which it went in suggested that the tearful woman was not entirely unprepared for the impalement. As it slid between her thighs Muriel opened them to receive it. Her head came up and she looked at Rhonda steadily as the penetration was completed.

Muriel groaned when Rhonda slid the dildo back out, and then slowly in again. The groan was not a protest. As before, the sexual nature of the stimulation apparently made her forget the pain that had preceded it. Evidently Muriel had mastered the masochist's trick of being aroused by the pain; the pleasure that followed the pain would be heightened by the contrast. Paul made a mental note to ask her on another occasion. He had already decided that there would be such an occasion, and this time Rhonda was not in a position to notice the physical consequences of his decision. Paul was, though. The cage constricted his cock and balls as they tried to respond to the sight of the present action and to the anticipation of his own encounter with Rhonda's dark-haired victim.

The fucking of Muriel went on, to the apparent satisfaction of both participants. Muriel moaned steadily as Rhonda thrust in and out. Rhonda embraced her victim, their breasts pressed together between their straining bodies, and she moaned as her half of the double dildo did its work in her own cunt. The pace grew gradually faster, Muriel's groans louder. Rhonda began to growl like an animal, a sign Paul recognised from his experience in bed with her: it was a sign of imminent climax. The climax itself was signalled by a prolonged 'Haaahhhh!' of pleasure. But she did not stop afterwards. The beating she had given Muriel seemed to have aroused her as well. She thrust deeper and more quickly, the dildo sliding into view, glistening with Muriel's juices, and then disappearing again. It reminded Paul of a black piston sliding in and out, the machine metaphor contributing to the excitement of the spectacle.

Muriel's tautly stretched body began to move in rhythm with Rhonda's thrusts as her own excitement grew. The ropes holding her hands over her head were digging into her wrists as she allowed her weight to come on to them. Her knees sagged as she thrust her hips forwards to allow Rhonda to fuck her more easily. The gag choked back her cries, but it was plain that she was having multiple orgasms as she was fucked.

Paul's excitement nearly kept pace with theirs, but he could do nothing for himself. Even without the handcuffs he would have been unable to join them – no matter how much he longed to. Sex was not primarily a spectator sport for him, as Rhonda knew very well. By keeping him on the sidelines she was adding to the torture she had begun in the parking lot at the restaurant. It did not help very much to believe that she would make it up to him. Sometimes she did, allowing him access to her body after torturing him. And sometimes she did not. The agony of not-knowing sparked his imagination and sent additional blood to his imprisoned cock.

Rhonda moaned again as she came. She seemed to be having her own multiple orgasms as Muriel groaned and shook. Muriel's hands were twisting in the air above her head, the rope taut between her wrists and the ceiling. Abruptly her knees gave way, leaving her hanging by her bound wrists. Even after Rhonda came again and withdrew from her, she hung by the rope.

Rhonda allowed herself (and Paul) a long look at the unconscious woman strung up from the ceiling before she moved to slacken the rope and allow her body to touch the floor. Muriel lay without move-ment. The only sign of life was the heaving of her chest as she drew in great draughts of air through her widely flaring nostrils. Paul guessed it had been an earth-shattering series of orgasms. He had never managed to make Rhonda pass out after making love to her. He wondered if he could make Muriel pass out after sex with him. It was an exciting thought.

Rhonda glanced at him for the first time since she had begun the punishment of her other victim. Her own breasts heaving, she asked him mockingly, 'How was it for you?'

Paul did not reply, but he thought that the dildo protruding from her belly made her more erotic than ever. He imagined its counterpart, thrust deep within her, and shivered. The contrast between its hardness and the sheer stockings she still wore excited him. But then almost everything about Rhonda excited him. It was too bad that she was so good at arousing him and so indifferent to his own satisfaction. He vowed again not to beg her for relief, knowing that sooner or later he would. She always made him beg, and he supposed that he enjoyed that aspect of it. It was not his usual position with the women he knew and bedded. The contrast, he decided: that was what kept him coming back to Rhonda.

This time Rhonda came to him, the dildo bobbing before her. She cupped his imprisoned balls and stroked his cock gently. She smiled as she felt it try to respond to her manipulation. 'Are your balls blue enough yet?' she asked teasingly. Without waiting for his reply, she asked, 'What do you think of Muriel?'

That was a loaded question. No matter what he said, Rhonda would use it against him, and he was in no position to resist whatever she decided to do – or not do. I'm like Muriel, he thought. I let her do whatever she wants with me. I allow her to make me helpless. I enjoy the process and the results of submission. She's a remarkable woman.

The remarkable woman was still teasing his cock and waiting for an answer.

'She's . . . nice,' he said non-committally.

'Just nice?' Rhonda asked, giving his cock a squeeze. 'I believe you feel more than that for her, don't you?' The last remark was addressed as much to his cock as to him. 'I think you were thinking about getting her into bed when I wasn't looking.'

Paul had never been a convincing liar. And Rhonda had a way of getting the truth out of most of her victims. All it took was the application of the right pressure, and she was holding one of his major pressure points in her hand.

He nodded, not wanting to say anything more. Good manners went a long way with Rhonda. False denials did not.

She nodded. 'I may let you couple later. Under proper supervision, of course.' There was no doubt as to whose supervision she meant.

The idea of bedding Muriel in Rhonda's presence was daunting. There could be all sorts of nasty repercussions if, for instance, they both enjoyed the experience too obviously. Paul normally approached sex with enthusiasm. Rhonda might not like to see such enthusiasm in him when another woman was involved. Although Rhonda had repeatedly said that she was not seeking a permanent partner, there was still a distressing amount of territoriality bred into every female, even her. And just now there was still the matter of the cock-cage and the handcuffs.

Rhonda released his cock and crossed to Muriel. Paul was glad she didn't press the matter – or his cock – any further. The dark-haired woman was showing signs of revival. Rhonda brought her bound wrists down in front of her and re-tied the crotch-rope around her waist. With both her captives helpless she went into the toilet to do those essential things women do after sex and torture. One of those essentials was not the removal of the dildo. When she re-emerged, Muriel was struggling to get to her feet. Rhonda helped her to rise and guided her over to the bed. There she bound Muriel's ankles and knees once more and laid her on her back.

Moving back to Paul, she loosened his tether from the door-knob and led him across to the bed as well. Rhonda being what she was, her bed was as special as her bedroom. There was a long length of chrome-plated machine chain fastened to one of the legs which she used for keeping her bedmates near by. She drew it out from beneath the bed and fastened Paul's tether to it. 'I guess it's safe enough now for you and Muriel to share a bed,' she said with a smile at them both. 'Enjoy one another's company while I watch the late news on television.' Irony was another of Rhonda's strong points.

Paul took the opportunity to look more closely at Muriel. The red marks were still angry-looking. Her breasts and belly were well striped. He imagined there were more stripes between her legs that he could not see. Rhonda had used her standard braided cotton rope to tie Muriel. The knots were out of her fingers' reach, a standard practice among careful dominatrices. The gag consisted of a scarf tied tightly between her teeth, presumably holding some sort of packing inside her mouth. Muriel's cheeks bulged. There was a second scarf tied over her mouth from nose to chin to hold the whole thing in place. The knots were behind her head. He debated whether to try to remove her gag so that they could at least converse, but Rhonda might not appreciate that. Muriel might well be too embarrassed to talk to a stranger who had just seen her beaten thoroughly and then made to come repeatedly. All in all, he decided, it was better to accept the conditions Rhonda had imposed – not that he could do very much about those she had imposed on him.

'Er . . .,' he began, 'are you all right? I mean, after the beating and all?' Not a promising start, he thought, but just what did one say to a woman one had just met at a ritual whipping session? A woman who, moreover, could not reply?

Muriel blushed but nodded her head slowly. 'Mmmfff,' she said, thrusting her chin towards him.

'Were you wanting me to take off the gag?'

Muriel nodded vigorously. 'Mmmmmm!'

He sat on the bed beside her. 'I might be able to, but I don't think Rhonda would appreciate it. Her displeasure can be, er, rather painful. And it's locked on. She always does that.' Paul was prepared to defy Rhonda in this, if only because he wanted to get Muriel's telephone number, but the consequences would also apply to her.

Muriel looked thoughtful, then slowly nodded. She lowered her chin.

Paul began an awkward one-sided conversation with the nude woman lying bound and gagged within reach of his hands – had they been free. Rhonda had known what he would do if he were left alone with the attractive stranger. Leaving him handcuffed in the face of such temptation was just her way of adding to his sexual frustration. And very effective it was too. Paul's cock pressed against its prison again and again as he strove to keep up the monologue.

'Rhonda does this quite often. She's really very good at it.' That sounded idiotic. He tried again. 'It looked as if you enjoyed it.'

Muriel grunted behind the gag.

Paul had an idea. 'I know you can't talk, but if I ask you a question you can reply – one grunt for yes, two for no. Is that OK?'

Muriel grunted once more, nodding at the same time.

'Oh, yes, how stupid of me. You can nod or shake your head too if you prefer. Now, where was I? I watched you while she whipped you. It looked as if you enjoyed it.'

Muriel blushed deeply but nodded her head too, slowly, as if reluctant to admit the truth of his observation.

Paul tried another approach. 'You needn't feel embarrassed in front of me. We're both in the same boat. Only,' he added with a sheepish grin, 'you've already had a dose of the whip, and I'm still waiting for it. Rhonda is in control of the two of us. I'd like to know how you came to be here, but that will have to wait for later. If you'd like, I can tell you what happened to me this evening.'

Muriel grunted once, and Paul launched into a recital that began with the receipt of the cock-cage and ended with his being led into the room by Rhonda.

Muriel listened with interest and, as he recounted their session in the park, with obvious arousal. He thought she might like him to perform the same service for her, but Rhonda had made that impossible. Later, he thought, when he could ask Muriel out on her own account. Her arousal was nevertheless an encouraging sign.

Rhonda chose that moment to return. 'What, you're not both at it like rabbits?' she asked brightly. 'Oh, I see. Someone has left you all tied up. And –' to Paul '– put you into a nasty cock-cage. How dreadful it must feel to be so close to temptation but be unable to succumb – as I've no doubt you both have been tempted. But I have come to save you both from surrendering to carnal desire. Or at least to carnal desire for one another.'

She still wore the strap-on dildo. Muriel looked at it with nervous anticipation, Paul with fascination. He had never seen Rhonda like this. The rubber shaft moved as she strode across to the bed. Paul wondered what the other end of the thing was doing to his . . . their . . . mistress. He felt a strange desire to touch, to stroke that rude shaft protruding from between her thighs.

It did not take a genius to guess what thoughts had been going through Paul's mind as he had sat next to a helpless nude woman. He wondered what Rhonda would do to him for thinking of bedding Muriel while he belonged, cock and balls at least, to her. It would no doubt be as ingeniously painful and pleasurable as the cock-cage had proved so far to be. Ruefully he thought of having Muriel or Rhonda (or both), and knew that his chances of having either in the near future were slim. Rhonda showed no sign of producing the necessary keys, or of turning herself or Muriel over to him.

Rhonda meanwhile was enjoying having two persons to tantalise at once. Paul's frustration and Muriel's trepidation seemed to please her. She spent some time just gazing at her two captives, allowing their uncertainty to grow. Her ability to make others squirm with anticipation or dread was well developed. It was what made her so sought-after as a dominatrix among her circle of friends. It required a certain patience and self-restraint, a willingness to postpone her own (and her victims') pleasure until the last moment, and so heighten both. She was looking patient just then.

Paul knew the look. It was going to take some time before he knew what she would allow him this time. His cock almost literally itched to plunge into her and pleasure them both. The dildo Rhonda flaunted only reminded him that it was where he wanted to be. He tugged futilely at the handcuffs.

Rhonda noticed. 'I think it would be a good idea to separate you two for a bit. To let you both cool down, as it were. Paul in particular needs some time to reflect on loyalty and good manners.' She unfastened the chain from the bed and tugged sharply on it. 'Come along!' she commanded cheerfully.

Paul struggled to his feet and followed her as she led him from the bedroom. In the living room the TV was still turned on. Some inane sitcom involving the characters' inability to achieve any kind of harmony, in bed or out. Their problem was one of custom and conscience. His was more tangible, and was likely to be much more effective in preventing anything happening between him and either of the two women in the apartment.

Rhonda indicated for him to sit on the couch. He did so with difficulty. Sitting with his hands behind his back was awkward, and the handcuffs dug into his wrists if he sat back. Rhonda paid no mind to his discomfort. It was her business to provide discomfort for her victims. It was their business to deal with it. She fastened the leading chain to the coffee table with a small padlock.

'Enjoy the entertainment,' she told him as she went back into the bedroom.

Knowing what was likely to be happening in the bedroom, Paul had a hard time concentrating on anything else but that. The TV paled into insignificance before the lurid image of Rhonda sliding that dildo into Muriel and fucking her stupid – which he knew she was quite capable of doing. The noises coming from the bedroom, mostly strangled grunts and moans from Muriel and louder groans from Rhonda, made his cock throb inside its steel prison. Auditor sex was exciting but essentially unsatisfactory. He squirmed on the couch, longing to be an active participant in the scene behind the closed door.

The noises went on for a long time. When they finally ended Paul was able to relax. He waited for Rhonda to emerge and perhaps release him for a bit of fun with her – or Muriel. She didn't come out. After two hours (timed by the changing programmes on the TV) he knew that she wasn't going to come. She was probably sleeping. He wondered if Muriel, bound and gagged as she no doubt still was, was sleeping as well. But it didn't matter. Rhonda was not going to release him any time soon, and Muriel couldn't.

Paul spent an uneasy night on the couch, sleeping and waking to try to find a more comfortable position. Finally he slid to the floor and sat with his back against the front of the sofa. In this position his hands were not pressed against the cushions, and he managed to doze off.

3

Breakfast À Trois

Morning-noises woke him: water running, the clink
of glassware, the rattle of a cereal box. Rhonda was
in the kitchen, still wearing her garter belt and
stockings and that dildo. The sight of her striding
around energetically excited Paul, but he didn't say
anything. Nor did Rhonda. He wondered where
Muriel was.

Finally, needing to go to the toilet, Paul broke the
silence. Rhonda smiled at his request and went into
the bedroom to get the key to the lead chain. She
emerged pushing Muriel before her and minus the
dildo she had (presumably) worn all night. Paul
wasn't sure that its absence was an improvement.
Muriel's hands were still tied down to her belly. She
still wore her gag, and her hair was mussed. She
looked even more attractive in her dishabille.

'Muriel has to pee as well. Let her go first while I'm
unlocking you.' Rhonda directed her female captive
towards the bathroom and came to unlock Paul from
the coffee table.

He got to his feet awkwardly and stood waiting for
Muriel to finish. She was taking a long time, and he
thought he might be forced to wet himself and the
carpet. Rhonda came to the same conclusion. Leading him by the chain, she made her way to the

bathroom door. Inside, Muriel was squatting awkwardly on the toilet and looking distressed.

'Can't wee?' Rhonda asked.

Muriel nodded dolefully.

Rhonda turned on one of the basin taps and began to rub Muriel's crotch. 'I sometimes find it hard to wee after a good fucking,' she told her captive. 'Just relax and it'll come.' She continued to stroke Muriel's labia and cunt.

Watching them, Paul knew that he was going to wet himself any second. He stood in the shower stall and with a strangled sound of relief he let go. It was embarrassing to have to wet himself before two witnesses. The warm urine ran down his legs. But he was relieved.

Over on the toilet, Muriel too was relieved. With what sounded like a moan of pleasure she urinated, the stream divided by the crotch-rope but nevertheless coming out with great force and running up Rhonda's arm as far as the elbow.

'There. I told you it would come. You just have to relax.' She changed hands and continued to stroke Muriel's labia and cunt. She washed the urine from the wet hand under the running tap and shook it dry. She used it to stroke Muriel's belly and mons.

Muriel looked wildly at her captor, shaking her head and making noises of protest through her gag. Which Rhonda ignored. Muriel squirmed and tried to stand. Rhonda casually pushed her back down on to the toilet, where she sat with her legs spread, looking uncomfortable and undignified. Since Rhonda was kneeling between her legs, Muriel couldn't close them to prevent what was going to be (they all knew it) an arousal *à la toilette*.

Still dripping with his own urine, Paul watched from the shower stall. His cock sent signals of discomfort as it tried to swell within its cage. Doubtless Muriel was aware of, and embarrassed by, his witnessing her undignified but unavoidable sexual arousal. His own arousal followed as a matter of course. Rhonda, he thought, could probably give a corpse one last case of tumescence. She was certainly unafraid and unabashed to do things that others (Muriel, in this case) found embarrassing.

'Come over here,' she commanded Paul, 'and take care of her tits. I need both hands for her cunt.'

Muriel shot an agonised glance at Paul as he obeyed. She shook her head mutely, no, no.

Seeing her anxiety, he hesitated.

Rhonda used one hand to grasp the chain attached to his cock and tugged him to his knees beside the toilet – and Muriel. 'Kiss her tits and bite her nipples. You know the drill,' she commanded.

He shot an apologetic glance at Muriel as he bent forwards. Careful, he told himself; don't overbalance. He wished that his hands were free so that he could feel her tits as well.

'Nnnnngggg!' Muriel said, shaking her head wildly. Her breasts bobbed and swayed. She strained to close her legs and to rise from her awkward squat.

'Sit still!' Rhonda snapped.

She sounded annoyed, but Paul could see her amusement. She liked to make people squirm, he knew. Perhaps Muriel didn't know that, but she was beginning to squirm nicely. Her full breasts, squeezed together by her upper arms, thrust out invitingly.

As Paul bent closer, Muriel looked at him appealingly. He shrugged his shoulders, trying to indicate that he was as helpless as she was. Which wasn't strictly true, his conscience reminded him. He could always refuse if he was willing to pay the price of refusing Rhonda. At the same time he knew he wasn't

44

going to refuse. Those breasts before him ached to be nuzzled. He ached (quite literally, in the more southerly regions of his anatomy) to nuzzle them. But first there was something else he could do for the frightened woman.

He bent close to her face and kissed her eyes. She closed them and seemed to relax slightly. He moved to kiss the side of her neck and her ear lobes. 'Do as she says,' he whispered in Muriel's ear. 'She isn't going to hurt you if you obey.' He had hoped that Rhonda would not hear or understand the whispered instructions.

She smiled ironically at him. 'Good advice at any time,' she said. 'If you followed it more closely you might not be wearing that cock-cage just now. Now shut up and do her tits like I told you to.'

Paul bent to those inviting bits of anatomy and licked the top of her right breast. Muriel gasped and her face reddened. Bending closer, he kissed the upper slope of her breast. Ideally he would have liked to cup and fondle her breasts while kissing them, but Rhonda had made that impossible. He continued kissing her while Rhonda stroked her between the legs.

Muriel made one last attempt to dissuade her tormentors before it was too late. Before, in fact, she had an orgasm and became unable to stop herself. She moaned and shook her head, no, no, no. Paul felt a pang of conscience, and another, sharper pang from his imprisoned cock, but he didn't stop teasing her nipples. Nor did Rhonda abandon her attack on Muriel's virtue from farther south. Just why she wanted them to stop was not clear to Paul. She was embarrassed, of course, but she had already overcome her inhibitions enough to seek out Rhonda. She had undeniably enjoyed last night's whipping and fucking. Presumably she had enjoyed what Rhonda did to her after Paul was safely chained to the coffee table. So why not just relax and enjoy this morning's attentions to her sensitive bits?

Muriel's doubts and protests did not concern Rhonda. Muriel had come to her, Muriel was still here, and she would do whatever Rhonda wished until she left.

Muriel's protests grew fainter as she became more aroused. Her breathing increased in tempo and depth as the two mouths worked their magic on her body. At first this was the only sign of her increasing arousal, but gradually her nipples grew erect and her neck and chest became flushed. Paul leaned further down so that he could nip that erect bud between his teeth. Muriel gasped and shuddered. Rhonda paused to push the crotch-rope deeper into her captive's cunt, pressing on her clitoris. Muriel moaned at the touch. Her bound hands jerked, pulling the rope still deeper into her sensitive flesh. It was almost out of sight between her labia, and must have been pressing hard on her clitoris. She moaned again, longer and deeper. Rhonda smiled at the reaction. While Paul bit and kissed her nipples, Rhonda bent to kiss Muriel's exposed cunt.

Muriel jerked and shuddered as her captor's tongue found her clitoris, and her weak head-shaking became academic. Paul guessed she had had her first orgasm of the day. When the next one came, not too long thereafter, she was utterly lost. She shuddered and groaned on the toilet seat as the wave of pleasure hit her. It was the best way to wake up. He wished he was in that position, but he kept working on Muriel's nipples as ordered.

Rhonda and Paul worked over her while orgasm after orgasm shook her body, while Muriel tugged at her crotch-rope and excited herself. A long time later she sagged exhaustedly in her seat, drawing in rasping breaths and moaning softly. Her body was covered with a sheen of perspiration. Her hair was matted and damp, and the slackness of her muscles suggested that she could come no more. Rhonda at last relented, signalling Paul to stop as well.

Rhonda helped Muriel to stand. Her knees showed an alarming tendency to buckle. Rhonda half led, half dragged her across to the shower stall and propped her against the wall. She turned the water on and let it soak away Muriel's perspiration and the odour of her sex.

Paul had to struggle to his feet on his own.

Awareness of her surroundings gradually came back to Muriel. She stood more steadily and turned to let the stream reach every part of her body. Her dark hair hung down over her face, but with her hands tied she could do nothing about it. She looked appealingly at Rhonda, who at length turned off the water and began to dry her helpless captive. Without untying Muriel's hands, Rhonda rubbed her body until it glowed. She dried Muriel's hair and brushed it into some semblance of order.

When she was done with Muriel, Rhonda signalled Paul to get into the shower. 'You smell of piss,' she observed.

Under the shower he got rid of the objectionable smell. Rhonda led Muriel away and he was left alone for a few minutes. Rhonda came back and dried him in his turn, leading him back to the breakfast area afterwards. There he saw Muriel sitting at the table with her hands still tied tightly down to her belly. The crotch-rope was tight between her legs, and must have been uncomfortable, for she kept shifting on the chair. Maybe she was trying to make herself come

47

again, though that was rather doubtful after her thorough seeing-to.

Rhonda fastened his leading chain to the table leg and removed his handcuffs. Paul gratefully stretched his arms and shoulders.

'Take off Muriel's gag,' she commanded him as he finished his exercises. She turned to make coffee and to get fruit juice, bacon and eggs from the refrigerator.

Paul untied the scarf holding the gag in Muriel's mouth. He extracted the damp and sour wad. It was a pair of woman's pants, most likely Muriel's own.

Muriel worked her jaws to ease the cramp from being held open for so long. 'Water,' she croaked.

Rhonda set a glass of orange juice on the table, signalling Paul to help Muriel drink.

Muriel blushed, but drank thirstily. She raised her chin when she had had enough. Paul set the glass down on the table, while Muriel tried not to look at anyone.

'Tell me when you want more,' he told her.

Muriel nodded mutely, blushing more deeply.

Rhonda broke up the situation by telling Paul to make breakfast. 'Your chain is long enough to reach the stove and the sink. Get busy. I like my eggs over lightly. Muriel?'

Muriel didn't want to talk. Rhonda asked again, more sharply.

Avoiding eye contact, she whispered, 'The same.'

Rhonda sat down with her coffee while Paul made breakfast for them. Paul and Rhonda ate heartily, Muriel timidly as they fed her. Rhonda dominated the conversation. Muriel said nothing, unless repeated flushes counted.

Rhonda cut through the awkwardness with characteristic decision. 'You,' she told Paul, 'can do the washing up. I need to have a shower and change my stockings.'

She left them alone.

The silence lengthened, becoming awkward. It was clear that Muriel was not going to end it. She was too embarrassed. It was up to him.

'Look, I know this is awkward, but it isn't going to get less so by keeping quiet. I told you last night how I got here. How about telling me your story?'

Muriel looked at him in alarm.

'OK. Maybe later. How about telling me the rest of your name? I promise not to blackmail you, but I would like to see you away from . . . here.' He nodded at the door through which Rhonda had gone.

Muriel summoned up a wan smile. 'Castle. Muriel Castle.'

'Of this city?'

'Of San Francisco.'

'You're working here, then?'

A nod.

'Doing what?'

'Bank manager.'

Paul was impressed. Not many women as young as Muriel appeared to be were bank managers. With her sitting naked before him, he perversely imagined her in the uniform of pin-striped jacket and skirt with opaque black tights. And perversely, the idea excited him. He was glad he was wearing the cock-cage, for his reaction might have put her off.

'I've just begun,' Muriel volunteered. 'But it's tremendously exciting.'

He wanted to ask, 'As exciting as Rhonda?' But he guessed that any allusion to her recent orgasms would make her dry up, and he wanted to get her telephone number before Rhonda came back to interrupt things. So he asked instead, 'Which bank?'

'Bank of Crescent City,' she replied after a short hesitation.

Paul guessed that she would not be eager to discuss her work in any depth. If word got around in banking circles of what she did for fun it would do her career no good. But he was satisfied. He could find her through her work if he didn't manage to get her telephone number. The rest of the breakfast time passed in desultory but not very revealing conversation. Muriel was clearly embarrassed by his presence, though Paul guessed that that was due more to what he had witnessed than to a dislike of him personally. Or so he hoped. Women with Muriel's peculiar bent were not exactly lying around for the taking.

Rhonda, dressed for the street and looking very attractive, returned to the breakfast table and announced that she was going out for the day. Paul, she said, would remain there to clear up. She produced a long chain with which she fastened him to the breakfast table by the cock-cage. Rhonda said as an aside to Muriel that he could reach nearly all of the apartment from there. She said as an aside to Paul (with Muriel an interested witness) that she expected it to be clean when she returned. Rhonda then untied Muriel and told her to get dressed. It was clearly a dismissal, though she did offer Muriel a lift home.

Muriel declined. She had her car outside, she said. She went into the bedroom to dress, leaving Paul and Rhonda to discuss personal matters.

Rhonda began by observing that he seemed rather interested in Muriel. He did not deny it. He knew that a denial so obvious as that would anger the dominatrix. Rhonda was not the jealous type, she said. She could not afford to be exclusive with her associates, as she called them. She really tried to give each one what they wanted from her – within the limits of her specialised profession.

50

They had been friends long enough for each to understand the other's needs and to tolerate their differences. In an earlier age Rhonda would have been called a courtesan. The censorious would have called her something less kind. Paul might have been called a playboy, for he had enough money to allow him to work only when he chose. He delivered yachts around the world for owners who did not like long sea voyages. Many envied him the work.

He had met Rhonda after one such delivery to the Caribbean. She had been entertaining the owner of another yacht in Bridgetown harbour and was about to fly back to New Orleans. Instead they had stayed aboard the yacht he had delivered, entertaining one another, for a further week. And they had met again back in New Orleans for further entertainments. Last night's meeting had been their first for nearly a month. Rhonda did not expect him to wait for her summons. Nor did he. Muriel might well be the next object of his interests. *He* rather thought so. It seemed like a good prospect.

'Be kind to her,' Rhonda told him ironically.

Muriel's return broke up the conversation. The two women left together and Paul was alone in the apartment. He set about clearing up the breakfast things and tidying the place. Rhonda would probably be out the whole day, but he would prefer to have the work done before she returned in order to leave the evening free for more rewarding activities. He dragged the chain into all the corners of the apartment, dusting and polishing the furniture and running the vacuum cleaner over the floors and rugs. Nevertheless, it was a long day. Rhonda had planned it that way, he knew, so that he would appreciate her return the more.

Rhonda had taken the keys to the cock-cage and chain with her. She was careful to ensure that her captives remained captive. Paul (and her other associates) appreciated her thoroughness, even when it meant that they had to wait for her.

4

Muriel at Work

Muriel usually rose early to give herself time to look at the mail and to have a leisurely breakfast. Also to prepare herself mentally for the day's responsibilities. She found the usual day's harvest of bills and advertisements and offers of 'free' credit. As a banker, she knew that there was no such thing. Her own bank made similar offers, and she knew that many people were hooked by them, getting themselves into debt in the belief that there really was a free lunch. It was part of her job to disillusion them when they couldn't pay. She didn't like the offers, and she liked the resultant rude awakenings even less. But – everyone was doing it.

She laid the collection on the breakfast table to sort through after a shower and the preliminary stages of the daily ritual of dressing. This morning, as always, she laid out her 'uniform' on the bed. The bank didn't exactly have a uniform, but their dress code prescribed the nearly ubiquitous striped suit – in her case consisting of a dark blue knee-length skirt and matching jacket. As it was spring, she chose beige tights. Winter meant black tights. Muriel preferred the shiny ones at all times, believing that they showed off her legs to advantage – though she didn't like to think of herself as dressing specifically to attract men.

At 28 she was beginning to feel guilty because she did not feel the nesting urge. Most of her friends and schoolmates had already nested, and bred. Some had even migrated to other climes and other nest-mates. She felt the vague guilt of the woman who had done neither yet. So far she had managed to stay clear of such career-unfriendly relations. To herself she admitted that her predilection for freedom and her penchant for bondage and domination, while they complemented each other, made her own mate more difficult to find. She had never managed to confide her secret desires to any of the men she had met so far. She had sought instead the services of women like Rhonda, on the assumption that another woman would be more sympathetic.

At the thought of her recent session with the dominatrix, Muriel felt a flush of pleasure and a flutter of excitement. She congratulated herself on having found an especially skilled tormentor, while regretting that she had not yet found a man to whom she could confide her needs. The thought of being dominated by a man thrilled her in a dark way that she found worrying. What if he didn't stop when he had bound her? In her deepest self that thought was exciting, while in her more prudent self she knew that such thoughts were dangerous. Like everyone else, she was aware of the many reports of women being found dead with the marks of sexual torture on their bodies. While dreaming of a dominant man who liked rope, she didn't want to become a statistic in the hunt for him. Rhonda was safer.

She laid out her underwear: conservative nylon/silk beige to match her tights. Muriel never wore cotton. Cotton was for old women, she believed. She liked the feel of silk against her skin. Muriel put on a shower-cap to keep her short hair dry and stepped under the water jet. She washed everywhere, especially her breasts and crotch, as they had received most of Rhonda's attention. There was no intention to wash away the marks of her sexual adventure. She liked to be clean all over all the time. The right man might come along at any moment, unannounced, and she wanted to be appealing to him. And the warm water felt good on her abused body.

Muriel looked critically over her body as she washed. The marks from the beating were fading but still discernible. Anyone who saw her in the nude would know at once what she had been doing. Her colleagues at the bank would be scandalised, she was sure. If they knew what the manager liked to do in her spare time, it would be impossible to control them. Her cunt was still deliciously sore and sensitive from Rhonda's wickedly clever upward cuts. Muriel shivered in remembered delight as she touched her sensitive skin.

She dried herself off and applied talcum powder. In her fluffy bathrobe Muriel went into the kitchen to prepare breakfast. As the coffee-maker bubbled she scrambled two eggs and made toast. While she ate, Muriel tackled the morning's post. Among the usual junk mail she found a personal letter. From Paul, it turned out. He had got her address somehow. Muriel felt a flash of annoyance, followed at once by a sense of mild pleasure: he had made the effort to contact her despite her discouragement.

The contents surprised and shocked her mildly by his sheer effrontery. 'Wouldn't you feel more comfortable if you wore stockings and a garter belt today?' he asked. It continued, 'And no pants?'

Muriel flushed at the idea of going naked – or nearly so – under her clothes. She didn't take the suggestions seriously. I don't have any stockings or garter belt in any case, she thought. And as for the other suggestion ... She put the letter aside and finished her breakfast.

Dressed in her 'uniform', and with tights and pants in place, she drove to the bank, enduring the rush-hour traffic as she did every day. She thought more of what Rhonda had done to her than of what Paul had more recently suggested. She intended to see Rhonda again. Preferably without Paul. Muriel felt a growing warmth between her legs at the memory of last week. Restlessly she shifted in the driving seat, her thighs making a whispery nylon against nylon sound. Her breasts felt hot and heavy, the nipples pressing against her brassiere. And all this, she thought, just from remembering her treatment at Rhonda's hands.

Am I a lesbian, she wondered? Certainly I've never felt so excited with a man.

No, she pushed the thought aside. It's just that a man has never done to me what she did. Her deeper self added, it's just that you've never let any man know what turns you on. You're a practising masochist, that's what you are. Muriel found that label more congenial than the other.

At the bank Muriel nosed her Firebird into the space reserved for her, and felt a small flush of pride to see her own name on the parking space. She locked the car and went to open the bank's front door. As usual, she was the first one there. As she unlocked the door, Sheila Graham and Mike Barrett arrived together. Muriel suspected that they were living together but, as neither of them ever said anything about it, she didn't ask. Living in sin, as it used to be called, was hardly a matter for comment now – except in the ultra-conservative circle of banks and bank managers, she thought with a smile. All the more reason to keep her own secret life secret. The three went into the bank and began the daily ritual of turning on the lights and arranging the cash drawers behind the counter. It was a small branch. There were only six people employed there, and the staff was due to shrink still further as the relentless march of automation made more and more jobs redundant. She went into her office, shut the door and began to go through the mail while waiting for the first security van to deliver the daily float of cash from central office.

When she checked her e-mail, there was another note from Paul: 'Well, did you wear a garter belt and stockings, Muriel?' So he had found her e-mail address as well. It wasn't that much of a secret, but it was not something she gave out carelessly either. Probably he had her telephone number as well by now. How long would it be before he called her? Not long, she surmised. Would she go out with him? Muriel wondered if Rhonda had released him from his cock-cage yet. The idea of a man going about with that thing on under his clothes amused her, as it had Rhonda. It might be fun to go out with a man who was utterly 'safe'. It might be fun to take him away from Rhonda, too, if a bit dangerous. Rhonda might not be amused.

Muriel went through the rest of her correspondence without finding any more letter-bombs from Paul. When the security van arrived she left her desk to open the vault for the deposit. As she walked to the vault she was suddenly conscious of the friction as her thighs rubbed together through the sheer nylon of her tights. She heard the whisper of nylon on nylon. It was not something she ordinarily noticed. Paul's two notes were probably responsible for the sudden sensitivity.

She worked through lunch and into the afternoon, conscious of a rising excitement. Her nipples erected themselves spontaneously several times, and she rubbed them once or twice with a mild pleasure. She felt warm between the thighs too, thinking of Rhonda and Paul. Muriel abruptly decided to leave work early. She was not getting anything done. Leaving Mike in charge, she drove to her favourite mall for a spot of retail therapy. The place was moderately crowded on this Monday afternoon.

She had nothing particularly in mind, and wandered aimlessly through several boutiques without buying anything. On impulse Muriel went into the Victoria's Secret store and bought a lacy garter belt and several pairs of sheer stockings, at the same time denying that her purchase had anything to do with the notes she had received. The garter belt was a dark cherry-red, the stockings sheer and shiny with a reddish tint, like those Rhonda had worn on the last occasion. They had seams up the back, like the ones she remembered her mother wearing. Muriel found herself blushing as she paid for her purchases. She imagined the salesgirl could read her mind. Angry with herself, Muriel left the shop and drove home.

She left her new purchases on the kitchen table and went to her computer. There she set about finding Rhonda's e-mail address. It was an experiment, she told herself. How much trouble had Paul taken to find hers, and what would Rhonda think of an e-message from a woman seeking another appointment so soon after the last? After nearly an hour, she still had no leads in her search. Apparently it was not as easy to find out someone's address as she had thought. Paul had taken considerable trouble to find hers, then. She did not fancy asking Rhonda. *If* she decided to take Paul away from her, she did not want the dominatrix to know of her plan. So when she called the number Rhonda had given her, she intended only to set up another appointment for herself.

Rhonda, however, was not at home. Callers were invited to record a message. Telephone-answering machines annoyed Muriel, especially now when she wanted to have another session very badly, but there was no other choice. Trying not to sound too anxious, or desperate, she asked Rhonda to return her call when she herself returned.

When she had left her message, Muriel suddenly realised that it would be relatively easy to find Paul's address, as well as his telephone number. The note that had arrived that morning lay on the kitchen table, under the bag containing her new lingerie. The postmark was local, and she knew his name. The telephone directory yielded several P. Grahams, as well as several Pauls and Peters. Muriel made a list of the most likely, but was reluctant to call any of them. Even if she hit upon the right one the first time, she could think of no reason for calling that would not make her seem to be pursuing him – especially when she wasn't.

The next morning Muriel put on her new garter belt instead of the usual tights. She rolled the stockings up her legs, smoothing them and straightening the seams with a delicious sense of wickedness. She looked at herself in the mirror, and was startled to see how erotic she looked. Rhonda had looked like this. The sight was almost enough to make her take them off and revert to her usual safe tights, but in the end she did not. As she dressed (including pants), Muriel was nevertheless conscious of the difference her new stockings made. With a last check to see that her seams were straight, she walked out to her car.

At the bank Mike stared at her legs for a moment longer than he usually did. Muriel strove, not entirely successfully, to ignore him and to pretend that there was nothing out of the ordinary. Having followed Paul's suggestion thus far, she felt a glow of excitement as a result. Muriel could not say why. Surely not just the stockings and garter belt? Yet she was conscious of the unaccustomed feel of the straps against her thighs and bottom. She felt the increased freedom without her usual tights. And she rather liked the surreptitious admiring glances from Mike and the other male member of staff. She imagined that they were lusting after her, not an unflattering idea, so long as they remained conscious of their stations. She was the boss and, alluring as she might be, they had to keep their hands off. In short, Muriel was enjoying the role of the tease, albeit in a mild way.

That evening when she returned home, Muriel had an e-mail from Rhonda, to whom she *had* given her address. Rhonda said that she was going to be busy for the next few days, but offered to lend Paul to Muriel if she wanted him instead. Rhonda said that she had been keeping him around the house and that she thought he might enjoy an outing. Rhonda did not say what she and Paul had been doing, and Muriel wondered, with a stirring of jealousy, if they had been fucking while she had been suffering (if that was the right word) mild excitement and frustration at the bank.

Rhonda offered to let her have him either 'safe', with cock-cage and handcuffs, or without. 'Be careful if you choose the latter,' Rhonda warned. 'He usually means business. Remember that he knows what you like.'

Muriel flushed as she remembered Paul watching her being beaten – and obviously enjoying the experience. She also wondered if Paul had got her e-mail address from Rhonda, or even if Rhonda had given it to him between bouts of wild sex and encouraged him to send those messages – looking over his shoulder and urging him on, in fact. Rhonda, she knew, was not bound by normal considerations of privacy or by delicacy of feelings. If she were, she would never have let Paul witness her in the throes of orgasm.

Rhonda might well have kept him in the cock-cage the whole time (Muriel preferred to believe that) while tormenting him by encouraging his fantasies about Muriel. In addition, of course, to frustrating his desires for Rhonda herself. Muriel was uncertain about the offer, and so she delayed giving an answer. It might be interesting to have a male slave around the house for a bit. Muriel had never before considered the idea. Now the thought excited her. If she kept him locked up as Rhonda did, Muriel could enjoy tormenting him with the sight of her while he was unable to do anything without her permission. And she would be able to consider whether she liked him well enough to date him, with a view to further developments. On the other hand, if Paul wore the cock-cage, there would be no fucking for her either. She would reply tomorrow.

On Wednesday morning Muriel woke in a state of mild excitement. This time, as she showered and powdered her body, she considered it from what she thought of as a man's point of view. She scrutinised her breasts for sag, and was pleased to find none. Her stomach was flat and taut, with that small double dome that spoke of well-toned muscles. It sloped away tantalisingly to her pubic mound and the swelling between her legs. Long full legs, narrow waist, widely flaring hips. The body of a mature woman, attractive, youthful, healthy ... eager. Yes. She would take Rhonda's offer. It would be an exciting adventure in her usually workaday life.

She called Rhonda, and was pleased to reach her this time. After the usual pleasantries they got down to the business of delivering Paul. Rhonda, it turned out, was going house-hunting the next day. Would that time do? Yes. Did she want Paul 'safe', or not? Safe, Muriel said with a lurch in her stomach. Rhonda accepted the condition without comment. Did she want the keys to Paul's handcuffs and cock-cage? Muriel hadn't thought about that. She hesitated.

Rhonda noticed her indecision. 'If you like, I'll bring them to the bank. I'll need to pick up a key to your place anyway so I can get him in. You can decide whether to take them home or leave them there, and he won't know what you decide, or whether you even have the keys at all.'

Rhonda's brisk, no-nonsense manner could be encouraging, if somewhat overwhelming. Muriel felt that it would be cowardly to admit any doubts to that decisive woman, and so she agreed. But she had to know one thing: 'How will you get him in without the neighbours seeing?' She broke off in confusion, not wanting to sound like a nervous prude.

'Leave all that to me,' Rhonda told her. 'See you this afternoon.'

She hung up, leaving Muriel wondering if she could go through with it. Too late now, she told herself. Nevertheless her stomach was full of butterflies as she drank her coffee.

Dressing, she decided against wearing stockings with seams. It might appear too much like flaunting herself to her colleagues at the bank. Muriel chose a pair of sheer, shiny black seamless stockings instead.

As she adjusted the garter straps Muriel once again looked at herself in the mirror. Still erotic, she thought with a certain tremulous satisfaction. As if to compensate for the more sensible stockings, she decided to leave the pants off today. No one but she would know. On the other hand, she would be reminded of her pantless condition all day. Maybe I'll take a pair in my purse, she thought, and then rejected the idea. Go the whole way, she told herself. If you're going to have an adventure, then have the whole thing.

She felt quite daring as she drove to the bank. If only the people who saw her could know that she was naked under her prim suit. No one in the streets or at the bank noticed, to her mingled disappointment and relief. Surely, she thought, they could at least see the difference in her demeanour.

The day passed at a snail's pace, to Muriel's distress. She decided a dozen times to call Rhonda and tell her it was all off, and each time her courage failed her. Then it was too late. 'A Ms Rhonda Stuart to see you,' her receptionist announced. 'She doesn't have any appointment. Should I tell her you're engaged?'

'No. I'll see her,' Muriel replied, hoping that Alison would not notice the quaver in her voice. Nervously, she stood to receive her visitor, unconsciously smoothing her skirt and jacket. There was a fine sheen of perspiration on her forehead which she wiped hurriedly with her hand.

Then Rhonda was coming through the door, smiling sardonically at her. She looked over the office curiously. 'So this is where you work. Do they know what you do when you're not on duty?'

The veiled threat shook Muriel. She made shushing motions with her hands, feeling the flush spreading to her face and neck. Her palms felt sweaty.

Rhonda's smile widened. 'No, I suppose not. I don't think it would do any good to tell them you like to be beaten with a whip, so I won't.' She managed to convey that she was doing Muriel a big favour – as she was.

Muriel made more frantic shushing motions.

'No pants today, I see,' Rhonda observed. In response to Muriel's startled look, she explained, 'No VPL.'

Muriel went red as a beet. 'Close the door, please!' she said.

'Do you like the cool air on your tush?' Rhonda asked, making no effort to do so.

Muriel normally felt secure in her office. This was her ground. She was the manager, the boss. Rhonda had taken all that away in less than a minute. She felt like a schoolgirl caught masturbating. Hurrying around the desk, she pushed the door closed, relieved to see that Alison was not in the hallway to overhear Rhonda. Nervously she checked to see that the intercom was turned off as well. Muriel was a nervous wreck, sweaty and flushed. Shakily she made her way to her executive chair and practically fell into it. Her knees were trembling.

Rhonda enjoyed the effect hugely. 'So how's the boss now?' she asked.

Muriel didn't reply. The silence stretched out. If she had known how awful this would be, she would never have agreed to meet Rhonda at the bank. Or anywhere else. She chastised herself. How naive I've been, thinking that it would be simply a matter of exchanging keys, perhaps a civilised cup of coffee and some polite but meaningless conversation. This was dreadful.

At last Rhonda relented. 'Don't worry. Your secret's safe with me.'

Muriel relaxed slightly, still eyeing her visitor warily.

From her purse Rhonda produced a small key ring, which she dropped on to Muriel's desk.

To Muriel, the clink as it hit the blotter sounded like a peal of bells. Everyone in the bank, she was sure, had heard it. And knew what the keys fitted.

'Handcuffs,' Rhonda explained, pointing to a silvery key with internal threads. 'You have to screw this into the hole on each side to release the locks. Unscrewing it locks the cuffs.'

Muriel flushed and looked at the door as if there were ears pressed to it from the outside. She wished that Rhonda would lower her voice.

Rhonda went on in conversational tones. 'These three small ones are for his cock-cage. They all look alike but they aren't. You'll have to try them until you find the right one for each lock. If you plan to let him plough you, that is. If you decide to keep his cock locked up, don't let him know you have the keys. It would be best if I took his clothes away with me. Even if you unlock him, he won't be able to go anywhere – unless you're also a transvestite who enjoys dressing in men's clothes and can lend them to him. Even so, I doubt if anything you might have would fit him.'

Thoroughly alarmed again, Muriel snatched up the key ring and hid the evidence of her perversion in the desk drawer. She made desperate shushing noises.

Rhonda declined to be shushed. 'Are you wearing stockings and suspenders today? I'll bet your tush feels the difference.'

Muriel's blush spoke for her.

'Stand up!' The command was abrupt. Muriel sprang to her feet instinctively.

'Lift your skirt,' Rhonda commanded.

Instead of obeying, Muriel tugged it tightly around her knees, holding it down at the same time.

Rhonda leaned across the desk and slapped her hard across the face, backhand and forehand. 'I said, lift your skirt!'

Her face flaming, from embarrassment as much as from the blows, Muriel slowly tugged her skirt up to mid-thigh. There she stopped, with a pleading look at Rhonda.

'Higher! All the way to your waist.'

Not looking at Rhonda, Muriel bowed her head as she inched the skirt higher, hoping at each moment that the other woman would relent.

Rhonda didn't. When the skirt was up to Muriel's waist, she inspected the bare skin and the enticing folds of her labia. 'Nice stockings,' she commented. 'Now sit down,' she ordered.

Wildly Muriel looked at her, beginning to pull her skirt down.

Once again Rhonda slapped her face. 'Leave it. Bend forward over the desk!'

Muriel looked as if she had not understood a word. This couldn't be happening here in her safe office.

'Bend over your desk,' Rhonda repeated menacingly. 'If I don't see your bottom in the air before I can count to three, I'll call your staff in here to see you. One . . . two . . .'

Reluctantly Muriel bent over her desk.

'Further,' Rhonda commanded. 'Grasp the front of the desk with your hands and hold on tight. Don't let go until I tell you. All right. Now spread your legs apart.' Rhonda lifted her own skirt to reveal her tights and pants – and to emphasise Muriel's nakedness. Slowly she removed her tights and pants while her victim flushed with fear and embarrassment. Rhonda knew that Muriel dared not disobey or cry out for help.

'Open your mouth,' she told her victim.

When she did, Rhonda stuffed her pants deeply into Muriel's mouth, gagging her. Then she picked up a metal ruler from the desktop.

'I imagine you can guess what this is for.'

Muriel shook her head wildly, no! This wasn't happening, not here in her own private office.

'Be still,' Rhonda commanded. She moved around until she stood behind her demoralised victim.

Muriel looked over her shoulder at her tormentor, pleading wordlessly for this to stop. 'Nnnnnngh!' she said.

Rhonda raised the metal ruler and struck Muriel across her bare bottom.

The hapless woman jerked erect and reached around with both hands to protect herself from further blows. The ruler cracked against her knuckles with agonising results.

'Hands on the desk!' Rhonda hissed at her. 'If you move again I'll tie you across the desk and beat you until you are red. And I'll leave you here for your staff to find.'

It was this last threat that broke Muriel's resistance. Tears streaming down her face, she bent over the desk and gripped the front edge so tightly her knuckles whitened. She hunched her shoulders and bowed her head as she braced for the next blow.

Rhonda beat her for what seemed like an eternity while she fought for breath and tried to remain quiet. Being seen by her staff was unthinkable. Muriel's head swam as her abused bottom went from white to red. It felt as if it were on fire when Rhonda finally stopped. Muriel couldn't believe the beating was over. For long minutes she gripped her desk, legs spread apart, shoulders hunched, tears streaming from her eyes. When she looked up at last, Rhonda once more stood in front of the desk. She hadn't heard or seen her move.

Rhonda laid the ruler on the desk and retrieved her panties from Muriel's gaping mouth. Calmly she put them back on, pulled on her tights and rearranged her skirt before sitting down in the visitor's chair.

'You can sit down now,' Rhonda told her victim. 'No. Leave your skirt as it is,' she added as Muriel made to cover herself.

The chair felt icy against her burning bottom. Her head was whirling. No one had ever assaulted her like that before, or made her do such outrageous things. Worse was to come, she knew.

'Spread your legs and play with yourself while we finish the arrangements,' Rhonda commanded.

Muriel looked at her incredulously. 'No, please, no,' she whimpered.

Rhonda rested a forefinger on the intercom. 'Shall I send for Alison so that she can take down my directions and read them back to you? You don't seem to understand what I want you to do.'

Wildly Muriel grasped the finger and pushed it away from the intercom. Her other hand disappeared between her legs as she shifted in the chair. She began to rub her labia while looking appealingly for signs of relenting.

Rhonda was relentless. 'That's it. When you start to get wet, you can slide your finger inside and tease your clitoris until you come. I imagine you'll be able to have quite a few satisfactory orgasms while we chat.'

Muriel doubted it, but she had no will to resist. Her bottom was still afire, and she had no desire to attract any more punishment. Nevertheless the stimulation of her sex had the usual effect. She relaxed gradually. She slid back in her chair and spread her thighs wide as she probed herself under the amused gaze of her tormentor.

Rhonda watched non-committally for long minutes, until she was satisfied that Muriel was becoming aroused. Then she went on with the conversation despite Muriel's obvious distress and embarrassment. 'I need a key to your door so I can slip him in. I just hope no one sees us. Handcuffs are so hard to explain convincingly.'

'In my purse,' Muriel said, her voice shaking. 'Take . . . the key ring. The brass key with the round he . . . he . . . head,' she gasped as the first signs of an orgasm made themselves felt in her belly.

'Shall I leave it under the mat when Paul is safely inside?'

'N . . . no,' Muriel stammered. 'Keep it. I . . . I have another.'

'Ah, then you might find me waiting for you one day when you come home from a hard day in the money-mines. Would you like that? I can bring along a nice riding crop to lash you with.'

Muriel made a strangled sound of protest. It was one thing to visit Rhonda's apartment for bondage and torture. It was quite another to talk of those same things in this antiseptic office. The protest became a groan as her finger slid inside her wet cunt to rub her clit.

'Ah, that's what I like to see,' Rhonda remarked, 'a woman who enjoys her work.'

Muriel's eyes slowly unfocused. She seemed oblivious to her visitor. A moan of pleasure escaped her, and then another, longer one. She shuddered with her first orgasm. When the first spasm had passed, she continued until the next. And the one after that. The office faded, became a private place of pleasure, all thoughts of work forgotten as she surrendered to her body's needs. Time stood still, though Muriel didn't.

Grasping her engorged clit between thumb and forefinger, she drove herself to orgasm again and again. The pain from her bottom became entangled with the pleasure from her belly. She was in a haze of lust in her own office. As she imagined Rhonda waiting for her with a riding crop, Muriel cried out with the ecstasy of her release.

A moment later the intercom buzzed. It was Alison. 'Are you all right, Miss? I heard a strange noise from your office.'

Muriel's head jerked up even as her body shook with her orgasm. 'Oh, God,' she gasped. She reached for the intercom switch, thinking furiously of a plausible explanation. Her hand stilled as she fought for control. 'I closed a desk drawer on my finger, Alison. That's all. I . . . I'm all right.'

Rhonda came around behind the desk while the conversation went on. She slid her own finger into Muriel's cunt and began to knead and rub the swollen clitoris.

Muriel struggled wildly for control, trying to force Rhonda's hand away so she could deal with the outside world.

Alison was still there. 'Are you sure? It sounded like something serious.'

'What could be more serious than pleasure?' Rhonda murmured sotto voce.

Alison was asking, 'Shall I come in?' as the next orgasm struck her boss.

'N . . . no. I'm all *right*,' Muriel insisted desperately, still trying to push Rhonda away.

Rhonda hung on doggedly despite the struggles of the other woman.

'Only, you've an appointment in fifteen minutes with Mr Armitage about a loan. I just thought I'd remind you.'

'Call him and ask him if he could make that thirty minutes, would you? I . . . I need more time to get things prepared.' Muriel hoped the lie would do. She was normally prepared long before any interview.

Alison clicked off as Muriel shuddered again under Rhonda's hand.

'Please, Rhonda, please don't make me do this. I've got to carry on as normal. I want to see you again. I want you to beat me and make me come, but not now, please!'

'Like this, you mean?' Rhonda squeezed Muriel's clitoris, smiling as the other woman came again with a groan and a shudder. But at the end of that one she did finally stop. She went back to her chair and watched as Muriel slowly recovered from her ordeal by pain and pleasure.

The intercom buzzed again. 'Mr Armitage says he's running late too, so he'll be by in a half-hour.' Alison still sounded worried. 'You're sure you're all right?'

'Fine,' Muriel replied.

She stood to pull down her skirt.

Rhonda told her to leave it as it was.

'Rhonda, I can't see a client like this!'

'Why not? Your desk has a modesty board,' she said, referring to the panel that stretched across the front of Muriel's desk from side to side and reached nearly to the floor. 'Wouldn't it be thrilling to interview a client with your skirt around your waist? I'm sure you could carry it off.'

'No, I couldn't,' Muriel insisted. 'Please let me get dressed.'

Rhonda produced two lengths of chain, two padlocks and two dildoes from her purse. 'All right,' she told Muriel. 'You can get dressed as soon as I've put these into you.'

Muriel went pale, shaking her head. 'The interview,' she said faintly.

Rhonda dug more deeply into her purse and came up with a small coil of thin nylon cord. 'Shall I leave you tied up here for the staff – or your Mr Armitage – to find?' Rhonda looked determined to carry out her threat. 'I could leave a note on your desk. Something along the lines of not interrupting the boss when she is having fun. I could say you asked me to tie you up and leave you here.'

Muriel went pale at the prospect. She gave in – as, she realised, both she and Paul had been doing all along with Rhonda. The woman was impossible to resist. 'No. Don't do that.'

'That's better,' Rhonda told her. 'This won't take long, and I know you'll enjoy the experience once you get used to it. Stand up now and come over here,' she commanded.

In a daze Muriel moved around her desk. She had used it so often as a barrier to hide behind. Now she felt defenceless.

Rhonda passed one length of chain through an enlarged ring on the other piece. Muriel saw that there was a similar ring each end of the chain. Next Rhonda locked the second length of chain around her waist. It fitted her tightly, and Muriel knew that she would be unable to slide it off over her hips. Dazedly she heard Rhonda's command to bend over and grasp her ankles, and dazedly she obeyed, looking fearfully over her shoulder.

In that awkward position Muriel was unable to prevent what happened next. Rhonda slid one of the dildoes into her cunt. She gasped as she felt the touch of it inside her and on her clitoris. She clenched her teeth on a whimper as she felt her body's response. She should have been worn out, but she knew that it would not take much to push her shuddering and screaming over the edge once again.

Rhonda withdrew the dildo, and pushed it against her anus. Muriel gasped, 'No!' as it slid past her anal sphincter, but Rhonda pushed it all the way home.

Muriel tried desperately to expel it. She had never felt so full back there. It felt terribly ... strange. Uncomfortable too.

Rhonda slapped her hands away when she tried to pull it out.

'Hold on to your ankles, or I'll tie your hands behind your back and leave you.'

Muriel grasped her ankles obediently. The second dildo, much larger than the first, slid into her wet cunt without any trouble. Once again Muriel groaned as she felt its girth and weight inside her. As the shaft rubbed on her clitoris she bit back a moan of pleasure.

But Rhonda had not finished yet. Threading the chain dangling between Muriel's thighs through rings on the base of each dildo, she locked it to the back of the waist chain with the second padlock, leaving Muriel plugged front and back and unable to remove the dildoes.

'Now you can get dressed,' Rhonda told her.

Muriel released her ankles and stood erect, the dildo shifting inside her and producing a pleasant friction. The one up her anus felt uncomfortable but not painful.

'Rhonda, I can't see anyone with these ... things inside me. Please take them out!'

Rhonda shook her head. 'You'll get used to them. I predict you'll even like them. Anyway, they stay in until you go home. I'll leave you now and get Paul settled at your place. You clean up and finish your day's work and go on home. See what develops. I'll see you both in two days' time. Have fun.'

'How can I have fun with these plugs inside me?'

Rhonda looked sharply at her. Muriel blushed. She realised that she had virtually confessed to wanting to have sex with Paul.

'How can you not?' Rhonda countered. 'But I'll leave the keys to you at your place. You can get loose as soon as you get home. Unless, of course, you learn to like being plugged in the meantime.'

Rhonda left with a smile. Muriel inspected the new internal arrangements and concluded that she could do nothing until she got home. With shaking hands she pulled down her skirt and smoothed the wrinkles as best she could. She went into her private wash-room to repair the damage to her make-up and hair. Refreshed, but acutely aware of her own internal arrangements, Muriel sat down in her chair. She shot to her feet as the dildo in her anus was shoved deeply into her. But she had to sit down. Interviews were always conducted that way. It would be awkward if she stood. She tried again, easing herself into the chair. Once again the anal dildo made itself felt, but she settled herself in as best she could.

She felt as if she had to shit, but knew she didn't have to. She squirmed on the chair, feeling awkward and full. The dildo inside her cunt shifted, rubbing her clit and producing the most disturbing sensations from her crotch. Muriel shifted again, and this time she had to bite back a groan of pleasure. No, she told herself, this won't do. She tried to find a neutral position as she prepared herself for the coming interview. There didn't seem to be one. The anal dildo stabbed her however she sat, and the one in her cunt stimulated her clitoris whenever she moved. It was a devilishly clever arrangement, and at any other time she would probably have appreciated it. She imagined herself alone, bound and gagged and stuffed as she was. That would be interesting. She guessed that she would be heaving and groaning and coming. Just now, however, there was the interview to get through. She hoped she could control herself until she could get away.

Mr Armitage, when he came, didn't seem to notice anything out of the ordinary. Muriel was exercising every ounce of her self-control to keep him from guessing that there *was* anything out of the ordinary. It made for a certain vagueness on her part, a preoccupation with internal matters when she should have been paying attention to the details of her client's proposals. She got through the interview somehow, grateful that this was only a preliminary to the final negotiations. It was a relief to get to her feet and see her visitor out. She didn't sit down again.

Alison, blonde, young, pretty, asked with concern about her finger. Muriel assured her with a rueful smile that she would live. The routine of closing time prevented further enquiry. Muriel walked to her car, conscious of her internal condition every step of the way. She had calmed down somewhat. The vaginal dildo no longer threatened to make her come with each movement, but it was definitely there, and she knew that if she concentrated on it she would have a hard time avoiding a public display of her arousal. The anal dildo was the real problem. As soon as she got into her car it stabbed her in the rear. Driving would require all her concentration.

She waved goodbye to Alison and Mike Barrett and drove out into the evening traffic. It seemed slower than ever. And then there was Paul waiting for her at home. Muriel half-hoped that Rhonda had been unable to get him into the apartment, or had changed her mind and taken him away with her.

Muriel drove to the nearest supermarket. She was low on food at home, and now there would be two mouths to feed. She parked and got out, stabbed by her dildoes with every step she took. She was sufficiently accustomed to the new situation now to experience a thrill of pleasure as the secret plugs moved inside her. Muriel glanced at the other women shoppers with a certain pity. She was reasonably sure that they had no such delicious secrets inside their bodies. She felt the signs of arousal and strove to ignore them. Food. Think of food. Don't think of . . . She whimpered softly as the interior fireworks moved a step closer. 'Nooo,' she moaned softly, 'not here, please, not here.'

She had no idea that she had spoken aloud, nor that anyone had heard her plea to her body, until a woman touched her arm and asked if she was all right. 'You sounded as if something hurt you,' her unknown interlocutor said.

Muriel blushed even as she reassured the concerned woman that she was bursting for a pee and was heading for the toilet.

'Oh,' she said, relieved. She explained to Muriel where the toilets were while Muriel teetered on the edge of an orgasm, wishing the other woman would just go away. Muriel almost screamed to her to leave her alone, just to go, but managed to look nearly normal. Eventually the woman stopped talking and left. Muriel was thankful to be let alone, but shopping looked like being an ordeal. Her body was going on about its subversive business, and she knew where that would end. The knowledge brought the moment closer. As she walked Muriel strove to keep her knees from buckling. The tide overtook her as she passed the fruit and vegetable counters. All those long phallic things reminded her vividly of her own phallic things. She clamped her lips together and shook with the waves of pleasure that swept through her body.

76

When she could, Muriel looked around to see if anyone had noticed her public orgasm. The shopping public seemed oblivious to her predicament. When she tried to walk on again, the familiar signs grew stronger.

She knew that she would never get the shopping done as she was. Muriel abandoned her cart and fled back to the parking lot, the dildoes stabbing her at every movement. The faster she walked the more her hips swung, and that exacerbated the problem. When she reached her car, Muriel could barely unlock it, so violently were her hands shaking. She dropped the keys and swore as she stooped to pick them up. On her hands and knees, the rough concrete biting into her knees through her stockings, she scrabbled under the car. And as she scrabbled, she came. This time she could not stifle the moan of pleasure as her body shuddered. Finally the wave passed, leaving her shaking and sweating.

The keys! She rose on shaky legs to unlock the driver's door and fell gratefully into the seat. The anal dildo made itself felt at once as she struggled to get her feet and legs inside her car. This time, the discomfort aroused her. In her present state, she realised, almost anything would arouse her. Muriel concentrated on getting the key into the ignition switch without dropping it. She started the car, and drove off with a screech of tyres as another orgasm shook her.

Alone inside the air-conditioned car, with the windows up, she could give vent to her feelings. Muriel moaned and swore. Rhonda had found exactly the right way to torture her – if torture was the right word for the pleasure that shook her all the way home.

5

Muriel and Paul

Muriel parked and hurriedly walked to her front door, anxious to get out of public view. She clung grimly to the keys, knowing what would happen if she dropped them again. And it did indeed happen as she struggled to open her front door, so that she entered her apartment with yet another orgasm shaking her body and her wits. She practically fell through the door, before pushing it closed and leaning against it as the climax racked her body. She was pale, sweating and badly shaken when her eyes focused again.

Paul was sitting on the sofa, watching her closely. 'I see that Rhonda left you with something to remember her by. I do hope that your trip home was enjoyable.'

'Enjoyable!' But in its way it had been. Muriel had to concede that the secret plugs and her public orgasms had been remarkably pleasurable – now that she was home safely. She looked at Paul.

He was naked, as Rhonda had promised. His wrists were held behind his back in handcuffs, and the cock-cage was locked in place, exactly as Muriel remembered it. But she suddenly realised that she had left *his* keys in her desk drawer at the bank in her hurry to escape the scene of her embarrassment. When she told Paul, he looked gravely at her.

'I'll have to go back to the bank and get them.'

'I see,' was all he said.

'First I have to get these things out of me.' Muriel staggered to the kitchen in search of her own release keys, saying over her shoulder to Paul that she would make coffee for them. She didn't want him to see her struggles to unlock and unplug herself. He was virtually a stranger, and she wondered how she had ever agreed to let Rhonda board him with her for the interim. But just then she had to get herself unplugged – before she had another orgasm. She felt weak and sweaty from the ones she had already had, worn out as if she had done a hard day's physical labour.

There were no keys in evidence. Muriel had expected them to be lying in plain view. She began to open drawers, the dildoes shifting inside her with each movement and threatening her with yet more in the way of internal fireworks. There was sweat on her forehead and dampness under her arms. There was wetness of another sort between her legs. Where were the keys? Muriel was dismayed at the thought that Rhonda might have taken them with her. In view of what had happened at the bank, it was not all that unlikely. She might even now be laughing at the idea of the two of them struggling through the next two days in enforced propinquity and total chastity.

Well, at least not total chastity. She had no doubt that the dildoes would keep her in a state of imminent arousal – when they were not actually driving her over the screaming edge of orgasm. Or did one become used to going around in public and private with both openings tightly plugged? She partly hoped, partly doubted it. Forty-eight hours of sexual orgasms was a daunting prospect. She would have to stay at home. She would never be able to control herself in public and, when she cracked, positively *everyone* would know her secret. She had never had such a series of shattering orgasms so close together. She would be exhausted if this went on for the next two days. And it would, if there were no keys.

The coffee percolator signalled that she had been searching for at least ten minutes without success. With trembling hands, Muriel poured two cups of coffee. In a shaky voice, she called through to Paul, 'Sugar and milk?'

'Both,' he said. 'Two sugars, please.'

The polite ritual seemed bizarre in the light of their joint predicament. Muriel carried the coffee things through on a tray, acutely conscious of how close she was to losing control again.

She held the cup for Paul to drink, and then took a sip from her own. 'I can't find the keys to my ... chastity belt,' she said with an attempt at lightness which she was far from feeling. 'Do you think Rhonda took them away for a joke? Did she say anything to you before she left?'

'No, but she did go through the apartment as if inspecting it. She likes to know everything about her ... associates. It gives her a sense of power over their lives if she knows where the dirty linen – or lingerie – is kept. And she's probably right about that. It's harder to resist someone who knows all about you. The keys could be literally anywhere. Look in the bedroom,' he advised.

Muriel drank some more of her coffee, and offered more to Paul, before she spoke again. 'Come ... with me,' she asked.

Paul smiled. 'Are you afraid the dragon lady is waiting to pounce on you?'

'It's no joke!' Muriel burst out. 'I feel as I'm going to lose control of myself ... my body ... at any

80

moment. I have to go out sometime. I can't stay at home the whole time, and I can't go out in public like this. And don't grin like that! It's not funny.' Her voice was shrill.

With a shrug Paul indicated his own condition. 'I was hoping for a wild day or so with you myself. I didn't expect this.'

Muriel felt the tears start. Angrily, she shook her head. She realised that she too had already accepted the possibility of sex with him. Why else allow Rhonda to leave him with her? He seemed to have read her mind, and she didn't like to admit the accuracy of his insight.

'Come along,' she told him as she headed for the bedroom.

Behind her Paul got awkwardly to his feet to follow. 'What did Rhonda do to you?'

As she searched, Muriel told him of her humiliation at the bank. 'Nearly the whole staff must be laughing at me now!'

'I don't think so. Only Alison heard anything, and that wasn't much by your account. And Rhonda is usually careful not to expose her ... associates. She's not that kind of sadist, though she is very good at making people suffer in other ways – as we both know.'

His assessment comforted her. Curiously she asked, 'Did she keep you ... like this ... the whole time?'

'Pretty much,' he admitted, 'though she did let me out now and again for, er, some exercise.'

Muriel looked sharply at him.

'Well, Rhonda is not exactly a chaste woman,' he replied to her unspoken question.

Muriel had to smile. 'And you're not exactly a chaste man either, are you?'

81

'Only when I have to be,' Paul replied, with a nod towards his cock-cage. 'I was sort of hoping to be unchaste with you.'

This affirmation of his desire for her made Muriel feel better. 'Why do you let her do these things to you?'

'Rhonda is not very resistible, as you've just found out. In theory you could have yelled for help when she threatened you with the ruler. Why did *you* submit to her?'

'Because I didn't want my whole staff to see the boss with her skirt around her hips and her ... private parts ... on show.' Muriel paused, and then went on with the real reason. 'And because I need sex with bondage and pain – just the sort of thing Rhonda is so good at.'

'Exactly. I like what she does too – and allows me to do – as a change from my usual sex practices. There are lots of people like us, but they dare not admit their desires – for much the same reasons as you were reluctant to yell for help at the bank.'

Muriel had been searching her chest of drawers without success for the keys to her chastity belt. There was no sign of them in the bedroom. She had already searched the kitchen. There was only the bathroom left.

Paul followed her as she led the way. In the bathroom she found the keys. They were in the toilet – a toilet whose water was distinctly yellow. She dared not flush Rhonda's urine away for fear of washing the keys away at the same time. Wrinkling her nose in disgust, Muriel fished them out and then rinsed and washed them in the basin before applying them to her locks. She raised her skirt to her waist as Rhonda had made her do earlier and unlocked the waist belt. It was not easy, as Rhonda had placed the locks behind her back. Eventually she got the first lock open. She was about to pluck the dildoes from her cunt and anus when she realised that Paul was watching with interest.

She looked up in annoyance. 'Go away! Haven't you any decency?'

'Not much,' he admitted. 'And you don't make it any easier when you're so prettily indecent. I like the stockings and garter belt. And the legs. And the rest.'

Muriel said no more, concentrating on extracting the dildo from her anus. It resisted, as if her body had accommodated itself to its presence. She grimaced as it came out, smelling strongly of shit. There were brown streaks all over the rubber shaft. Muriel dropped it into the basin with disgust. The other dildo slid out more easily. Its removal left her feeling distinctly empty – but more in control. She pulled her skirt down and washed the dildoes, then her hands.

'I'll have to go back for the keys now. I'm afraid you'll have to wait until I get back. Is there anything I can do for you before I go?'

Paul said no, and Muriel locked the door as she left. The drive back to the bank was uneventful. The keys were in her desk drawer. Muriel looked around the scene of her subjugation with different eyes, knowing that the place would never be the same again. Her sanctuary had been violated. She took the keys and locked up again. This time, when she stopped at the all-night supermarket, she was able to shop without losing control. As she shopped, Muriel realised that she was delaying her return home, where she would have to deal with Paul. She shook herself mentally and finished the task.

Paul was waiting as before on the sofa. Without any ceremony Muriel unlocked his handcuffs and cock-cage.

'Thank you,' he said when he was free.

There were red marks on his cock and balls where the cage had pressed against his skin. 'Does it . . . hurt?' she asked.

He shrugged it off. 'Only when I see a pretty woman.'

'Let's make supper, then,' Muriel said, hoping to establish some sort of normality in their bizarre situation.

'Only if you take off your clothes too. It's hardly fair, is it, if you keep them on.'

'Certainly not!' Muriel's reaction was instinctive. After a moment's consideration she concluded that false modesty was undignified. Silently she began to undress. It was the defining moment in their relationship. She had accepted him as her lover-to-be, or lover-on-trial.

'Leave the stockings and garter belt, please. I like the look.'

Muriel remembered the stockings and garter belt Rhonda had worn throughout her own ordeal. She guessed that they had been mostly for Paul's benefit – a small concession to his desire when he could do nothing about the otherwise naked woman who controlled him.

Dressed in nothing but the stockings and garter belt, Muriel cooked steaks and French fries while Paul set the table and made the salad. It was companionable if bizarre. She rationalised her sudden intimacy with Paul, a relative stranger, as a sort of rebellion against Rhonda and what she had done that day. Muriel had no intention of not seeing Rhonda again. She knew of no one else who would give her the dose of pain and ecstasy she needed.

As they ate, they exchanged concise life stories. Paul, it turned out, was wealthy and did not have to work every day. He did not say exactly how he had achieved this enviable status. It explained why he was free to indulge his own taste for domination for a week or two whenever he felt like it. Muriel, essentially one of the working classes, found herself vaguely resenting his independence even while she envied it. What might she do if she were free to see Rhonda for a whole week – or longer? The idea excited her. She asked him what he did when he was not letting Rhonda control his life.

'I enslave young women in my turn whenever I find a willing one. What else would a civilised man do?'

Muriel's heart felt as if it were being squeezed. She had dreamed so often of finding someone – some man, that is – like Paul, while at the same time she had feared letting any man have that kind of power over her. And now here he was. But she said nothing. Later, she told herself. When I know him better. Then her common sense told her that he already knew of her penchant for bizarre sex. He had seen her with Rhonda. He knew what had happened to her that very day. And he knew that she had been excited by both experiences. She flushed all over.

'And would you like to . . . enslave me?' she asked in a shaking voice.

'Well, I *am* between slaves, as it were. But the important question is, would *you* like to be enslaved?'

Muriel was silent while her heart pounded so loudly in her own ears that she wondered he did not hear it across the table. 'I . . . I don't know.' She felt as if she were choking on excitement.

'Well, let me know when you do,' he replied. 'In the meantime we can enjoy the two days Rhonda has granted us. Did you know that she left a bag of her own equipment in the hall in case we wanted something more bizarre than the missionary position?'

'I was . . . rather preoccupied when I got here. Do you know what's there?'

'Not exactly, but my experience with Rhonda suggests it would shock the neighbours if they knew. So we won't tell them.'

Muriel nodded thoughtfully. Suddenly she dropped the thought of delaying the inevitable any longer. 'Coffee, tea or me?' she asked with a boldness she did not entirely feel.

'What would you do if I chose coffee?' Paul asked with a grin.

'I'd kill you,' she retorted, matching his grin. She rose from the table and held out her hand. When he took it she led him towards the bedroom.

6

The Day After

The next morning, dressing for work, Muriel felt
deliciously wicked. And sated. Paul still lay in bed,
watching her as she chose one of her prim suits from
the wardrobe.

'I'll cook tonight,' he offered.

'You don't have to,' she told him, 'but that would
be nice.'

'I need something to do. It will be a long day when
I can't go anywhere.'

'Did you find the day long when you were waiting
for Rhonda to come home?' It was a loaded question,
she knew, but could not stop herself from wondering,
from wanting to compare herself to his other woman
– or women.

When he shook his head, Muriel felt a flash of
jealousy which, she realised, was unjustified. She had
just met him, just admitted him to intimacy. She had
no right to expect him to say that after one night with
her (during which they had done several things which
would have shocked at least the missionaries) he had
forgotten his former lovers. *She* had not forsworn
Rhonda. She should not expect him to do so. But
logic and fairness were no match for the surprising
jealousy she still felt. With resolution she vowed not
to let it show – if she could.

'I'll have a surprise for you when you get back. When do you usually get home from work?'

With a sudden access of frankness, Muriel told him, 'Usually about six o'clock, but I'll try to make it sooner today.'

'Good. Just to remind yourself of this evening all day, why don't you wear those stockings with the seams today? I'd like to think of you wearing them.'

Muriel put the stockings on, conscious of him watching as she smoothed them up her legs and straightened the seams. She snapped the garters to the stocking tops. She didn't wear any pants. Yesterday had been decisive. She looked up for his reaction.

'Too bad you have to wear anything else,' Paul told her. She sat on the side of the bed and leaned across to kiss him. The kiss grew hands and tongues, threatening to make her late. Reluctantly she drew back to finish dressing and put on her make-up. Even with her former occasional lovers she had never let them see her repairing the damages of the previous night. It gave her a curious sense of intimacy with him. As she left, Muriel felt positively light-hearted, eager for the day, as well as for the coming evening. The feeling persisted through the day. Mike's occasional lingering looks at her legs cheered her up too. Only in her office did she feel a lessening of the sense of well-being – until she reflected that this was the sort of thing that Rhonda could do again whenever she wished. And I'll learn to like that too, Muriel admitted to herself with a flush of excitement. Alone in her sanctuary, she imagined herself tied to her chair awaiting punishment from Rhonda. Or Paul. He had asked her about enslavement. Should she let him have all of her? Flushes and flutterings and anticipations made the day fly by for her.

And at the end of the day, alone in her private washroom just prior to locking up for the night,

Muriel again repaired her make-up – for Paul, she realised with a flush of excitement. She lifted her skirt, unsnapped the garters from her stockings and straightened the seams before going back to her place and to Paul. Satisfied that she looked as attractive as possible, she collected her car for the drive home.

The apartment to which she had returned alone every day had a new air. It was definitely occupied. The smells and the feel were different. Paul was cooking. When he heard her come in he emerged from the kitchen wearing one of her aprons. Muriel smiled at the incongruity of a man in an apron. A man, moreover, who had an erection. It was flattering to think that it was a response to her arrival.

He advanced to plant a quick kiss on her mouth. 'Hard day at the office, dear?' he asked with a smile.

Muriel too smiled at the inversion of the traditional roles, although her own career plans were emphatically not limited to cooking and keeping house.

'Go and get erotic while I finish the supper,' he said as he returned to the kitchen.

Paul had moved the pile of 'equipment' that Rhonda had left for their mutual pleasure to the bedroom. Her heart beat faster when she saw the riding crop. Drawn irresistibly, she picked it up and swung it experimentally, getting the feel of it, its heft and suppleness. Her chest tightened and her breath grew short as she imagined it landing on her exposed and helpless body. Rhonda had included rope and an unusual inflatable ball that Muriel thought might be a gag. It fitted into her mouth, and when she gave the attached pump a squeeze or two, it swelled alarmingly, forcing her jaws apart and trapping her tongue beneath it. She released the pressure and removed the thing. There were handcuffs and leg-irons. Chain restraints of several sorts. Yesterday's chastity belt and dildoes were there, as was a leather helmet that would cover a person's entire head and face. Muriel was fascinated as she went through the pile. Paul might want to use this stuff on *her*.

And she might . . . want him to. She undressed down to her stockings and garter belt, glancing again at the collection on the bed. What all the best-dressed slaves wore, she thought, and felt her heart lurch. Muriel started for the door, and then turned back, seized by a sudden impulse. From the collection she selected a pair of leg-irons for examination. Unlike the handcuffs Paul had worn, these were adjustable to fit ankles of various sizes. Hers, for instance. She stooped to close them snugly around her ankles, regarding herself in the mirror on the wardrobe door. Not bad, she thought. Exciting, in fact. The next obvious step was handcuffs. She chose a pair that were the twins of the leg-irons, only smaller, obviously intended for wrists. Hers, for instance. Muriel locked one of the cuffs snugly around her right wrist. She was about to secure the other when she changed her mind. She brought her hands behind her back and fumbled the open cuff around her left wrist. When it closed, she was helpless.

Just how helpless was brought home to her when she tried to open the bedroom door. In the end she had to turn her back to it before she could grasp the knob properly. She walked through her familiar sitting room wearing the unfamiliar manacles, feeling an unfamiliar but rather pleasant excitement.

In the kitchen Paul was busy at the stove and so did not at first notice her. When he did, he smiled broadly and came to take her in his arms. The kiss grew hands again – his, of course. Muriel was shaken by the touch of his hands on her helpless but obviously eager body. His erection poked rudely into her belly through the apron.

'You've decided, then?' he asked, when the kiss at last ended.

'I'm . . . still thinking about it,' Muriel temporised. 'We'll see.'

'All right.' Paul returned to the stove to put the meal on the table. 'I'll feed you while you think it over. Sit down.' He held a chair for her.

Her wrists felt uncomfortable, trapped between her back and the back of the chair. Paul deftly lifted them over the chair back and arranged them so that they dangled behind it.

'Better?' he asked.

She nodded.

'It takes some getting used to,' he told her.

She nodded again, barely trusting her voice not to betray her excitement.

He set the table. Muriel watched. It was bizarre, being waited on by a man while she herself was helpless. Paul had prepared a meal of chilli con carne and baked potatoes. There was a tossed salad of lettuce, tomatoes, spring onions and grated cheese. There was wine, too, one of the few bottles she kept around the house for those special occasions that never seemed to occur. This seemed to be one of them. He had set candles on the table, a romantic touch she appreciated when he lit them and turned out the lights. The candle-light on bare skin, his and hers, was seductive. This was seduction, although who was seducing whom was not clear.

Paul fed her and himself. The food was delicious – or was it simply the atmosphere of eroticism that made it so? For this was an erotic scene: helpless naked woman being fed by helpful naked man. Soft light, good wine, no visitors expected, bedroom handy. Muriel relaxed and let it flow over her, discovering that, in handing herself over to Paul (at

91

least for the evening, she insisted to herself), she had to allow him to do everything for her. To her, as well, she realised with a shiver. But that would come later.

Not too much later, some different part of her said. She did not want to be given too much time to change her mind and retreat to her former mode of existence. At least I'll see where this leads, she told herself, reflecting wryly that Eve might have said something similar on the first night.

The meal over, Muriel suggested with a flush of excitement that he stack the dishes in the sink: 'First things first,' she added.

'And you're the first thing?'

Muriel nodded, struggling to her feet and heading for the living room. A few minutes of fondling would be nice in the way of foreplay. So long as he wasn't just after her body – nice though that might be for a start.

Paul followed. When she made to sit on the sofa, he stopped her by taking her arm and pulled her towards the bedroom.

Muriel noticed that the flagpole was up. He obviously wanted her body, but she did not resist the bedward course as much as her mother might have wished. And how might her mother have reacted to her preference for bondage and pain with her sex? Shock and horror would best describe it.

Paul had her sit on the side of the bed. He sat beside her and took one of her breasts in his hand. He bent to kiss the nipple.

'Ummmm,' Muriel sighed. The handcuffs kept her from participating any more actively in what she knew would end with sex. Wild, abandoned sex, she hoped, all inhibitions cast aside.

Paul was using his teeth and tongue on her nipple, and Muriel surrendered herself wholly to the sensations flooding through her. Her cunt grew wet and her legs parted. Paul got up and knelt between her thighs, never removing his mouth from her breast. His hands stroked her thighs through the sheer nylon stockings. The sensation was quite erotic. She was glad she had adopted stockings and garter belt – and left her pants off. So much less trouble getting down to business, she thought as she teetered on the brink of orgasm. Muriel would have liked to stroke his erect cock, but the handcuffs prevented her. She tugged restlessly at the steel bracelets, moaning in pleasure and frustration. She had never been helpless with a man because of her fear of what might happen, but she was finding this occasion more pleasurable (and less fearful) than she had imagined. When Paul switched his mouth to her cunt, Muriel whimpered with eager response. His hands stroked her thighs and legs while his tongue and teeth stimulated her labia. And then his teeth found her engorged clitoris.

Muriel bit back a scream, shuddering with pleasure. Her next orgasm destroyed her control. Her scream rang through the apartment, and she didn't care who heard her. 'Oh, God, Paul. Come inside me now. Please!' She realised that she was begging him to fuck her, but she didn't care about that either. Paul rose and lay down on the bed on his back. His cock stood up and Muriel stared at the instrument of her impalement with a quivering eagerness. She stood on shaky legs and awkwardly lay beside him. He reached over and pulled her above him. His legs went between hers, trapping the chain that joined her ankles beneath them. He helped her to sit up and then to kneel astride him while he guided his cock into her. Then he made her lie fully above him, impaled, her breasts and nipples pressed against his chest. With her hands held behind her back Muriel's full weight lay on him, and she groaned as she felt him stir inside her. Her breasts flattened against him.

Paul reached around her to hold her handcuffed wrists with one hand. His other arm went around her waist and pulled her tightly against him, his cock fully inside her now.

Muriel screamed again, all control lost as she struggled for yet more penetration, wriggling her hips and trying to rise and fall so as to make his cock slide in and out of her.

Paul caught her rhythm, and they rose and fell together, his cock gliding into her deeply on the upstroke. Muriel thought she would pass out. Grimly she fought to remain aware of what was happening between her legs and in her belly – and found the task much easier than she had imagined. Being helpless for the first time drove her wild. Muriel screamed and moaned as he fucked her. She pulled at her chains, stimulated even more by her complete helplessness. She was completely under the control of this man whose cock impaled her so deliciously.

Muriel passed out when she felt him spending inside her.

When she awoke, still impaled, her hands still chained behind her back, she didn't at first know where she was or what had happened to her. She opened her eyes, saw Paul lying beneath her and sighed with pleasure as her memory came back. 'No one ever made me pass out before,' she told him in a soft whisper. 'Thank you.' She kissed him on the mouth, relishing the handless kiss and the cock inside her.

'Rhonda did,' he reminded her.

'Well, no *man* ever did,' she retorted. 'Stop fishing for compliments.'

Paul raised and lowered his hips experimentally – more of a question than an invitation.

Muriel responded by moving her own hips. She sighed as his cock slid back into her.

Agreement reached, Paul began slowly to arouse her again. There was no foreplay. He held her atop him as before, one arm around her narrow waist, his other hand clasping her manacled hands. Muriel found the latter exciting. It reminded her of her helplessness, and that turned her on again. They fucked slowly, rocking now where earlier it had been more like riding a bucking horse.

Muriel whimpered with the first climax. She closed her eyes and laid her head on his shoulder. He brought her to climax again. She couldn't spread her legs any further because of the leg-irons, but she imagined herself staked out naked with her legs wide apart. On some deserted beach, perhaps. The prisoner/slave of some strange man who would force her to respond in ways she had never imagined possible. Oh, God, she thought, this is the real thing. There's a man inside me and I can't escape whatever he wants to do to me.

That wasn't strictly true, of course. Paul had not gagged her. She could scream for help. But the idea of being found naked and in chains by her neighbours was off-putting. Besides, she didn't want any help beyond what would bring on the next orgasm, and they were both capable of supplying that – Paul with that maddening in-and-out glide, and she with her vivid mental images of herself as his captive woman.

This time Muriel did not pass out from the pleasure. This time was slower and curiously satisfying even though it lacked the sharp peaks of pleasure that had marked her first series of orgasms. This time she was more aware of the slide and the pressure inside her cunt and against her swollen clitoris. This time Muriel concentrated on each orgasm as a separate and valuable thing. This time seemed to go on forever, long and slow and delicious. And this time she slipped off to sleep after Paul had come inside her a second time. When she woke, Paul lay motionless beneath her. She was still helpless in her chains, but she felt content. She did not want to think of the moment when he would have to let her go. How nice it would be to spend whole days, weeks perhaps, as the captive of some man. Perhaps of this man. No need to go to work, no need to leave the house. Unable to leave the house, a deep, mysterious part of her suggested. The idea of indefinite periods of captivity and arousal and satisfaction was alluring. Muriel was glad that she still had most of the night to relish her captivity before the demands of the next day intruded.

She slept that night in chains, waking from time to time to shift against Paul. Her sleep was fitful. In the morning she felt gritty-eyed and stiff but curiously happy.

Paul freed her so that she could shower and dress. Once again he watched her.

'Will Rhonda come to take you away today?' she asked, not wanting to hear the answer.

'Probably,' Paul told her. 'But that needn't mean the end of the world. While I'm ... away, you can consider the question of slavery and the prospect of further nights like the last one. When you have decided, let me know. I am not Rhonda's steady. Nor does she get jealous. Well,' he amended, 'she hasn't so far. But I am willing to bear her displeasure if it means more nights like the last one.'

Muriel was cheered by his matter-of-fact approach to sexual relations – with her. She chose a clean pair of stockings, making a mental note to buy more on her next visit to the shops. This time she left her pants off without having to think of it.

'Watch out you don't stand over a hot air duct. Marilyn Monroe got to be a sexual icon for a whole generation just by standing in the wrong place at the right time.'

Muriel finished dressing, and then came the awkward moment of departure. It felt very strange to leave Paul – or indeed any man – alone in her apartment. 'I suppose you'll be gone when I get back,' she said half-questioningly. She regretted not being able to look forward to another night of what she called privately 'torrid sex'. The phrase came from the movies, and was just purple enough to make her feel overly dramatic. But it expressed her feelings accurately enough.

Paul nodded. 'Cheer up. It won't be forever unless you decide to make it so. I just don't know exactly when Rhonda will let up on me.'

'Can't you just . . . walk out?'

'Well, yes. But Rhonda is not that easy to walk out on once you've let her gain control. You've noticed the matter of the clothes. I have to wait around for her to collect me.'

'Would you like me to get something for you to wear? You could make your escape then.'

'Better wait for Rhonda. We both need to keep on her good side, but thanks for the offer.'

'I suppose she will make you wear that . . . cage again?'

'Probably.'

'Why do you let her do that?'

'Why did you put on the handcuffs and leg-irons last night?'

Muriel had no answer to that. She went into the kitchen to make breakfast and check through the letters and the e-mail. Paul followed a few minutes later. The contrast between her fully clothed (except for her pants) and Paul naked made her feel awkward. They ate in silence. When it was time to go Muriel felt even more awkward. How do you bid farewell to a stranger in whose arms you have just spent the night?

She solved the problem with a muttered 'thank you' and a kiss on the cheek. She went to her car feeling very queer indeed, conscious of having crossed an important divide in her life without being sure how to continue with the parts of it that had not changed. The parts that *had* changed presented even more of a problem.

7

Rhonda's Summons

When she got home Paul had gone. So had the pile of equipment that Rhonda had left at her place. Muriel had been hoping subconsciously that he might be there, or that at least the chains had been left. She would have liked to practise a bit with them – get used to the idea of being a captive. But that was now out of the question.

That evening she attended her German class as usual. The instructor was going through the differences between the formal *Sie* and the familiar *Du*. 'Try to use the familiar form whenever you can,' he suggested. 'You need to get familiar with both forms and with the differences in the verb forms they require.' He was a handsome man whom she had marked down as a possible for the future. At any other time she would have addressed him in the familiar *Du*. That evening she had trouble seeing why she had thought of doing so. She had her mind on Paul and her night in chains nearly the whole time he was attempting to make conversation. Her repartee, in German or in English, lacked its former sparkle. He was puzzled and hurt. Muriel was vaguely regretful, but could not erase from her memory the jingle of chains and the shattering orgasms of the previous night. Would this outwardly nice man like to enslave her, as Paul had expressed it? What would he think if she mentioned her preference for *die Handfesseln und die Ketten*? Would he enjoy keeping her in chains as his sexual toy? She thought not, but in any case she was not going to ask him. He too was a professional, a lawyer. Lawyers were supposed to keep their clients' information confidential, but she wasn't his client. Did the same rule apply to mistresses/girl-friends/sex slaves? Too risky to find out. He moved in the same circles as she did. They had several mutual acquaintances.

Muriel spent most of Tuesday in meetings at the head office, fearing that her lack of pants (almost a habit by now, barely a week since she had first heard the suggestion) would be detected. Her skirt might blow up over her hips, or inexplicably drop to her ankles, and *everyone* would know her darkest secrets instantly. She felt as if she had a sign on her bottom: 'No pants. Lift skirt for a view of a bank manager's behind.' Her bosses would not understand. Even if they did, they would not tolerate a person with her views, unless she were the mistress of a person strong and powerful enough to ignore the scandal. And there weren't many like that.

Wednesday she spent thinking that she had dreamed the whole thing. When she was in her office the memory of Rhonda's visit, the beating and the threats was strong, but elsewhere it seemed unreal. At home Paul's presence was less strongly felt. Rhonda, she concluded, had the stronger personality. But what if they had both forgotten her?

All along she had been hoping subconsciously that Rhonda would let him go and that he would call her. When he finally did ring – at the bank that Wednes-day just before closing time – she learned that

Rhonda was still keeping him around. Muriel wondered what they were doing that made such a protracted association necessary – and pleasurable at least for Rhonda. Paul seemed to be bearing up pretty well under the regime of enforced celibacy – if indeed that was what was happening. Rhonda might well have let him out of his cage for her own pleasure. And his, she thought with a strong sense of jealousy and resentment. He had been on her mind ever since their night of torrid sex. She was looking forward to some more time in the torrid zone.

Muriel did not like to ask (though she was burning to know) exactly what they were doing. She herself had been going to work pantlessly in stockings and garter belt every day. She had begun to lift her skirt (when she was sure she would be undisturbed) in her office, and was becoming used to the sensation of her bare bottom on the chair as she sat at her desk. But she was feeling strongly like a woman scorned as Paul spoke of their activities. Rhonda, it turned out, had settled on a new place with characteristic suddenness. She was in the process of moving in, helped, it appeared, by Paul and several other unnamed persons. Muriel gathered that it was a mixed group, and that they were not wholly engrossed in moving furniture and chattels from A to B – or from town to countryside. They were themselves chattels, Muriel guessed. She felt her stomach go hollow as she imagined what they did when they were not toiling for Rhonda's benefit. They were probably toiling for her pleasure – and their own. Muriel felt ever more left out.

This empty feeling was soon dispelled. Paul went on to tell her that Rhonda wanted her to join the work party. And had commanded him to inform her of what she was to do. Thus reminded of last week, she replayed in her mind's eye Rhonda's previous visit to her sanctuary, and shivered at the memory. She also anticipated the next visit, and shivered again. Would the dark-haired dominatrix really tie her to the chair and leave her for the staff to find? The idea became more attractive (and less frightening) the longer she entertained it. And so long as it remained merely a fantasy.

Paul's voice broke into her fevered day-dream. On Friday afternoon, he told her, she would be picked up and driven to Rhonda's new house. She would not need to bring anything. Everything would be provided. She should expect a messenger around six o'clock in the evening. Would she be at home? Yes, she would, she said with a flutter of excitement. Follow the instructions of the messenger, he said. Rhonda had stressed this above all else. 'You know how she likes us to follow orders,' Paul said. Muriel's spirits rose when he added that he was looking forward to seeing her again.

That Wednesday evening she had gone home in a fever of anticipation. On Thursday she went shopping. She bought the new stockings she had promised herself, and a silky green garter belt and matching bra; also a matching slip and pair of pants to complete the set. Friday passed with the swiftness of a geriatric turtle. Muriel went around the bank in a haze. A haze of lust, she told herself, smiling both at the illicit thought and its aptness. Mike spent a gratifying amount of time staring at her legs, despite Alison's black looks. Muriel straightened her seams nearly every time she went into her office, imagining her appearance among the strangers helping Rhonda. By closing time she was giddy with excitement. She drove home in her Firebird and in the same haze of lust, smiling wryly each time she thought of her inner turmoil.

There was a note among her mail from (she assumed) Rhonda. It said, 'Have a quick shower and get dressed. You will be contacted soon.' All very enigmatic. Threatening, if you weren't expecting this sort of cryptic message. Muriel followed the instructions, putting on the new green lingerie and a clean pair of stockings. She made sure the seams were straight as she snapped the garters to the stocking tops. On impulse she put a spare pair into her handbag. She went through to the kitchen but was too nervous even to make a cup of coffee. Stop acting like a schoolgirl on your first date, she told herself. She sat on the edge of a chair and crossed her legs. The whisper of nylon against nylon sounded loud in the stillness of her empty apartment as she restlessly swung her foot to and fro.

The sound of the doorbell startled her. Muriel looked around wild-eyed, then recalled herself. This was what she had been waiting for. Nervously she stood and smoothed her skirt over her bottom and thighs. Her knees felt shaky as she walked to the front door. Pull yourself together, she told herself angrily, but she couldn't.

A strange woman faced her as she opened the door. She had long blonde hair and was pretty rather than stunning. She couldn't have been more than Muriel's own age, and was dressed, similarly, in a business suit. She looked like a fellow professional, maybe secretary to someone with whom she might have to do business. But the clothes said more than 'secretary'.

The woman looked at Muriel closely, then turned her face down to study a photograph she held. When she looked up again, she smiled. 'Ms M Castle. I'm Valerie Sanderson.'

'Wh– who?' Muriel repeated woodenly.

'Rhonda sent me to collect you,' the woman replied. 'Can I come in? I need to prepare you for travelling, and that's best done indoors.'

'Prepare me?' Muriel felt a thrill of fear at the idea of being 'prepared' by this stranger. She didn't move.

Valerie Sanderson held up the photograph she was carrying. It showed Muriel naked and strung up at Rhonda's apartment. It had obviously been taken sometime during her session with the whip. Who, she wondered fearfully, had taken it? Her next thoughts were even more frightening. Were there others? And where were they? Would she be blackmailed? Threatened with exposure? Ruined professionally and socially? Photographs like this had so many possible uses.

Ms Sanderson was growing impatient. 'Look, I get asked to pick up people like you all the time for people like Rhonda Stuart. Stop stalling. Let me in and let's get on with it.'

'People like me?' Muriel snapped angrily. 'And just what kind of person do you think I am?' Her indignation must have sounded as false to her visitor as it did to her.

'I don't think. I *know.* You're one of those freaks who like to be tied up and whipped before sex. A masochist, if you like the ten-dollar word instead of the more frank description.'

Confronted with this daunting woman, Muriel was on the verge of closing the door and retreating into the safety of her apartment. Just then her next-door neighbour, Mr Santos, drove up and parked his car. He called hello to her with a wave.

Ms Sanderson, noting this byplay, said, 'I could always go ask your neighbour if he knows the woman in the photograph.' She made as if to turn away.

Muriel grabbed her arm hysterically. 'No. Don't do that. Come inside.'

'That's better,' said Ms Sanderson, stepping inside and closing the door as Muriel retreated backwards into her living room.

'Ms Sanderson . . .' Muriel began shakily.

'Call me Valerie,' she replied with a menacing air. 'We'll be seeing one another too often to be formal all the time. I might even come to you for a loan.'

The idea of being asked for a bank loan by this woman was frightening. 'Loan' might mean blackmail. And how could she refuse if Ms Sanderson – Valerie – threatened to show more of those damning photographs to her staff? Mike Barrett would be interested, for one. Her own bosses would take an interest as well.

Valerie set down her handbag with a heavy thud. 'Lift your skirt, bend over and grasp your ankles,' she commanded.

Muriel remembered all too well the last time she had heard the same peremptory command. 'N . . . no. No. I don't want to do that.'

Valerie extracted a gun-like object from her handbag and showed it to Muriel. 'Do you know what this is?'

Muriel knew a taser when she saw one. She had one in the bottom drawer of her desk at the bank, and had taken the required training courses as part of the bank's security and anti-theft programme. She hoped she would never have to use the stun gun. She nodded dumbly.

'Good,' Valerie said. 'I don't want to have to demonstrate it to you. I'm just a collector of people like you. I'm not a sadist.' She sounded contemptuous of both masochists and sadists. She laid the taser aside and took out the two dildoes, the chain and the locks that Rhonda had used on her victim only last week.

Muriel stared at the instruments of her torture and her ecstasy with dread and a dull excitement. Tangled emotions made her knees weak. She knew what those dildoes would do to her.

'Lift your skirt,' Valerie commanded again.

Muriel lifted her skirt slowly, as she had for Rhonda, looking for signs of relenting. There were none. Valerie gestured impatiently with the anal dildo. Muriel lifted her skirt to her waist and bent over to grasp her ankles. Her anal sphincter tightened reflexively, though she knew that that would only make things harder.

'Little Ms No-Pants, I see. You must have been looking forward to this all day. Nice stockings, too,' Valerie remarked. 'I'll bet you like to wear them when Rhonda beats you. People like you are often such exhibitionists.' Changing tack, she asked, 'Where is the bathroom?'

Muriel indicated with a nod.

Valerie set the chastity belt down on the sofa. 'Don't move,' she ordered as she went towards the door.

Muriel felt awkward, exposed, degraded – and excited. She remained bent over while Valerie went into the bathroom. The taser lay on the sofa. She could turn around, grab it and have the other woman at her mercy by the time she returned. But she did not. She felt as if her knees would give way by the time Valerie returned with a jar of petroleum jelly. She set it down beside the dildoes. She brought the chain over and locked it around Muriel's waist, as Rhonda had done. The lock closed behind her back. The other piece of chain, the one that would go between her legs and hold the plugs inside her, hung down almost to her ankles. Oh, God, she thought, get it over with.

Valerie was in no hurry. She seemed to delight in making her intended victim sweat with shame. 'I guess I won't need much lubrication on this,' she said with a thin smile, gesturing with the vaginal dildo.

Muriel recognised the thick black rubber shaft that would fill her. She said nothing.

Valerie's finger slid inside her and came away gleaming wetly.

'All excited, aren't you,' Valerie said mockingly. 'You're the proper little masochist.' Valerie slid the dildo into Muriel's cunt.

Muriel bit back a moan of pleasure as it slid home.

'You like that, don't you?' Valerie gave the shaft a shove and a twist.

Losing control, Muriel moaned aloud. She watched in helpless fascination as Valerie smeared petroleum jelly liberally over the anal dildo. When she approached Muriel's exposed arse-hole with the glistening shaft, she closed her anal sphincter more tightly. The touch of the shaft made her jump.

'Hold still,' Valerie commanded. 'You know this is part of it, and we both know you like what's going to happen to you.' She sounded grim and angry.

Muriel wondered if Valerie was feeling left out, and concluded that the tough woman who was doing all this to her probably was into straight sex only. The contempt for 'people like her' could only come from a straight-sex person. Perhaps from a strictly no-sex person. Muriel knew that such women existed, but she could not understand their anger and aversion.

The shaft pushed its way past her sphincter in a slow glide, the jelly easing its passage into Muriel's back passage. She moaned involuntarily, not wanting Valerie to know how exciting this all was. She tried to concentrate on the pain and humiliation. She found little of the former, and was greatly excited by the latter.

Valerie was threading the chain through the eyes on the outer ends of the dildoes. There was a brief tug, the cool silvery chain was pulled tightly into her crotch, and the second lock closed behind her back with an ominous click. Muriel felt the chain pressing into her cunt, touching and rubbing against her clitoris. 'Ohhhhh,' she sighed.

'Stand up now, slut,' Valerie ordered. 'And lower your skirt.'

The chain eased a bit as Muriel stood erect. She tugged her skirt down and smoothed it into place with trembling hands, acutely conscious of the plugs inside her. They shifted whenever she moved. She clamped her lips together to stifle her moan of pleasure.

'Get your purse and come with me,' Valerie said, placing the taser in her own purse and replacing the lid on the petroleum jelly.

Muriel's arse-hole felt greasy – and deliciously stuffed.

Valerie led the way to the door, as Muriel tried to steel herself to appear in public with her internal secrets. She locked the door, and followed the other woman to the car-parking area. In the visitors' section there was a black van with tinted windows. They were nearly opaque from the outside. Muriel was relieved to know that she would be fairly well hidden during her trip into weekend captivity.

Valerie unlocked the doors with the radio transmitter. The lights blinked and the horn beeped briefly. She gestured for Muriel to get in. She herself went around to the driver's side and slid behind the wheel.

At once Muriel experienced the uncomfortable stabbing from her anal dildo as she shifted uneasily on the seat. Her movements, however, caused the vaginal dildo to shift deliciously in her cunt. The chain, tightened by her seated position, bit into her clitoris.

'Comfy?' Valerie asked mockingly as she started the engine.

Muriel did not reply. The windows might have been tinted, but from inside they appeared alarmingly transparent. Nerves, she concluded, not really believing the reassurance. The back of the van, behind the front seats, was empty. There was carpet on the floor of what must have been the freight area. Muriel fastened the seat belt.

Valerie turned out of Muriel's apartment complex, heading east.

'Where are we going?' Muriel asked.

'To Rhonda's new place,' Valerie answered succinctly. 'But I suppose you knew that already. It's in the Florida panhandle, and we'll be on the road for a long while. When we get on to the Interstate, I'll pull over and make you more comfortable for the trip.'

Muriel recognised the irony, and shivered at the prospect of a long trip in captivity. Valerie turned on to Interstate 10, heading east. They drove in silence for a space. Muriel's thoughts were churning, and her body felt hot and itchy. She sat uncomfortably looking at the monotonous vista of swamp and willow trees sweeping past outside the speeding van. The post-rush-hour traffic rolled past in a steady stream.

Valerie said, 'We'll let the traffic thin out. It wouldn't do for the general public to see what I'm going to do to you.' The courier put a Joni Mitchell CD into the player and the two women listened as the Canadian singer told the story of Michael From Mountains, and sang sadly of the down side of clouds. Muriel liked the music, reminding her as it did of her girlhood and young womanhood. She didn't dream then that she would now be listening to the same music on her way to a masochistic weekend in the Florida wilderness.

After several miles Valerie signalled and pulled into a rest area. Muriel guessed that she was about to be made 'more comfortable'. There were several other cars already parked, their passengers stretching their legs and using the toilets and buying snacks for the journey ahead.

'Out,' Valerie ordered tersely.

They joined the other motorists, Valerie jauntily, Muriel uneasily, half afraid that her novel internal arrangements would cause her to betray her secret, as they had nearly done in the supermarket. She walked stiffly, saying nothing, as Valerie went first to the toilet.

'It might be a good idea to use the facilities while you can,' she said darkly, 'it'll be a long trip.'

Muriel found it awkward to pee with the dildo in place. She was glad that she had managed to shit earlier. The anal plug made it impossible now. The pressure against her clit made her moan softly as she dried herself.

Valerie was nowhere in sight when Muriel came out of the toilet. She walked back to the van as naturally as she could, anxious to get out of the view of other persons. Illogically, she imagined that her bizarre desires were branded on her forehead, and that everyone would recognise the signs of her deviation. Mothers would look and gather their children away from this impious young woman. But no one took any notice. Nevertheless, she was glad to be back in the darkness of Valerie's van.

Valerie herself came back after about ten minutes, carrying a bag of doughnuts and several tins of Coca Cola. She offered them to Muriel, whose throat seemed as tightly closed as her stomach seemed full. It was excitement, she knew. And apprehension and anticipation. She managed a swallow of Coca Cola but refused all else. Valerie ate and drank with gusto. Finished, she gestured for Muriel to get into the back of the van. Outside the tinted windows a few people still walked about, and Muriel was afraid they would see what they were doing – or at least guess. Valerie seemed unconcerned. She was busy taking long lengths of thin nylon cord from the glove compartment. She laid it to hand on the front seat. There was a leather helmet among the equipment, with an inflatable rubber mouthpiece that Muriel knew would expand into a gag.

'You don't need to tie me up. I won't make any trouble,' Muriel said desperately. The idea of travelling for hours bound and gagged was frightening. So was the possibility of being seen as she was bound.

Valerie laid the taser suggestively on the seat.

Muriel climbed into the back of the van. There was not enough headroom for her to stand upright.

'Kneel,' Valerie said. 'Hands behind your back. Palm to palm.'

Muriel looked appealingly at her captor, shaking her head.

Valerie picked up the taser.

Muriel knelt and brought her hands behind her.

Valerie tied her wrists tightly, taking all the slack out of the rope and tying several knots, all of them placed carefully out of reach of Muriel's fingers. For good measure she tied Muriel's thumbs together as well.

Muriel tried her bonds and found them inescapable. The tying of her thumbs made her doubly captive.

Valerie used more of the thin cord to tie her elbows together. She pulled them until they nearly touched.

Muriel had never before been tied in this way. She was surprised by how closely her elbows came together. When she tried to move her arms she found that she could not do more than lift them slightly away from her back. The tying of her elbows pulled her shoulders back and made her breasts stand out prominently. Under other circumstances Muriel would have found the effect bold. Now she found it erotic, another stimulating aspect of bondage.

'Even if you managed to get your hands free,' Valerie said conversationally, 'there's no way you can get at the ropes around your elbows. But don't worry. You won't get your hands free. I know what I'm doing, you see.'

Muriel, trying to wriggle out of her bonds, saw. Her breasts almost ached to be touched, but Valerie made no move to do so. Instead she began to fit the leather helmet over her captive's head. She remembered the helmet Rhonda had left at her place when she had loaned Paul to her. This might have been its twin. Perhaps Rhonda had lent her helmet to Valerie for this job. Muriel saw that there were foam rubber eye-pads to cover her eyes on the inside. Foam rubber went over her ears too, but Valerie was not satisfied with that. She produced a pair of ear-plugs and stuffed them into Muriel's ears. The world abruptly grew more silent.

'Open wide,' Valerie commanded. She pushed the gag into Muriel's mouth and pulled the helmet over her head. Darkness descended. Valerie pulled the laces tight, and Muriel experienced for the first time the excitement of having her head compressed inside a tight helmet that deprived her of sight and hearing muffled her. When Valerie inflated the gag, she was also deprived of speech. 'Unnnggg!' she gasped, excited and dismayed at its effectiveness. It filled her mouth, forcing her jaws open and trapping her tongue beneath it. She knew that no one outside the van would hear, no matter how loudly she tried to scream.

Muriel felt a stab of fear and excitement. That was becoming a familiar mix for her. She was in utter darkness, unable to speak or hear. Her hands and arms were tied tightly behind her back, and she was plugged front and rear with rubber shafts she could not remove. All the elements of her darkest fantasy were coming true.

But Valerie was not finished yet. Roughly she pushed Muriel, causing her to fall heavily on to her side.

The rough treatment disoriented and frightened the captive. Valerie pulled Muriel's legs straight and tied her ankles together with more of the nylon cord. She raised Muriel's skirt, exposing the tops of her thighs, and tied her legs again above and below the knees. She pulled all the cords tight, cinching them with turns between her victim's legs. The thin cords bit into her flesh beneath the sheer stockings.

Muriel tested her bonds and found her legs effectively welded together from thighs to ankles. She shifted awkwardly, rolling on to her stomach on the carpeting. The air felt cool and strange on her exposed, bound legs.

Valerie bent Muriel's knees, then used more of the cord to tie her ankles and wrists together, making her wrists and ankles nearly meet behind her back. Thus hog-tied, she was completely helpless. No amount of struggling produced any slack in her bonds.

Valerie let her pull and tug and thrash about until she grew tired and sweaty. 'OK,' she said when Muriel lay quietly, 'now you know you can't get away. But don't let that stop you from trying. Most of the women I transport for Ms Stuart manage several orgasms as they struggle. The dildoes inside you will probably help if you learn to shift them effectively. That's why she supplies them. She's not the complete sadist. Now I'm going to turn you on to your side before we get moving. But wriggle as much as you like on the way.'

Valerie sounded as if she were gloating. Muriel, helpless, felt excited and afraid. The result was an overall tingle of anticipation.

Muriel moaned as Valerie rolled her on to her left side. The dildoes shifted and stabbed her in all her sensitive places. Oh, God, this is *it*! My fantasy is coming true. So why am I frightened? She couldn't answer the question, except to believe that the fear was a part of the fantasy, and would somehow heighten the pleasure. There were many hours and hundreds of miles in which to test her theories, her bonds and her dildoes.

Valerie moved from her side. She felt, rather than heard, the engine being started, and the van begin to move. But she could not see or hear any of these things. The road noise was likewise inaudible, though Muriel knew that it should be quite loud to anyone lying on the floor. Either there was extra sound insulation under the carpet on which she lay bound and gagged, or her ear-plugs were very effective. Muriel was experiencing nearly total sensory deprivation. Feeling and smell were all that were left to her. She had no idea of their progress or of how long she had to go. Several hours, at least, if Valerie's estimate was anywhere near accurate. She contemplated lying helpless for hours at a time. Could she do it? But then what choice did she have? Her captor could leave her like this for as long as she wished. She could not get free, no matter how hard she struggled. She knew

114

this, but she also knew that she would struggle. All captives did, in all the best movies. She imagined how she would look to a filmmaker, her wrists, thumbs and elbows tied together behind her back, her legs exposed to her crotch in her seamed stockings and tied at ankles, knees and thighs. Hog-tied. A faceless head, a gag. Sexy, she imagined. Appealing, she hoped.

Experimentally, Muriel wriggled, bringing her legs up as far as she could towards her bound wrists, then straightening them as far as her hog-tie allowed. She raised and lowered her hips, twisting as she did so. The dildoes made themselves felt. Thus encouraged, Muriel repeated her wriggle. Better. She felt a tingle of excitement as she imagined herself struggling and coming. Making herself come by struggling. It was a new idea. Now was the time to try it out. No one could see her. No one knew where she was. No one would look for her. There was nothing else to do. She was completely helpless in her tight bondage.

Another tingle of excitement, accompanied this time by a more positive feeling from between her legs and in her anus as the dildoes and the chain did their work. She struggled harder, tugging against the ropes, pulling against her hog-tie, squirming on the carpet, sightless, deaf, speechless. Better yet. The van went around a curve, and the motion rolled Muriel on to her stomach. She thrust backwards and forwards with her hips, feeling a definite flutter of arousal in her belly. Encouraged, she threw herself about more energetically, heedless of the fact that Valerie was probably listening to the noises she made.

Another turn rolled her on to her side again. Muriel bent at the waist, drawing the chain tighter against her clitoris. Ah! Definitely a flash of pleasure. She repeated the movement, and the flash came again. Muriel began a rhythmic series of hip thrusts and leg bends that made the dildoes move inside her and the chain in her crotch tighten in a most satisfactory manner. The cords bit into her wrists and arms and legs as she struggled. She came suddenly, lights flashing behind her blind eyes and roarings coming to her deaf ears. She knew that she was whimpering and moaning, making as much noise as she could with the gag in place. It didn't matter that the lights and the roaring were imaginary, or that her whimpers were muffled by the gag. She was coming, jerking in her bonds as she was borne helplessly across country. Though she could not see it, Muriel knew that outside it was growing dark, adding another layer of secrecy to her abduction.

Muriel imagined the hundreds of vehicles that shared the road with them that evening, the drivers and the passengers, men and women and children, all of them oblivious to the fact that in *this* anonymous van an attractive woman, a bank manager, lay bound and gagged and struggling as she drove herself to orgasm after orgasm. The idea of her isolation, her helplessness and her anonymity added to her excitement. She came and came, moaning and jerking and becoming ever more excited.

But no one is superhuman, and Muriel eventually wore herself out. She drowsed, lying on her side in a sweaty heap, rolling gently as the van took the shallow curves of Interstate 10 towards Florida.

When she woke again, nothing had outwardly changed. She was still bound and gagged and plugged. The thought flashed through her mind that she was being borne helplessly across several state lines. She was being abducted, apparently against her will. If any state policeman stopped them and looked into the back of the van, he would see a woman captive. She hoped fervently that Valerie was obeying the speed limits. She wanted no investigations, no embarrassment, no headlines. She just wanted to get safely to Rhonda's place where more delicious tortures undoubtedly awaited her.

Inwardly, though, there was a profound difference between the professional woman who had sought Rhonda for a beating, and the same woman who now lay bound and gagged in a dark van, driving herself to orgasm with the idea that she was helpless to prevent anyone from doing whatever they might wish to her. That was wildly exciting, the fear forming a background to the sexual aspects of her bondage.

Muriel struggled again, with the same results. She could not escape, but she could make herself come wildly by trying. She tried enthusiastically, picturing herself being transported through the dark countryside. More flashes of pleasure in her belly and anus and crotch rewarded her efforts.

Once again Muriel exhausted herself. The sweat between her bound legs made the stockings slippery. The well-greased dildo in her anus moved as she heaved and jerked, the chain sawed at her clit and the dildo in her cunt made her feel stuffed to capacity. This was, if not heaven, then at least a passable substitute.

Worn out, Muriel drowsed again. This time, when she awoke, the cords that bound her felt like lines of fire on her skin. This time she was aware of her bondage on another level. These fiery lines reminded her that she must have been bound for a very long time. Her struggles had made the cords dig into her skin as she heaved and jerked. This unrelenting pressure of their bonds was something that *real* captives felt. Muriel knew herself then to be a real captive. Valerie might not release her. This might be a real abduction. Because of her position, Muriel knew that she was a prime target. The bank had sent her on security, anti-terrorist and anti-abduction courses. They had warned all their managers of the danger of being taken for ransom, or as a means of robbing their branch banks. Most banks kept very little actual cash on hand, having learned the hard way of how it attracted thieves. But the robbers often had a fixed belief in the availability of money at any bank. It would be ironic if her own bizarre desires had landed her in a spot of genuine (rather than imaginary) trouble. The thought was like an icy shower.

All her heated fantasies of torture and beating and wild orgasms suddenly seemed crazy, the frivolous dreams of an innocent in the real world. The real world was about money and, to someone who (supposedly) had access to large amounts of it, bondage was likely to be for other than merely sexual reasons.

Muriel moaned into her gag and renewed her struggles to get free. In her sudden panic she forgot the futility of her previous attempts. She forgot that her captor was sure to notice any success she might have, and would thwart the attempt at once. She could only think of escape. So she struggled wildly once again, tugging against the cords that held her captive, thrashing on the carpeted floor of the van and rolling from her stomach on to her side and back again as she overbalanced with the van's motion.

But as she fought the tight cords her body betrayed her again. The dildoes shifted and stabbed her in her sensitive places. The chain tightened against her clitoris. Her sweaty legs rubbed together as she tried to break the hog-tie rope. And she came. Her body had its own agenda, which she was powerless to control. Muriel keened with pleasure even as panic drove her to struggle harder. Indeed the panic was adding to her sexual arousal. Moaning and shuddering, Muriel's body betrayed her again and again.

And at the end she was still bound as tightly as ever. She was even more exhausted than before, but she fought to stay alert. Falling asleep seemed too much like giving in. Yet once again her body betrayed her. As she fought to stay awake she felt herself coming yet again. And as she came she moved closer to exhaustion. In the end she had to lie still and rest, and so sleep stole over her.

Valerie woke her from her tortured sleep. Muriel was conscious that the van had stopped as soon as she woke. Valerie's hands were busy undoing her bonds. Muriel felt the rope joining her wrists and ankles slacken and then fall away. With a groan she straightened her bound legs. She was lying on her stomach in the back of the van, still helpless despite the removal of the hog-tie.

Valerie dragged her by the ankles until Muriel felt her legs dangling over empty space. She knew that Valerie was taking her from the van, and she panicked anew, fighting the cords that dug into her skin and making protesting noises behind her gag. Where were they? she wondered frantically. Was Valerie taking her out in public bound and gagged? It took some moments for her to realise that that was unlikely. Perhaps they had arrived at Rhonda's place, but, if so, why was it only one person who was moving her? Where were the others? And was this necessarily still Valerie? Might the woman who had collected her have turned her over to her real abductors? The thought frightened her into stillness.

Muriel felt fingers deflating the gag and unlacing her helmet. Her eyes refused to adjust to what little

119

light there was after so long in utter darkness. For a moment she thought she was blind, then she saw the moon. A wave of relief swept over her, so that, when Valerie – it was still Valerie – helped her to sit up, she almost sobbed with relief. Muriel sat with her bound legs dangling over the back bumper of the van and her feet touching the asphalt of a rest area. It was fortunately deserted at this hour. Her damp and wrinkled skirt was nearly up around her waist, revealing the tops of her stockings and the straps from her garter belt. Muriel felt exposed and degraded.

'Well, Ms M, did you enjoy the ride?' Valerie asked as she stooped to untie Muriel's legs. 'It certainly smells like it. You smell like a whorehouse on a Saturday night. You must really like being tied up.' Valerie's bantering tone held overtones of mockery.

As the cords fell away Muriel felt pins and needles in her legs as the circulation returned. She felt weak and light-headed but said nothing to her captor.

'Cat got your tongue?' Valerie asked. 'I'd have thought you would be glad to babble after such a long silence. Most of the other people I collect are talking non-stop as soon as I take the gag out.'

Muriel remained silent.

'Don't try to stand just yet,' Valerie warned her. 'And don't try to run away. The taser is rather painful. Anyway, your legs wouldn't hold you up after being tied for so long.'

'How long?' Muriel asked shakily. 'And where are we?'

'She can speak!' Valerie said in mock surprise. 'We're still on the road,' she continued, 'but I need a pit stop and I guessed that you might like one as well. It wouldn't be very nice for either of us if you pissed yourself. Some of my people do.'

As she spoke Muriel felt a strong urge to pee. It had been several hours since the last one. As she fought to control her bladder Muriel remembered her safe apartment. It seemed even more desirable than ever as she sat bound in the darkness of she knew not where.

Valerie let her rest for a few minutes more, during which the urge to pee grew stronger.

'Please let me go to the toilet,' Muriel said finally, reluctant to plead with her captor. 'Otherwise I *will* . . . piss myself.'

Valerie helped her to stand. Her high heels, so familiar to her as part of her everyday dress, seemed like skyscrapers. She teetered and Valerie caught her before she fell. Muriel's knees were shaky and her legs felt as if they belonged to someone else. The stab of the dildoes inside her almost made her lose control and wet herself. Silently she fought her internal battle as Valerie led her into the trees that ringed the parking area. Once inside their shadow Muriel felt safer. At least no one could see her. She moved awkwardly over the uneven ground. Lacking the use of her hands and arms, she felt as if she would fall at any moment. She was grateful for Valerie's steadying hand, though she didn't want to say so.

Valerie lifted her skirt and helped her to squat, and Muriel felt an immense relief as she emptied her bladder. The chain in her crotch diverted the stream, and Muriel felt some of it strike her ankles and run down into her shoes, but she said nothing. That was infinitely better than lying for hours in a puddle of her own urine.

Valerie removed her pants and panty-hose and squatted beside her to add her own urine to the considerable puddle. She sighed in relief as she stood and replaced her clothing. As Valerie smoothed her skirt down, Muriel was doubly aware of her own relative nakedness. Valerie helped her to stand and wiped her crotch dry with a tissue.

'Would you please pull my skirt down too?' Muriel asked. She was mortified when Valerie shook her head.

'I'd only have to raise it again when I get you back to the truck. Doesn't it give you an added thrill to be nearly naked in public? People like you often like the humiliation – and the danger of being seen.'

Muriel shook her head but did not ask again. She was silent as Valerie led her back to the truck. Valerie offered her water, and she drank gratefully, nodding in silent thanks. She remained silent as Valerie replaced the helmet and gag and ear-plugs. She submitted tamely as Valerie tied her ankles and knees and thighs with the thin cords. Despite the possibility that she had fallen into the hands of a real abductor, Muriel felt illogically safer in her dark silent world. It was coming to seem like a normal condition. Any change represented uncertainty. She tested her bonds and found them reassuringly tight and inescapable.

Valerie used Muriel's bound legs as a lever to move her captive back into the van. She retied Muriel's ankles to her wrists.

Once again Muriel was left with feeling and smell as her only sensory inputs. She felt the door slam, felt the vibration as Valerie started the engine, and felt her body roll slightly as the van returned to the road to continue the long journey. This time she slept. Her earlier struggles and orgasms had drained her energy. As she was borne through the night, Muriel dreamed lurid dreams of abduction and sexual release and utter helplessness. Waking, she found that her dreams were real, and she was content. She slept again.

8

Waking up at Rhonda's

Muriel woke when she felt hands on her body once
again. It was evident that there was more than one
person handling her. The hands untied the cord
joining her wrists and ankles but left her bondage
otherwise unchanged. She was picked up like a sack
of potatoes and slung over someone's shoulders. She
inferred that it was a man, unless Valerie was a lot
stronger than she appeared. There was a thrill of fear
at the knowledge that there was a man around. Her
naked cunt and her raised bottom seemed suddenly
more vulnerable, the dildoes in her cunt and anus
suddenly more noticeable as they shifted inside her.
She got the impression that she was being carried into
a house, and then up a staircase; she was deposited
on a bed on her side and the hands went away. She
waited for new developments, but there were none;
she was alone. Panic set in again, and she struggled
anew to free herself from the bonds that had defeated
all her efforts till now. Silently she jerked and tugged
and rolled from side to side. This time, free of the
hog-tie, she could bend and straighten her legs.
Nothing had any effect. In the movies the captive
usually managed to wriggle free. This was not a
movie.

Her body betrayed her once again. Her struggles
made the dildoes move in their intended fashion, and

she was keening again as wave of pleasure rippled through her helpless body. She continued to struggle, but now more for the pleasure than for any hope of freeing herself. Gradually she realised that she did not want to be free if being bound produced such bliss. Muriel surrendered herself to her body's pleasure with enthusiasm.

More hands woke her some indeterminate time afterwards. They rolled her over on to her back, pulled her bound legs to one side and sat her up on the side of the bed. She moaned as the anal dildo pushed deeper into her. The same hands (she surmised) unlaced her helmet. Light flooded in and dazzled her eyes, so long accustomed to utter darkness. She closed them quickly. When the gag came out, she worked her sore jaws and croaked, 'Water.'

The hands went away. Muriel sat on the side of the bed with her feet on the floor. She opened her eyes experimentally. Still too much light. She closed them again. The hands came back, holding a glass of water to her lips. Muriel drank thirstily. This time, when she opened her eyes, she was able to recognise Paul.

He set the glass on the bedside table and returned to sit beside Muriel on the bed. He rested his arm around her shoulders and drew her against him. She relaxed as much as her tight bonds would allow and enjoyed the twin sensations of being held by a man and by the cords in which she had travelled to meet him. He had said that Rhonda wanted her to join the work party, but Paul said nothing about the dominatrix. Muriel did not miss her. It was nice to have him to herself, to be his captive in a secluded place. Her desire to be tied up and handled by a man looked as if it was about to be realised. The dildoes made themselves felt as a pleasant fullness inside her. The main effect was excitement rather than the fear she had expected at being held captive. I'm growing unfaithful to Rhonda, she thought as she leaned into his embrace. Less dependent on her, she corrected herself. Paul put the fingers of his free hand under her chin and raised her face to be kissed. His lips covered hers and she felt herself melt with desire. The kiss drew out, Muriel trying to press herself against him despite being immobilised by the cords binding her arms and legs. 'Mmmmm,' she moaned.

But pleasant as this arrangement was, there were some things that wouldn't be denied: cramped limbs and a full bladder, for example. The rising excitement made the latter problem more acute. Muriel felt herself leak suddenly. She clamped down but drew back from the kiss. The urgency of her need broke the spell.

Paul drew back too, and looked at her questioningly.

'What's the plan for me?' she asked, shrugging her shoulders and lifting her legs to indicate her tight bondage. 'I've been tied up for a long time, and I would like a shower, and I'm about to piss myself.' Muriel blushed at the coarse word that came so casually to her. I must be responding to present company, she thought. Rhonda was as blunt in her speech. Paul used four-letter words equally casually. And she was intimate with both of them.

'Luckily I can do something about that,' Paul said as he stooped to untie her legs.

As the cords loosened and fell away, Muriel felt the by-now familiar pins and needles in her legs. Looking down at them, she saw that the cords had made deep red marks in her skin. One of her stockings had a run in it. If that was all the damage from a night on the road in bondage, she could live with it. She tried to stand up but her legs gave way. She fell back on to the bed and nearly overbalanced. There was another warning spurt from her bladder.

'The bathroom, Paul. Please!' she wailed. 'I can't walk, and I'm about to wet myself.'

He lifted her from the bed and carried her quickly into the bathroom. There he held her erect while he lifted her skirt. He sat Muriel on the toilet an instant before the dam burst.

The relief resembled a minor orgasm, Muriel thought, as she emptied herself into the toilet. The chain between her legs divided the stream, so that some of it ended up on the floor or running down her legs.

'Ahhh,' she sighed as the river dried up. She sighed again as Paul dried her and wiped her clean. Being tied helplessly made it necessary for someone else to do even the most intimate things for her. That was a nice feeling.

Paul seemed to take longer than necessary about drying her. In fact, he was not drying her at all. He was stroking her labia and cunt. His fingers touched her clitoris, and she felt herself grow warm at once. He pushed the dildo deeper into her cunt. Muriel moaned, knowing that she was going to come if this went on much longer.

She had enjoyed the trip in the van and the effects of the dildoes inside her, but now she wanted something different. The real thing, in fact, and it was not a million miles away. Unless Rhonda had left him 'safe'.

'Paul,' she asked urgently, 'are you wearing the . . . thing? Rhonda's cage?' She hoped he wasn't. She was tied tightly, wholly in his power, and she felt a strong need to be had just then.

'No, as a matter of fact. Is that important?' he asked teasingly.

'Then can you get these ... things out of me and replace them with something more ... satisfying?' Muriel was too aroused to feel embarrassed by her need.

'I can probably do that too.' He helped her to stand. 'Legs OK now?'

Muriel nodded. She followed willingly as he led her back to the bedroom. She stood with barely concealed impatience as he removed her skirt. Since he made no effort to untie her wrists, elbows and thumbs, he could not remove her blouse and bra. He had to be content with unbuttoning the former and unhooking the latter, leaving Muriel standing in her stockings and garter belt with her breasts sticking out of her open blouse. She looked more erotic for the dishabille. Paul paused to kiss her again. When Muriel responded, the kiss grew longer, and she felt the dildoes stir inside her as her internal muscles contracted. With a gasp she drew back. 'Can you do anything about ... this?' She indicated her chastity belt by pointing with her chin and thrusting her hips forwards.

Paul produced the keys and unlocked her. He removed the chain from her waist, and withdrew the dildo from her sex. He laid it on the table beside the bed.

Muriel blushed when she saw that it was wet with her internal lubrication. Not many men would have taken that so casually, she thought. The dildo in her anus was another matter. She tried to expel it, but it didn't want to come out. Seeing her struggle and her embarrassment, Paul signalled her to bend over and pulled it out for her. Like the other dildo, this one was covered with her secretions, but they were not nearly as pleasant as the smell of her sex. Nevertheless Paul handled it casually, wiping off the shit before laying it beside its mate.

Muriel gazed for a long time at 'her' dildoes before she could meet Paul's eyes. She was relieved when he smiled.

'Sex and torture are sometimes messy,' he said lightly.

Muriel nodded. 'Now that the torture's done, could we get on with the sex?' She sat on the edge of the bed, watching in mounting excitement as Paul undressed. His erection spoke loudly of his own desire. Muriel couldn't take her eyes off it. 'I guess that means you like me,' she said shakily.

'It's a dead giveaway, isn't it?' He sat beside her and drew her down until they were lying side by side on the bed, facing one another. He kissed Muriel again, firmly on the mouth, before he rolled over on to his back and pulled her atop him. He helped her to straddle him, and then to raise her body so that he could guide his erect cock into her.

Unable to use her hands or arms, Muriel nevertheless struggled to help, spurred on by her own situation. This was what she had enjoyed so much at their first encounter. Then she had been only handcuffed. Now, even more tightly bound, she was that much more excited. Excitement seemed to be in direct proportion to the degree of her helplessness. The penetration, when complete, almost caused her to pass out from sheer pleasure. She clung grimly to consciousness. This was too good to miss. This was what she had been longing for, even while she had feared to make the attempt. Now all those fears seemed foolish. Even though Paul could do anything to her, even though she was powerless to stop him, she felt no fear. Only pleasure at having come to this moment. When he slid into her, Muriel cried out with the joy of it. Strange, she thought, how the mere friction of certain body parts could produce such supreme excitement: the friction of her bound wrists as she struggled against the cords that held them; the tension in her bound elbows; the slight movement of her bound thumbs; the more profound friction of Paul's stiff cock against her clitoris and vaginal walls.

Most importantly, there was the tension set up by her fantasies and her fears. Muriel, unlike many (perhaps most) women, was close to having her wildest fantasy fulfilled. Heedless of whoever might hear, she screamed when the first orgasm shook her, shuddering as the pleasure shot through her. Again and again she gave vent to her excitement and fulfilment. When she felt Paul spurt inside her, Muriel did pass out for a moment.

She regained consciousness still lying atop him, bound, helpless, sated. Paul looked at her quizzically, lifting an eyebrow and squeezing her bound wrists.

'Yes, I think I'd like to be untied now. I need a shower and another visit to the toilet,' Muriel said in reply to his unspoken question. 'I can barely feel my hands and arms.'

Paul rolled to one side so that she slid to the bed. He got up and helped her to sit while he undid the knots that held her. The cords binding her wrists, elbows and thumbs had been in place for longest and had made even deeper marks. Like her legs, her arms refused at first to obey her. They tingled and burned as circulation returned. The ache in her shoulders eased a bit with the removal of the cord, but she would have to wait a bit before she could move her arms and ease it entirely. But she had come through her first long-term bondage session well. She even decided that she would like to repeat the experience soon. Not right then. At least not until she had cleaned herself up and seen to personal needs.

'Throw your clothes out and I'll put them in to wash,' Paul said as she got up from the bed.

In the bathroom she undressed, smelling the odour of her damp clothing for the first time. Paul was right – it all needed washing and ironing. She opened the door and threw it into the bedroom. She used the toilet and then the shower to make herself presentable to the others Paul had told her would be here. The telephone invitation had implied as much.

When she came out, her clothes were gone, and so was Paul. Now she could not leave even if she were free of all restraint. She saw that it was nearly noon. The shadows of the pine trees in the back yard were very short, but the sunlight had that brightness of still morning about it. She had slept through the morning in her bonds, unaware until now of the passing time. There was no one else in view. No, wait, there was someone emerging from the pinewoods behind the house. It was a naked woman. Muriel didn't recognise her. Probably one of the other guests Paul had mentioned, unless Florida had gone in for public nudity. The sight of the strange woman naked in broad daylight both reassured and disturbed Muriel. She guessed that she would be expected to be similarly unclothed, both inside the house and out. But at least there appeared to be no nosy neighbours – as far as she could tell. She did not relish the prospect of yet another set of naked photos of herself.

Muriel watched the woman cross from the woods to the house. When she disappeared from view, Muriel was about to leave the bedroom and seek the others. Best to get the introductions over as soon as possible, she reasoned, before she lost her courage. But, before she could leave the room, Paul returned. She was both glad to see him and relieved that she could postpone the awkwardness for a bit longer. Besides, there were several questions on her mind.

But first, he had brought something for her to wear. It was not much, just a pair of stockings and a garter belt. Muriel knew by now that he favoured those accessories, just as she now did. She sat on the bed to put the stockings on, and then stood to clip the garters to the tops of the stockings. They reached nearly to her crotch, and were sheer and shiny. Most erotic, in fact. Dressed to thrill, Muriel sat down once more on the bed and invited Paul to join her.

'Could we talk a bit before I have to meet anyone else?' When he nodded, Muriel began with the most important matter: just how many people would she be meeting, and who were they? Paul thought for a moment, and Muriel feared that he was about to reel off a list of strangers.

'There's Rhonda, of course, but she's hardly a stranger. Ted Miller and Chloe. An unattached female called Zenobia who I think either works for Rhonda or is taking lessons from her. She will arrive today. There might be one or two others. The invitation was open-ended.'

OK, Muriel thought, four, maybe six, people. I think I can handle that. Next question: 'What about Rhonda? About you and Rhonda, I mean. Won't she be jealous . . . or something?'

'Or something,' Paul agreed. 'But would you let her get between you and this morning? It's . . . complicated. She seems to be professionally jealous. I mean, she acts the part of the jealous and angry mistress when it suits her purpose with an individual client. For example, she kept me chained for nearly twenty-four hours after you'd left her apartment. She was paying me back for too obviously coveting you. No doubt you also saw how she enjoyed tormenting me when I could do nothing about it. Remember how she made me kiss your tits and nipples while she fondled your cunt. You were sitting on the toilet ready to burst with the pleasure, and she knew I wanted to do much more than that to you.'

131

Muriel flushed, whether with embarrassment or satisfaction he could not tell. Paul decided not to tell her what he and Rhonda had done the next evening. *Muriel* might be the jealous type. Instead, he reminded her of Rhonda's part in setting up their first meeting. 'She knew what you . . . what *we* would do when she made the arrangements.'

Muriel flushed as she remembered Rhonda's visit to the bank. She had seemed angry then, even if she had later gone on to arrange the tryst with Paul. Rhonda might well be planning to take revenge for that now.

'Does she know . . . we've been . . . at it? Here? In her new house?'

'Maybe. Probably. She knows what most people would do in these circumstances. Do you want to ask her?'

'No!' The word burst from Muriel. 'She . . . scares me. I need what she does, I like it very much, but she can be a bit . . . overpowering.'

'Her strongest point,' Paul agreed. 'But don't worry. It spoils the moment. Next question.'

This time Muriel hesitated, debating how best to phrase the matter she had been thinking about off and on since Paul had casually mentioned slavery. Finally, 'What does a . . . slave girl have to do? I mean, is she kept prisoner all the time? Does she get beaten or tortured? What about my job?' She flushed at the inadvertent shift from 'she' to 'me'.

'Are you applying for the position?' Paul asked with a grin that caused further blushes.

'Well, asking for a job description, anyway. How can anyone know about a job when she doesn't know what it involves?' There, she had taken the plunge. She had not planned to 'apply', but she felt relieved now that the negotiations had begun.

Paul lay down on the bed and pulled Muriel over until she lay alongside, half on and half off his body. He settled her against him and put an arm around her shoulders. 'Well, here is the job description you need.'

What followed made Muriel blush and sweat with desire by quick turns as she imagined herself in the role that Paul outlined. Slavery, he told her, was like any other relationship. Either partner could end the arrangement, and there were no legal constraints except those applied to ordinary people who decided to end their partnership. Mostly there were financial matters to sort out – who got what, as in any property settlement. Since slavery was not a legal matter, there were no legal formalities to undo as in a normal marriage. 'Basically, it amounts to a dominant and a submissive partner agreeing to accept those roles with each other and with anyone else that they agree to let into the relationship.'

'Rhonda, for instance?' Muriel asked.

'Yes, Rhonda,' he agreed. 'It might be rather difficult to keep her out.'

Did she plan to give up her sessions with the dominatrix? Muriel admitted that she did not. 'Nor do I,' Paul said. They agreed that they would share Rhonda between them. 'But don't let her hear you say it that way,' Paul said with a grin. 'She likes to think that she is doing the sharing.'

Slavery, he told her, was not an exclusive relationship – not monogamous like marriage. Each partner was free in theory to have other liaisons, although emotional ties and dependencies sometimes got in the way of excursions from one to another. 'We just have to see how it goes,' Paul said.

Each was free to have his/her career/job as inclination and financial needs dictated. 'So you can go on being the bank manager by day and the slave girl by

133

night and on weekends if you want it that way. We both know something about what the other likes in the way of bondage and sex play, and that's a good thing to agree on and to develop. That's about all there is to it,' he said.

Muriel wanted to know if Rhonda would go along, that is, continue to see both of them as she had been doing. It seemed important to her that Rhonda be there whenever needed.

Paul did not think that that would be a problem. 'Rhonda has never demanded exclusive rights to any of the people she sees regularly. I don't think she can afford that if she has to deal with as many clients as I believe she does.' He paused. 'So do you want to go ahead with it?'

Muriel replied that she would like more time to think.

He agreed. 'How about a bit of bondage right now?' he suggested. 'Or something else? Sleep? Sex? Food? An interview with her downstairs?'

Not the last, Muriel said. 'I'm tired after all that's happened, so could you make me comfortably uncomfortable in bed and leave me to rest a bit?'

'Certainly,' Paul said. 'Lie on your back and spread your arms and legs.'

He used the cords that had bound her on her journey to tie her wrists and ankles to the four bedposts. He covered her with a light blanket. He drew the curtains and kissed her before leaving the room.

Alone, Muriel tested her bonds and, finding them tight and suitably inescapable, settled down to catch up on lost sleep. It was a superior way to rest, she thought as she drifted off.

Muriel woke up feeling rested and hungry. It was apparently late afternoon, judging by the light coming through the drawn curtains. She tested the ropes that held her once more and wondered what she should do to attract attention. She was not gagged, but it might be indelicate to shout for someone to release her. Suppose Rhonda came? With riding crop? And with Muriel spread so conveniently in the bed? She could not rid herself of the idea that Rhonda might resent her affair with Paul. What Rhonda might do to her produced a delicious shiver of excitement.

So Muriel kept silent, occasionally tugging against the ropes to remind herself of her helplessness. Between times she considered becoming Paul's slave girl. The idea appealed to her, especially the thought that she would not have to give up the official job she had fought for. The idea of spending her days bossing others and her evenings and weekends in bondage was exciting. It would be a delicious secret, and she liked the idea of keeping this secret from her colleagues. It would lend a spice of danger to her life – as well as the other sort of spice.

Muriel could do nothing else but lie in the bed until someone – Paul, she hoped – came to release her. She dozed and woke, dreaming of slave girls in chains. Most of them had her face. When Paul came for her, she was beginning to feel both hungry and excited.

'Food first,' he told her as he untied her. 'After that, we'll see.' He was still naked.

'What about . . . clothes?'

'You're already wearing more than everyone else here – except for Rhonda. She's wearing just her professional gear, so that doesn't count. But we might be able to find you a pair of shoes.' He opened the wardrobe and invited Muriel to choose for herself. There was an assortment of shoes available, all of them high-heeled pumps.

Muriel thought it odd that Rhonda should have such a collection. Looking more closely, she noticed that all of the shoes had ankle straps. Some of the straps were lockable. With a tingle of excitement she chose a pair of the latter, looking at Paul for his reaction.

He gave an approving nod. 'Rhonda favours those for her associates. The locks are in that carton on the shelf.'

Muriel put the shoes on, kneeling to buckle the straps around her ankles. In the carton she found an assortment of brass padlocks with their keys in place. She chose a matching pair and opened them. Without having to be told, she handed the keys to Paul before snapping the locks closed. Now she would have to wear the shoes until she got the keys back. She didn't expect that to be very soon.

Paul put the keys on the bureau before opening yet another wardrobe. This one contained bondage gear – obviously Rhonda's collection. 'If you still feel underdressed, I might be able to find a pair of handcuffs for you. Would you like leg-irons as well? Or would you prefer to be tied up again?'

Muriel gazed silently but with rising excitement at all the many different ways there were to make people – her, specifically – helpless. She swallowed and said, 'I think handcuffs for now,' in as steady a voice as she could manage. 'And leg-irons if you can manage them.' As she surveyed the collection, one object struck her immediately: what appeared to be a single, rather thick cuff made of chromed steel. 'What's that?' she asked Paul.

Paul took the mystery object from its hook. Muriel caught her breath on a gasp as he showed it to her. 'It's a pair of hinged handcuffs,' he explained as he unfolded them. 'They're much more severe than the ordinary kind. No chain means they are rigid. The wearer would not be able to unlock them even if she had the key.' He demonstrated the operation and showed Muriel that the hinge allowed only the slightest of movements. 'Want to try them?'

Muriel nodded, not trusting herself to speak. Her chest felt tight and her breath short. She turned away and brought her hands together behind her back. He closed the cuffs snugly around her wrists, double-locking them. 'Oh!' she gasped in surprise as she tried to move her hands. The rigid cuffs were much more confining than the ones she had worn, for example, when she and Paul had enjoyed their first encounter. She struggled with them for a moment before giving up.

In the meantime Paul had selected a set of leg-irons for her. Muriel shivered when he fastened the irons around her ankles, over her stockings. These too he double-locked. The keys went on top of the bureau, out of Muriel's reach so long as her hands were cuffed behind her back.

Paul himself selected a leather dog collar. As he buckled the collar around her neck, Muriel couldn't resist asking him if he wasn't gilding the lily. 'I wouldn't want to be overdressed,' she said.

'Let me worry about that. This is what all the best-dressed slave girls wear, anyway. Good practice for you. Rhonda has asked me to meet Zenobia at Bradenton airport so I'll have to leave you here for a while. But don't worry. There are others here in case you need anything. You know where the bathroom is. Outside there is a hall. Turn right and go down the stairs if you want to eat. The kitchen is at the back of the house, and there will be someone there to feed you. Or you can see the rest of the house first if you prefer. It's not very interesting on this floor – just more bedrooms.'

He kissed Muriel on the cheek before leaving her to decide her next limited course of action.

9

Muriel Descends

Left alone, Muriel wandered again to the window. There was no one in sight outside the house. The shadows told her that it was late afternoon. Her stomach told her the same, adding that something to fill the void would not come amiss. There was not really much choice: remain here until someone came for her, growing hungrier in the meantime, or explore the house and maybe find something to eat. She chose the latter. Paul had left the door open, perhaps realising that it would be difficult for her to open it herself with her wrists handcuffed behind her back. Muriel went out into the hall and turned right.

She descended the stairs carefully. A fall would be serious without her hands to break it. The stairs ended in a large reception hall with rooms opening off both sides. One of them appeared to be a dining room with a long table and seats for a dozen or so people. The table was not set. The room on the other side of the hall contained several items of furniture that suggested it would eventually become a lounge or sitting room, but they were not arranged in any recognisable pattern. Rather they looked as if they were awaiting someone – Rhonda, most likely – to impose order and create a room instead of an empty space. Muriel looked around the door into the room and saw a steel cage. It appeared to be bolted to the floor, and was large enough to contain at least one person if he/she did not insist on lying down full length.

Amid the ordinary surroundings it had a starkness to it that took her breath away. Muriel at once imagined herself locked into that cage and waiting in trepidation the dominatrix's arrival. The prospect shortened her breath and tightened her stomach. Muriel looked more closely at the cage. It was solidly constructed of round steel bars welded to flat bar framing. Like a miniature cell, in fact, open on all sides. Or like a cage in a zoo, designed to display whatever – whoever – was inside. The flooring was wooden, thick pine planks sanded smooth and varnished. At the top, horizontal steel bars formed a roof. The door stood open as if inviting her to step inside. The key was in the lock.

Muriel wandered around the room, the soft clinking of the chain that joined her ankles the only sound as she moved with short, careful steps. In her rigid handcuffs she moved through light and shadow, like a ghost, handless though mobile, looking at someone else's things without being able to make any impression on them. She passed through another set of double doors into a room that was obviously intended to be a library. Its walls were lined with empty shelves, and there were numerous boxes stacked on top of one another – books looking for a home. Muriel felt like an intruder amidst the oppressive silence. A sense of unreality stole over her. What was a bank manager doing wandering through a strange house, nude and in chains? Her office might as well have been on another planet, her job a feverish dream. The steel bands imprisoning her wrists and ankles alone reminded her of her earthly existence.

She wandered back into the room with the cage, and started in surprise when she saw Rhonda seated in an armchair. She wore a tight corselet or leotard of leather, black tights and black high-heeled shoes. A riding crop lay across her thighs. She looked the complete dominatrix, lithe, beautiful, menacing. The smile she gave Muriel was enigmatic. It suggested whips and pain . . . and glorious release.

'Did you enjoy the trip here?' she asked.

'It was . . . interesting,' she replied. 'Do your guests often arrive as parcels?'

'Many of them do,' Rhonda replied. 'Many of them ask to be delivered that way. In your case, I had to guess what would be best. I'm glad I guessed correctly. Valerie told me that you spent a good part of the trip struggling and having fun.'

Muriel flushed at the accuracy of the account. How much else had Valerie told Rhonda? But all she said was, 'I'm hungry. Is there anything to eat?'

Rhonda stood, looking more formidable in her professional dress. She laid the riding crop on the table and picked up a chain dog lead. Snapping it to Muriel's collar, she gave a tug and led her out of the room. They went towards the back of the house, Muriel struggling to keep up with her captor. The kitchen was beyond the dining room she had seen earlier. It was at least twenty feet long and nearly as wide. The blonde woman whom Muriel had watched crossing the back yard was there with a plate of sandwiches and a large pitcher of iced tea. Muriel's stomach rumbled, and her throat felt parched. She did not like to think how long it had been since she had last eaten.

'Muriel, this is Chloe. Chloe, Muriel.' The introductions were handled as if there were nothing out of the ordinary. Chloe was blonde. All over, Muriel

141

noticed. She had green eyes and a figure to envy. 'Chloe is here for the next week or so. She's spending her annual vacation with us,' Rhonda explained, without explaining what Chloe would be doing, nor who the 'us' might be. 'Now, how shall we go about this?' Rhonda continued. 'Shall we leave a sandwich and a bowl of iced tea on the table for Muriel, or would it be better to have her eat off the floor?' Rhonda sounded matter-of-fact.

Muriel did not relish eating like an animal, but she could do nothing about it. Rhonda handed the lead to Chloe and told her to decide how the problem should be handled. The problem, meanwhile, remained silent while her fate was decided.

Chloe shrugged and grinned when Rhonda was gone. 'Sit down and I'll feed you. It's the best I can do in the circumstances.'

'Won't Rhonda be angry?'

'She might, but that doesn't worry me. I'm going to be whipped no matter what I do, and I can hardly wait.' She pulled out a chair and turned it sideways on to the table. She set another one for herself facing it. 'Sit,' she told Muriel with a grin.

Muriel sat. Chloe sat facing her, and proceeded to feed her a sandwich a bite at a time. Muriel ate hungrily. The iced tea went down quickly. As she ate, she mused on the irony of being fed like an animal. She doubted whether she could have eaten unaided.

'Thank you,' she told Chloe at last.

'Got to keep up your strength for the athletics ahead,' Chloe told her cheerfully.

Muriel suddenly found herself looking forward to the rest of the programme chez Rhonda.

'How do you know what Rhonda is going to do?' Muriel asked as Chloe fed her the sandwich.

'Well, the way she's dressed should be a clue. When she's in that tight leather panty-corselet with black

142

tights and high heels – what I call her inaccessible mode – experience suggests that she is planning to do something rather severe to someone not so inaccessible. Notice anyone else dressed as she is? No? So then can you guess who she is intending to do things to? Besides, while she's dressed like that, it would be difficult for anyone to do anything to her – even if they wanted to, which I don't. And no one comes to Rhonda without expecting something severe and probably painful to happen to them. It's what she does. We're all expecting it. Or at any rate *I* am.' Chloe shivered with excitement as she contemplated the near future.

Muriel twisted her hands against the rigid handcuffs, savouring her own helplessness as she imagined Rhonda dealing with her. As Chloe had said, that's why they were both there. Her colleagues would be startled if they knew what the boss did for pleasure.

Rhonda, striking in her professional gear, returned for her two charges. 'All filled up?' she asked cheerfully. Without waiting for a reply she gestured for them both to stand. 'Battle stations,' she announced. 'Muriel, you'll do as you are, but I must do something about you, Chloe. Can't have naked females at large.' Chloe looked eager to have something 'done about her'. Muriel felt a hollowness in her stomach despite the food.

Rhonda took rope from a drawer and proceeded to tie the blonde woman's hands together in front of her body. When she was done, she took the free end of the rope between Chloe's thighs and pulled it tight. Chloe hissed as the rope was drawn into her crotch. Muriel remembered how it had felt when Rhonda had tied her that way. She recalled the pressure of the rope on her clitoris, envying Chloe the experience. Rhonda tied the rope around Chloe's waist. Her hands were pulled down tightly against her belly and her breasts were squeezed between her upper arms. They jutted invitingly. Rhonda stepped back to admire the effect. 'Very nice,' she remarked. She picked the riding crop from the table and flicked it across Chloe's breasts. Chloe jumped as the blow landed, leaving a white line across her nipples that slowly turned a dull red.

'That's better,' Rhonda announced. 'Chloe, you go first, as you know the way. I'll be right behind you with Muriel.'

Chloe went out of the open door and crossed the back porch. Rhonda grasped Muriel's lead and prepared to follow. Muriel was appalled at the idea of going outdoors in the nude. Rhonda tugged on the lead. 'Rhonda, I can't!' she said despairingly. 'Suppose someone sees me – us? I'd die of shame.' Wordlessly Rhonda dropped the lead. Muriel felt instant relief. She was safe from prying eyes.

Walking behind Muriel, Rhonda lifted the crop and struck her across her bottom. Muriel hissed in pain, but Rhonda was not through. She struck Muriel repeatedly, across her bottom, on the backs of her thighs, on her calves. Muriel was driven out of the door and across the porch, stumbling and crying as she was forced out into the bright sunlight. 'Rhonda, please!' she cried. 'Please stop. Don't make me go out there!'

'You're already out there, as you call it. Just keep going.' Rhonda kept using the crop to drive Muriel before her. 'The sooner you get into the trees, the sooner you'll be out of sight,' she offered by way of encouragement. 'Look at Chloe. She's not worried about being naked.'

Muriel, however, was; yet she could do nothing about it. She jerked futilely at the handcuffs but there was no escape for her. And Rhonda was implacable. Muriel was driven stumbling across the endless expanse of lawn, trying not to trip on her leg-irons, trying to escape the lash and the thousands of eyes she just knew were enjoying her humiliation and her nakedness. She did not know how she could ever face anybody again. What if her colleagues at the bank knew that their boss was being driven naked across a lawn? They would never respect her again. The whispers would reach head office. She would be ruined. Weeping, Muriel went on, Rhonda encouraging her every few steps with the whip. She felt as if she were on a stage, on display, humbled before everyone. The feeling lasted forever.

Finally they were among the trees, the forest gradually growing thicker, hiding her from the imaginary spectators. Muriel felt a little better. She tried to walk more slowly, but Rhonda continued to lash her. Her bottom and legs felt as if they were on fire.

Rhonda suddenly shifted the target. As Muriel took a careful step she felt the lash come up between her thighs. It landed on her cunt, and she screamed with the pain. She screamed again as the lash landed a second time. Muriel stopped and tried to clamp her thighs together to protect herself. Rhonda at once resumed beating her across the bottom and the backs of her legs. She had no choice but to go on. And when her legs parted, as they had to if she was to walk, the lash occasionally found its sensitive target again. Muriel screamed aloud as she was struck, not caring now who might hear her distress. No one seemed to. Rhonda drove her onwards. Muriel stumbled on, fighting her handcuffs and the leg-irons, pleading for respite.

'Such a noise! I would have gagged you if I'd known how loudly you would scream.' Rhonda, however, did not seem worried by the noise. She could have quietened her at once simply by stopping the lashing. Instead she kept it up.

Muriel was driven deeper into the woods, moaning and screaming under the lash. She tugged and jerked futilely at the handcuffs. She lost track of time and place. The woods seemed endless. Rhonda showed no sign of tiring. The pain and humiliation would go on forever.

'Are we having fun yet?' Rhonda asked as the crop landed once more on Muriel's cunt.

'Fun!' Muriel shrieked.

'Yes. You know, the old warmth in the belly, little flickerings in the cunt as you warm up? Like you did at my apartment. Would you like it better if Paul was here? Would you come if you had an audience?'

Muriel had not connected this lashing with the other one. That one had indeed been 'fun', as Rhonda had called it, though the word seemed inadequate to describe those internal earthquakes. Then, however, she had sought out Rhonda in the privacy of her apartment, knowing and partly expecting what would be done to her – and eager to get on with it. This was entirely different – driven through the woods, in danger of being seen by strangers, reported to her directors as a deviate, lashed between her legs on her most sensitive parts. That first time Rhonda had paused to arouse her before continuing the lashing. And then she had shoved that enormous dildo into her and made her come again and again. She had fainted at the end.

Rhonda pushed the stiff whip between Muriel's thighs and rubbed it backwards and forwards over her labia and clitoris. 'Oh!' Muriel cried in surprise. And 'Ohhhh!' as the unbearably pleasurable friction continued. The memory of the pain and humiliation

146

faded as the arousal continued. Muriel felt the fire in her abused legs and bottom and cunt as a background to the enjoyable rubbing of the whip between her legs. The pain faded into a pleasant warmth.

When Rhonda withdrew the lash and sent it stinging against her cunt again, Muriel shrieked in pain and surprise. She nearly fell to the ground. But Rhonda was stroking her again, the stiff leather handle against her clitoris, and the waves of pleasure were rising again to engulf her. As Rhonda alternately outraged and pleasured her, Muriel became progressively more aroused. What began as alternate pain and pleasure gradually became more enjoyable. The pain became an adjunct to it, heightening her excitement as she waited for the next probing between her thighs. Maybe if I concentrate on that, she thought, the rest will fade away. Think positive, she told herself.

Rhonda struck her again. Muriel concentrated, and was rewarded by a definite flicker in her belly. She imagined herself growing wet inside. I can almost feel it, she told herself. She glanced down and saw that her nipples were erect, and took heart from that sign too. Muriel began to anticipate her first climax. Rhonda struck her again, and she moaned with excitement.

A sudden blow across her breasts and nipples woke Muriel from her reverie. A red line grew as she watched, stupefied. Rhonda struck her again, stinging her erect nipples and drawing a groan of mingled pleasure and pain from her. Then the whip was between her legs again, and she was going to come!

Rhonda withdrew the whip and struck her across the bottom. 'Move!' she ordered.

Muriel couldn't believe her ears. She had been on the very edge of an orgasm. It was building in her belly, weakening her thigh muscles and threatening her knees with collapse, and now the pain had come back. But she had to believe her body. After the pleasure, the renewal of pain was more searing than before. Or so it seemed to her, driven like an animal, fighting her handcuffs and the reactions of her own body. Was this what she had come for, this endless pain and the teasing approach to release? Yes, she whispered to herself. Yes. Only, she would like more of the carrot and a bit less of the stick. Muriel groaned with frustration as she braced herself for the lash's return.

And so, alternately lashed and stroked, Muriel was driven deeper into the woods. She caught a glimpse of Chloe, standing still and looking back at her. Chloe gazed longingly at her. The look on her face said plainly that she would like to exchange places. Chloe was tugging at the rope that ran from her bound hands and back through her crotch, seeking her own release even as Muriel sought hers. 'Ohh!' she moaned as the stiff whip rubbed her clitoris once more.

The march went on endlessly, Muriel teetering on the verge of orgasm and always just failing to achieve it. She felt as if her whole body were afire, promising release and then drawing back from it. It took all of Rhonda's skill to keep her at that pitch.

Suddenly the shape of a barn loomed up before her clouded vision. The rain of blows ceased. Muriel stopped, tottering on her legs. Rhonda grasped her lead and tugged her forwards, towards the dimly seen building in the deep woods. Muriel cried out, 'Please, please let me come . . . make me come. I can't stand this!'

'Of course you can,' Rhonda told her. 'You can't always have what you want, you know,' she reproved her weary captive. 'Think of how much better the next time will feel after you've had some time to anticipate it.'

Anticipation was just what Muriel felt, a terrible foreboding of screaming orgasm, and she wanted it now. 'Nooo!' she moaned. 'Now. Please, now!'

Rhonda pulled her into the barn and attached the lead to a hook set in the wall at head height. 'Later,' she said to her desperate victim. 'Watch and enjoy.'

Chloe was already inside, standing in the centre of the large space. It was gloomy after the bright sunlight outside. And rather dull after the earlier fireworks. However, as her excitement ebbed, Muriel became aware that this was not a conventional barn. There was a forge and metal-working shop occupying the main part of the ground floor. As her eyes became accustomed to the light and shadow Muriel also noted that there were various projects in progress. All of them looked as if they had something to do with her own interest: B&D and sexual torment. The extensive collection in the house from which her own chains had come was made up of finished objects. Here there was an air of experimentation. This was a place where new restraints were tried out, perhaps being custom-made to individual requirements.

Rhonda was talking to a tall stranger who stood near the back entrance to the barn. She beckoned him to follow her. As he came closer, Muriel tried unsuccessfully for invisibility. 'Ted, this is Muriel. She's new to our scene and might enjoy seeing some of your creations. Muriel, this is Ted Miller, our resident blacksmith and creator of custom restraints to the trade.'

Ted Miller was tall, very tall. He had blond hair and dark eyes that swept appraisingly over her. He was broad across the shoulders and narrow at the waist. As befitted a blacksmith, his arms and hands were very large. Muriel felt intimidated, as well as embarrassed. Rhonda seemingly intended to introduce her to a whole circle of people on whose discretion she would have to rely if her secret was to remain secret. Secrets unshared were the safest.

'Glad to meet you, Muriel. Welcome to the circle of deviants and freaks that Rhonda presides over. It's always good to meet a new devotee.'

He sounded nice enough, polite and interested, even if he was speaking about things Muriel had hoped to keep private. Politeness demanded that she acknowledge his greeting, even if circumstances made nonsense of such rituals. She could not offer him her hand, for one thing. He did not comment on it; nor did he mention her chains or the red stripes that covered her body. Muriel had the feeling that nothing would disturb these people. The most bizarre occurrences were their everyday experience.

Rhonda was talking again. 'Muriel is going to watch as we give Chloe what she has been wanting. Then maybe we'll let Muriel enjoy a bit of the same if she behaves herself. Would you like to start with Chloe? She's about to wet herself with excitement.'

Chloe did indeed look anxious. Her out-thrust breasts were agitated with her rapid breathing, and she made little nervous, aimless movements as she awaited their attention. She smiled tensely at no one in particular.

'The whipping frame, don't you think?' Ted asked. 'Chloe liked that the last time.'

Rhonda nodded agreement. Chloe flushed as they led her to one side of the cleared floor. Against the wall stood a tall frame made of aluminium piping. It was in the form of a triangle, the two long pipes meeting at the top and then diverging again to allow a rope to be thrown between them and secured out of the victim's reach. There was a shorter pipe across the bottom, completing a tall isosceles triangle. A flat plate was welded to the top surface: a place for the victim to stand. Ted and Rhonda lifted the frame down from a hook and moved it until its base was resting some distance from the wall and its top leaned against the side of the barn. It looked out of place, the modern welded frame in the rustic setting of the barn. Out of place, but very efficient and intimidating. Chloe seemed eager rather than frightened. Muriel felt a hollowness in her stomach as she contemplated what they were going to do to Chloe – and then perhaps to her.

Rhonda was untying the rope that held Chloe's hands against her belly as Ted stood ready to catch it and throw it over the top of the whipping frame. Between them they secured Chloe in place, her bound wrists high over her head and her ankles tied to the lower corners of the frame. She was stretched tightly, her feet resting on the flat plate: held quite immovably.

Ted and Rhonda drew straws to decide who would lash Chloe. Rhonda won – or lost. She picked a short-handled whip with a stiff grip and what looked like a dozen knotted leather thongs, each about a foot long. Chloe glanced back over her shoulder as they made the final preparations for her chastisement. Muriel, attached to the hook across the floor, felt even hollower as she too watched and awaited her turn. It appeared that Ted would do her. She had never been beaten by a man before. A stranger would lash her all over and she could do nothing to prevent it. She shivered in the increasingly familiar combination of fear and anticipation.

'Put her out of her misery,' Ted said to Rhonda. 'You can see that she's been waiting for this all morning.' Rhonda gave him a quick smile of ac-knowledgement as she took her place behind Chloe. Ted crossed to Muriel. 'This is something to watch,' he told her as he unfastened her lead from its hook. 'Come closer so you can see what is happening.' He led her across to stand to one side. From there Muriel could see how tightly Chloe was tied into the frame – and how she trembled in anticipation of the lashing to come. Ted held the end of her lead as Rhonda let the thongs run through her fingers. She was going to have to watch this, even if she felt like running away. And she was going to have to endure her own torment soon after that. Muriel hoped that the reward would be worth the punishment.

Rhonda drew back her arm to begin the whipping when Ted called her to wait. He dropped Muriel's lead and took Rhonda to one side. They talked briefly, Ted doing most of it, Rhonda listening and then breaking into a broad smile. She nodded agree-ment with his idea and they returned to the two waiting victims. Rhonda spoke to them both.

'Ted has just had a wonderful idea. He suggests that we do you both at once. So we are going to make some changes. Muriel, we are going to take off your handcuffs and leg-irons and tie you face to face with Chloe. To induce you both to enjoy the experience we are going to add a double dildo. That should make wriggling more enjoyable, don't you think?'

Muriel blanched as her own moment of truth was brought forward, but there was nothing she could do about it. Rhonda went to fetch the dildo-harness while Ted fastened a rope to the top of the whipping frame. The rope was attached to a block and tackle suspended from the rafters overhead. He pulled on the rope; the frame with Chloe attached rose to the vertical and then swung free in the air. The frame and its attachee swung giddily, pendulum-like, turning at the same time. Gradually the wild movement slowed down, and Chloe opened her eyes. She looked dizzily around.

Rhonda came back with the dildo harness. She went to Muriel and without ceremony slid one of the dildoes into her cunt. Not surprisingly, it went in easily. She was wet from her earlier lashing and her anticipation of more. Rhonda buckled the harness on to her. When she was done, Muriel felt stuffed on the inside and protruded rudely on the outside. Rhonda grasped the protrusion and gave it a quick push and pull movement, causing Muriel to close her eyes and murmur lingeringly, 'Ohhh.'

'Muriel looks pleased,' Rhonda announced as she moved the dildo in and out. Muriel's knees began to feel weak.

Ted meanwhile had tied two ropes to the lower corners of the whipping triangle and secured them to two of the posts that held up the loft. Now the triangle, with Chloe firmly attached, was likewise held firmly from swinging. 'Did you bring along the keys to Muriel's handcuffs?' he asked.

'As if I'd forget a detail like that!' Rhonda said, producing the keys on a string around her neck. She unlocked the handcuffs and leg-irons.

Together they marched Muriel over to the suspended frame and forced her to mount it. Ted moved the dildo several times. Muriel sighed once more. He slid the other end into Chloe, who made similar sounds of satisfaction. As the taller of the two, Ted tied Muriel's wrists and flung the rope over the top of the frame. He pulled the rope tight and tied it off out of the reach of either woman's hands. Rhonda secured her ankles to the lower corners of the triangle.

Chloe and Muriel, practically eye-to-eye, were now likewise joined by the dildoes. Chloe wriggled, producing the required in-and-out motion that excited them both. Muriel did the same. They smiled at one another.

Rhonda noticed, as she always did. 'What a wonderful idea! They like it! So do I.'

Ted smiled at the tableau. 'I guess they're ready now.'

Rhonda picked up the whip and took up a position behind Chloe. She struck the blonde across her bottom. Chloe jerked forwards. 'Aieeee!' she said. 'Ummmm,' Muriel replied. Several more blows followed, with similarly dissimilar reactions. Rhonda paused. 'Ted, why don't you take another whip and do Muriel. That way they get the same treatment. Democracy in action, and all that.'

He did, and thereafter the screams and the moans were more equally distributed, though it took some time for the screams to turn into moans of pleasure as the whipping continued. The frame moved slightly as Chloe and Muriel jerked and shuddered and wriggled. Muriel assumed that Chloe was feeling as she was: painful lashes compensated for by the action of the dildoes. This lashing was far more pleasurable much sooner than the earlier one. Although it was impossible to reach her cunt or breasts with the whip, Ted did manage to lash her on the anus. That sent a jolt through her. She screamed whenever he found that target, but the thrusts from Chloe did a good deal to make the sensation bearable. When she came, Muriel threw back her head and screamed aloud. The lashing continued unabated through that orgasm and through the ones that followed. Muriel lost track of time as she screamed and came and the lash rose and fell on her back and bottom and the backs of her legs.

154

Chloe's screams and moans formed a background to her own. Chloe's jerks and thrusts provided the stimulus for Muriel's orgasms – as she presumed her own had done for her fellow victim.

Eventually she hung from her wrists, her legs barely able to support her. Chloe, opposite, was in the same state. Muriel managed a weak smile. Chloe winked back. Neither knew where Rhonda and Ted had gone, nor when they might return to untie them – or perhaps to lash them again.

Every move she made was transmitted to Chloe, and vice versa. It occurred to Muriel that they could steal a bit more pleasure while their captors were doing whatever captors did when they had done with their captives. As she thrust forwards with her hips, Muriel saw her partner in suffering jerk. Chloe opened her eyes and gave a slow conspiratorial smile. The two women then found their rhythm and began to move faster and faster, driving one another over the top without the spur of the lash. It took longer: for one thing, they were tired from the earlier orgasms. For another, they felt like naughty schoolgirls, taking forbidden liberties while the grown-ups were away, knowing that they might be punished if they were discovered. The forbidden-fruit effect added to their pleasure while it inhibited their activity – though not for very long. Muriel began to keen deep in her throat as she felt another orgasm building in her belly. Chloe was not very far behind. Together they managed to pleasure one another several times.

When they stopped in exhaustion, there was applause from the shadows. Ted stood smiling at them. 'Well done!' he said approvingly. Rhonda was not in evidence. Muriel wondered if she would have been so approving. Probably not. Rhonda might well have plied them with the whip as punishment for stealing pleasure without permission.

Ted did not look like untying them, and Muriel did not like to ask. She was learning that freedom was granted by the captors. It was not good form to ask to be set free. So she and Chloe hung in the whipping frame, breath slowing and bodies cooling. There was nothing to prevent them from doing it all over again when they had recovered – provided Rhonda stayed away. Muriel found herself wishing for her continued absence. Chloe looked like being a willing partner in crime.

Rhonda, meanwhile, had gone back to the house, leaving the two women to Ted. The whipping had excited her more than she cared to admit, and she had gone to meet Paul when he returned from the airport. She wanted to talk with him, and she hoped that eventually he would provide the release for her own tensions. She walked through the empty house seeking him, her heels tapping on the wooden floors. He should have been back by now with some interesting questions.

Paul was seated in the cage-room. There were no lights lit, and in the growing dusk he was hidden in the shadows. From the shadows he asked what had happened to Zenobia Salvaggio. 'She never showed up,' he said.

'That's because there was no Zenobia,' Rhonda replied. 'I needed you to be away for most of the afternoon, so I invented an errand for you. Come up to my bedroom and I'll explain it to you.'

Paul was piqued at the deception, but then Rhonda was offering an explanation in the place where she most often compensated him for impositions. He followed her up the stairs, admiring the way the tight leather garment outlined her trim figure. He was struck yet again by how provocative she managed to look while wearing clothing that discouraged all approaches.

Rhonda led him into her bedroom and turned on the bedside lamp. The soft light made her even more attractive. 'Unzip me,' she told Paul.

Conversations that began with those magic words often led in interesting directions. Paul unzipped the leather corselet and worked it down her legs. She stepped out of it and waited for him to remove her tights. This intimate service was intended to excite him. It did. Rhonda smiled at the evidence.

'I should have made you wear the cock-cage,' she said lightly. She sat on the bed and patted the mattress, inviting him to sit beside her.

'Now, Zenobia,' she began. 'I needed to have Muriel to myself this afternoon. She will tell you what we did, and whether she enjoyed it. It looked to me as if she did, even after what you two did this morning. Muriel is remarkably resilient, though I suspect she may be feeling, ah, a bit shagged out by now. You can talk to her tomorrow. Tonight I want you here.'

That kind of invitation was hard to resist.

'Do you like her?'

It was a dangerous question no matter how he answered, but Paul thought that the truth was too obvious to someone like Rhonda to deny. He nodded.

She smiled. 'I thought so. And, no, I am not taking revenge on her for that. I like her too. I wonder what you think about admitting her to our . . . circle.'

'I think she would enjoy that. And, no, I am not thinking wholly with my cock.'

'But it does have something to do with your decision?' Rhonda patted the instrument in question fondly. 'No matter. I agree. I think you should be her sponsor, the one to prepare the way and to pop the question.'

'I've already done something like that. She's thinking about becoming my slave, but she doesn't know yet about the rest of the group. I don't think that will be any problem when I've had some more time to work around to the main question. If she takes the first step, I can introduce the rest of the family, so to speak.'

'And you will work very hard at that?' Rhonda said with another smile.

'Moderately hard, anyway.'

'Good. Now you need to work very hard on me. I am difficult to please, so use all of your persuasive skills, please.'

He did. Rhonda was pleased, and so was he. For them both, the vanilla sex most people consider routine was a different experience. Afterwards they went down to the kitchen to make supper. Naked lunches (and suppers, and breakfasts) were the rule around Rhonda.

Back in the bedroom, Rhonda asked Paul to tie her up before they made love again. This was not her usual routine, but she insisted. Paul tied her to the bed in the classic spread-eagle pose, her naked body stretched tautly between the bed-posts. As an afterthought, though she had not asked him to, he gagged her, the ball-gag filling her mouth and buckled tightly behind her head. Rhonda clearly expected Paul to mount her at once. She was aroused, her nipples erect and her breath short and ragged. She raised her hips invitingly and grimaced around the ball that filled her mouth. It might have been intended for a smile of invitation.

Paul looked at her for a long time, admiring her body and aroused by her helplessness. Rhonda was very rarely in this predicament. Reluctantly he turned away and made for the door. When she realised that he was going to leave her there, Rhonda protested as loudly as her gag allowed. 'Nnnnnngggghh!' she yelped, bouncing on the bed and tugging at the ropes. Paul knew that this temerity would have to be paid for later, but considered the exercise well worth the expected retribution. Sometimes it was nice to give Rhonda a taste of her own medicine, lest she forget what it was like to be on the receiving end. He considered giving her a taste of the lash, but he had a better idea. He would balance the scales by allowing Muriel the opportunity to lash Rhonda.

Her wrath would then descend on someone else as well, but Muriel did not have to take the chance. However, she might like it. He would let Rhonda have the full treatment, he thought, as he closed the door on the struggling, angry woman. He went in search of food and drink, an excuse to fill the time while Rhonda learned the joys of anticipation and denial. It was not easy to refrain from such an inviting prospect as sex with his helpless mistress. Making angry love had a certain appeal.

Back at the barn Muriel still hung in the frame with her fellow sufferer, swaying slightly as it moved, drowsing and waking. At one point she noticed that it was dusk. It had been a long day. How long would they be left bound and joined as they were? She had begun to think of lying down, though not necessarily on her own. There were no lights in the barn, and so she was surprised to find Ted standing quite near to Chloe, behind her back. Muriel guessed he had come to free them. So she was even more surprised when he came closer and Chloe jerked awake. The shared dildo stabbed Muriel as her fellow captive moved suddenly. Her eyes were wide open but unfocused.

'Ohhhh,' she sighed. Ted stood close behind her now, and Muriel realised that he was guiding his cock into Chloe's anus. Chloe didn't seem to mind. She wriggled and shifted to accommodate him, incidentally causing Muriel to focus sharply on her own penetration. When he was fully home, Ted began the characteristic in and out thrusts. The frame moved in time to his rhythm. Chloe sighed again. Muriel did as well, the dildo stirring her fully awake and aware. She tried to imagine how it felt to Chloe, doubly penetrated. Probably something like the time Rhonda had left her at the bank with the two dildoes inside her. That had been a moving experience. Being fucked while doubly penetrated must be an even more moving one. Chloe certainly seemed to be enjoying it. She moaned loudly, and Muriel felt herself pushed closer to full arousal by the dildo inside her. Economy of effort, she thought before her excitement engulfed her: one man pleasuring two women. How nice. And then she had her first orgasm. Only a small one by her usual standards, but it was a start. It all depended on how long Chloe and Ted could hold out.

They held out for some considerable time. Muriel became more excited as the dildo continued to move inside her. Her next orgasm was much longer and better. The idea of being aroused by a woman's movement against her combined with her inescapable bondage to keep her aroused. She came as her partner did the same. At some point Muriel found herself kissing Chloe as her excitement mounted, and had time to wonder at the attraction of kissing another woman so intimately. Am I a lesbian as well? she wondered. Whether or no, she found the whole process exciting. So exciting, in fact, that she came again. The dildo moved inside her as Chloe responded to her double impalement. The idea of herself being thus penetrated excited Muriel too. The kiss drew out as both women came, swaying in the frame as the last of the daylight went, squirming and jerking as Ted too came at last.

After that, he finally untied them. Both sat down on the floor to recover from the beating and what came afterwards. Ted went off to make some supper for them.

'Your stockings are ruined,' Chloe remarked.

Muriel looked at the sheer nylons she had put on that afternoon. 'Oh, well. It was in a good cause,' she said philosophically. And so am I, she thought. Ruined if I get found out, and ruined for straight sex for the rest of my life. She wondered how she had survived so long without this necessary ingredient.

They ate at a long table with Ted, all very companionable and naked. Muriel wondered if she had the energy to take on Ted that evening, and surprised herself with having the thought at all. Probably not. But tomorrow would be another matter. That night they all slept in the same bed over the workshop.

It was just as well for Muriel that she slept well, because in the morning she became the object of Ted's attention. Helped by Chloe, he strung her up by the wrists in the frame and administered a beating which made the last one seem mild. The lash stung her bottom as it landed. Muriel jerked forwards, away from the blow, grunting in surprise. Ted struck her repeatedly, covering her bottom and back with red stripes before moving down the backs of her thighs. When he reached her ankles, Muriel was bathed in sweat, her body tense and trembling from the pain. She struggled against the ropes and against screaming. She was panting, her breasts rising and falling rapidly as she drew in great shuddery breaths.

Ted moved around in front of her and struck her heaving breasts. At that Muriel's control broke and she screamed aloud, heedless of who might hear. Of course, no one did. Once again the awareness of her isolation came to her: no one was going to come to her rescue. That excited her. Ted continued striking her breasts and nipples. Her nipples hardened and erected under the rain of blows, evidence of her perverse excitement. When Ted moved down to her stomach and belly and the fronts of her thighs, she was conscious of a mild disappointment. Her screams had gradually subsided as he struck her less sensitive areas.

Then he sent the lash straight up between her legs. Muriel howled as the whip landed squarely on her exposed cunt. As the lash struck her repeatedly between the thighs, Muriel screamed and jerked futilely against her bonds. Soon she was sweating once again from the pain, weeping and pleading with him to stop, when she felt the first stirring inside her cunt. Her body shifted gears as the lash rose and fell. As it had on the previous day when Rhonda had driven her through the woods, her body transmuted pain into arousal and, she knew, it would eventually reward her with an orgasm despite the pain of the preliminary stages. Muriel hoped he would continue. Rhonda had brought her through pain to the threshold of pleasure before stopping. The repetition of that process had left her begging for release – a release that Rhonda had denied. Only when they had reached their destination had she been allowed her release. The walk through the woods had been an exquisite torture as Rhonda had toyed with her. She desperately wanted Ted to finish the process.

Apparently he did too. He continued to lash her as she howled in pain. He could see that she was becoming aroused as he lashed her breasts and cunt and belly. Muriel was moaning as much as screaming, writhing and jerking in the frame. When she came the scream was clearly one of pleasure. Muriel shuddered and jerked as the lash brought her to orgasm again and again. Her screams filled the space and she lost all track of time. The sweat ran down between her heaving breasts and down her straining thighs. She gasped for breath between screams.

Some indeterminate time later she realised that the whip had gone away. Muriel hung in her bonds, swaying slightly in the frame. She was alone, as far as she could see, twisting her head from side to side. The day was bright outside the dark barn. Bird song and a gentle breeze came to her as she waited for Ted to return for her. Would he beat her again? Or would he shove his cock into her anus as he had done with Chloe the day before? Muriel shuddered with a dark delight at the thought, even as she took stock of her sore body and tired muscles. What had become of her? In only a few weeks she had become a different person. She was much happier, for one thing. Sex had become such a vivid experience since she had submitted herself to Rhonda and Paul. And to Ted. Sex with several partners, not all of them male, now seemed quite normal. The slavery that Paul had offered seemed much more attractive when it included days like this.

Muriel hung for a long time in the barn alone. At last she heard a slight sound behind her. She tried to turn far enough to see who it was but could not. The frame held her fast. She felt someone touching her anus, and she tightened her sphincter in response. Nevertheless, a slippery finger penetrated her from behind. Muriel yelped as it slid into her. Her visitor worked it around several times, while her muscles tried to expel it, and then it went away, leaving her feeling strangely empty. When the finger returned, it repeated the same performance in her cunt, from behind. That was more pleasant. Muriel moaned softly as it massaged her clitoris and explored her sex. Finally it too was withdrawn, much too soon in Muriel's opinion, but there was nothing she could do about it.

'Who is it?' she asked. There was no answer. She repeated the question. No reply. She became gradually aware that whoever had come to her had gone away again. Muriel tugged at the ropes in vain. She was not going to get loose without help.

After perhaps half an hour of futile struggle she became aware of an itching, burning sensation in and around her anus. A similar sensation started to grow in her cunt. She squirmed, trying to make it go away, and jerked once more at the ropes. She wanted to scratch the itch. It grew. Her hips twitched backwards and forwards as she tried to relieve herself. Soon she was trembling and sweating. She moaned in desperation as the itching and burning grew inside her. Muriel felt as if she would go mad with the sensation. She had to scratch, but could not. This was a torture as real as the lashing she had endured, but it promised no relief.

Muriel felt her breasts tightening, the nipples growing erect as she struggled. She could not believe that her body found *this* exciting. It was torment. She could do nothing to relieve herself.

'Help!' she screamed. And again. No help came. Muriel was drenched in sweat from her struggles as she grew more desperate. She needed something to stuff inside her to get at this maddening itch. A cock would do. Two of them. Or two dildoes. Anything she could use to relieve herself. And then, as if in answer to a prayer, Chloe came through the front door. Muriel cried out, 'Help me! I can't stand this!'

'Can't stand what?' Chloe asked, making no move to help. 'You've been tied up before. You even liked it when Ted beat you. I watched.'

The effort to explain her predicament was almost too much for Muriel. Red-faced, squirming, she implored Chloe to do something to relieve the intolerable itch. She thrust her hips forwards to indicate the affected parts.

Chloe nodded at last. 'I understand now. But it will go away on its own after a while.'

'I can't wait that long!' Muriel screamed. 'Do something now! Please! I can't stand this.'

'What do you want me to do?'

In exasperation Muriel screamed at her to shove something – some two things, actually – inside her and scratch the itch.

'That will only make it worse,' Chloe told her. 'And you'll probably come as well. You look tired out. You should rest.'

Muriel shook her head rapidly to clear the sweat from her eyes. 'I don't care! Just do something!'

'Are you sure you want me to shove dildoes into you?'

'Stop being obtuse and *do* something!' screamed Muriel in desperation, jerking once again at the ropes.

Chloe made as if to turn away. Muriel begged her not to go. 'At least untie me so I can do something for myself.'

'I'm not allowed to untie you. That's Ted's job. He's up at the house talking to Rhonda. Anyway, she is the one who makes the rules. You'll have to ask her when she comes.'

Muriel moaned in frustration.

At last Chloe took pity on her. 'I suppose I can get a dildo or two for you,' she said as she walked behind

Muriel. The helpless victim struggled with the ropes while Chloe rummaged around out of her sight. When she returned she had strapped the dildo harness around her waist, and evidently was feeling the first benefits from the dildo inside her. The one intended for Muriel stuck up rudely from her crotch. In her hand she held another rubber shaft, obviously intended for Muriel's back passage. The helpless woman stared at it in fascinated horror.

'I'll never get that inside.'

'You won't have to. I'll do it for you,' Chloe told her.

'No, you don't understand,' Muriel cried. 'It's too big!'

'Wait and see,' Chloe replied as she dragged over a stool. She climbed on to it and without more ado guided the dildo into Muriel's cunt.

The effect on Muriel was immediate. As the rubber shaft slid into her, she began a desperate series of rapid jerks that moved it in and out of her cunt. The relief was delicious.

Chloe reached around behind Muriel and thrust the second dildo against her anal sphincter. Muriel wailed a desperate 'No!' and clamped down to block the penetration. Chloe thrust slowly but relentlessly, timing her pushes to the frenzied jerking of Muriel's hips. Gradually the shaft slid into her anus, lubricated by the cream that was causing the itching. She tried to evade the anal dildo but found herself blocked by Chloe, who thrust her own hips forwards to prevent escape.

Doubly impaled, Muriel shuddered and moaned. 'No! Noooo!'

'Yes,' Chloe insisted, and there was nothing that Muriel could do. The blonde matched her movements to Muriel's, so that the dildo slid in and out of the captive. At the same time she managed to make the second dildo slide in and out of Muriel's anus. Muriel jerked and bucked but could not escape. And the dildoes *did* relieve the terrible itch. They did more than that, of course, but it was some time before Muriel became aware of the other effects. At first it was a relief just to scratch.

Gradually she realised she was becoming aroused by the twin dildoes, as was Chloe. Held rigidly and inescapably in the whipping triangle, Muriel felt the familiar heat in her belly and between her legs as the blonde woman fucked her. With a moan she leaned forwards and covered Chloe's lips with hers, her tongue searching her captor's mouth and her erect nipples tight against Chloe's own. Muriel surrendered herself to the double pleasure of scratching and fucking. Chloe was apparently satisfied with just the one. She pulled Muriel against her with her free arm, while her other hand continued to work the dildo in Muriel's anus.

Muriel felt dizzy with the spasms of pleasure that shook her. The itch was being scratched in the best way possible. Muriel felt Chloe shudder with her own orgasm, and once more was amazed to discover that sex with another woman could yield so much pleasure. This time, she did not worry whether she was becoming a lesbian. She concentrated on the fun girls could have together.

When Chloe withdrew, Muriel hung from her bound wrists, the second dildo still in her anus. Shortly she felt Chloe sliding another dildo into her sex. Muriel looked down to see the blonde woman strapping the harness around her waist. The position was now reversed. The dildo Chloe had stuffed herself with now stuffed Muriel. She looked down at the dildo that protruded from between her own legs, while she clenched herself around the two that now penetrated her. It was a deliciously wicked sight and feeling, even if she was tied helplessly and could do nothing with the twin shafts.

Chloe, however, could. And did. Moving behind Muriel as she hung in the triangular frame, she grasped the anal dildo and began to move it in and out. Muriel gasped as the shaft slid home and then was withdrawn. Chloe was going to make her come again. Desperately, she shook her head. 'No. Don't. I can't take any more.'

'Of course you can,' her captor retorted. She kept the dildo moving, and Muriel groaned as she felt her body begin to respond again. It was as if she stood to one side and watched herself being manipulated, while at the same time she felt the result of the manipulation. When Chloe reached around with her other hand to move the dildo in her cunt, Muriel whimpered helplessly with rising excitement. Whatever she might think, her body had its own agenda.

Chloe took her through one slow orgasm. Muriel stiffened in her bonds as the slow wave rolled through her, moaning softly as she came.

'There,' Chloe said soothingly, 'I knew you could do it.' And she continued to work the twin dildoes.

Muriel's next orgasm was shorter and sharper. She let out a long groan this time, pulling against the ropes while her body swayed in involuntary rhythm with the movement of the dildoes. She screamed as the next orgasm shook her. Her knees gave way and she slumped in her bonds, but even then Chloe was not done with her. Muriel lost track of how many times she came. At the end she was exhausted, whimpering, pleading with Chloe to stop.

Which she eventually did. She left the dildoes in place, however, a reminder to Muriel of what could be done to her yet again. She untied her captive's wrists from the frame and tied them again behind her back. Only then did she untie Muriel's ankles and help her down from the frame. Muriel swayed, and would have fallen had Chloe not caught her and steadied her until she could stand unaided.

Using the whip, she then drove Muriel back through the forest, switching her across the bottom or the backs of her thighs whenever she showed signs of slowing down. The dildoes moved and shifted as she stumbled along, the dildo protruding from between her thighs and bobbing as she walked. Both the shafts inside her sent disturbing signals to her weary body: it could all happen again. And, near the house, it did. Muriel fell to her knees on the path, moaning as the familiar sensations spread from her cunt and anus. She toppled to the ground, the dildo inside her cunt stabbing her as she fell.

'Ohhhhhh!' she moaned.

Chloe waited until she grew still before helping her back on to her feet and driving her along.

When they reached the house Muriel felt as if she could not take another step.

Paul came out to help her up the stairs and into the bathroom. There he supported her while Chloe untied her and removed the dildoes. The warm bath that awaited her felt heavenly. They put her to bed and she slept.

Paul woke Muriel. It was late afternoon. 'Come along to see Rhonda. She's been waiting for you.'

When she entered the bedroom, Muriel saw at once the aptness of his words. Rhonda was indeed waiting, but not very patiently. The sight of the dominatrix tied to her own bed was most unexpected. The sounds that emerged from behind the gag were definitely demands to be set free this instant. Muriel's first impulse was to do just that. Paul's hand on her shoulder held her back.

'If you remove the gag, you'll never get a word in edgewise. She's been waiting all night.'

Muriel caught sight of a riding crop lying beside the helpless dominatrix. She was being invited to converse with Rhonda via the whip. With some surprise, she felt a rising desire to do so, she who had never before inflicted pain. It must be a result of her own recent ordeals, Muriel told herself, even as she moved hesitantly to take the crop from the bed.

Rhonda watched her approach narrowly, and her eyes widened at what she saw in Muriel's expression. She shook her head slightly at her former captive who made no reply, merely advancing to stand beside the bed and its helpless, angry occupant.

The anger seemed to turn to trepidation at Muriel's silence. Paul, watching Rhonda's expression, wondered just how she would take to being beaten as she had beaten him and Muriel, among others. Not too well, he guessed, judging by the apprehension in Rhonda's face and by the general aspect of drawing-in as she prepared for the lash. Muriel's expression was more difficult to read. She seemed withdrawn, even as she hefted the riding crop and laid it across Rhonda's breasts.

Rhonda winced at the touch but remained silent. The gag had something to do with that, but more likely, Paul guessed, it was pride that kept her from trying to stop Muriel from whatever she was going to do. Victims, 'associates', were allowed to beg. Not dominatrices. Or at any rate not this one.

Muriel came to an abrupt decision. She raised the whip and brought it down across Rhonda's breasts. The crack of leather meeting flesh was loud in the silent room. Rhonda jerked against the ropes holding her wrists and ankles to the bedposts, and drew in a gasping breath.

Muriel gazed curiously down at her victim as she raised the crop for another blow. Rhonda seemed to brace herself for it. Muriel struck her again, across her nipples this time, and this time Rhonda moaned at the pain, jerking frenziedly at her bonds. Muriel raised the whip for another blow. Thus began a systematic beating that left Rhonda gasping and with tears running down her cheeks. Muriel struck the upper and lower slopes of her breasts, her nipples, the taut expanse of Rhonda's stomach, and her belly. Red stripes began to appear in the wake of the lash. Rhonda was moaning steadily, pulling against the ropes as she tried to escape the stinging cuts. When Muriel struck her cunt, Rhonda went wild. She would have screamed but for the gag. As it was, she went rigid, arms and legs straining, back arched, her body a taut bow. Muriel struck her cunt again, to the accompaniment of loud but muffled howls, presumably of pain. Did Rhonda know the trick of turning pain into pleasure? Muriel had only learned it recently. Perhaps not, judging from her reactions. Those muffled sounds indicated protest rather than release. Muriel laid the whip down. Rhonda looked relieved. Slowly the tautness went out of her muscles as she realised that the ordeal was over.

Muriel, naked like the dominatrix, climbed on to the bed and arranged herself in the sixty-nine position over Rhonda. She had never gone down on a woman before, but she felt compelled to do so now, aware of a desire to give Rhonda pleasure. Perhaps to show her that not all transactions had to involve pain and humiliation. But no one would have guessed that from Rhonda's reaction. If anything, she found the

171

prospect of Muriel's mouth on her body more alarming than the whip had been.

'Ooooo!' she cried, trying once more to escape. Muriel stopped to look around at her, seeing revulsion in Rhonda's look. Whether Rhonda didn't like the lesbian touch, or whether she had an aversion to taking her pleasure from one of her 'associates', Muriel could not tell. But she didn't stop, remembering Rhonda's refusal to heed her own pleas the day she had humiliated Muriel in her own office.

Rhonda's hips jerked as Muriel bent once again to her cunt, licking and kissing the labia and nipping the bud of Rhonda's clit as it swelled from the stimulation. She knew Paul was watching. Perhaps it was the same knowledge that made Rhonda averse to cunnilingus. Muriel kept her mouth fastened to Rhonda despite the other woman's heaving and bucking, and eventually Rhonda made a small moan of surrender as the teeth nipped her clitoris. Muriel slid a finger into Rhonda's cunt, and discovered the first traces of lubrication. Satisfied, she began to move the finger in and out, wishing she had a dildo to use instead. Doubtless there was one near by: this was after all Rhonda's place, but she did not want to stop to find it. She continued the oral and digital stimulation of the captive woman with the means at hand.

Rhonda's will to resist weakened gradually. She moaned and shuddered as another orgasm rippled through her. Muriel waited for a moment, allowing Rhonda to enjoy the release, and then continued to arouse her. Rhonda still made muffled sounds of protest, in the interval between orgasms: Ooooo! Eeeese! Muriel brought her to climax once again, and the protests turned to moans of release. At last it was all too much for Rhonda. Muriel felt her body relax, and then go taut all over as she came again. This one

172

was for real. The moans were clearly signs of pleasure. Rhonda was shaking and her cunt was wet all through. The first shudder was followed by another, a long one, or perhaps several peaks in succession. The dead giveaway was that at the last Rhonda wet herself, the golden stream rising in a shallow arch from her crotch and soaking her thighs and the bed. And Muriel, who caught most of it in the face. But she never faltered. She kept Rhonda at the peak for a long time after the deluge, until the helpless woman slumped in exhaustion in her bonds.

Muriel rose from the bed searching for a towel or a tissue. Paul handed her a box of Kleenex, with which she wiped her face. Rhonda lay with her eyes closed and her face averted. Was she trying to hide herself from these witnesses who knew of her arousal, or was she just tired?

'Come on, Muriel,' Paul said. 'You can shower while I call Ted and Chloe to take care of Rhonda.'

Rhonda immediately returned to the present with a howl of protest. A long wail that must have meant an emphatic no. She jerked at her bonds in a frenzy.

'I believe she doesn't want to be seen,' Paul said. 'Wouldn't you like Ted and Chloe to help while I help Muriel?'

More wails, much shaking of the head from the bound woman.

Muriel went into the en suite bathroom to clean herself. She wondered if Paul had staged the previous scene for his own reasons – a payback for things Rhonda had done. She herself felt somehow even with Rhonda. When she emerged he had gone and Rhonda was still tied to the bed. She looked pleadingly at Muriel, jerking at the ropes around her wrists and trying to talk around the gag. The appeal was plain enough. Muriel sat on the bed beside the captive. She brushed Rhonda's long hair from her face. Moved by a sudden impulse, she bent to kiss her forehead, her eyes and her cheeks. Rhonda went taut at once, but gradually relaxed. Muriel untied her wrists and helped her to sit up. Rhonda at once began to work on the gag, and Muriel thought it might be a good idea to be absent when she got it off. Rhonda could easily untie her own ankles.

Paul was waiting in the hall. He led Muriel to her room. 'Time to get back to New Orleans,' he told her. Her clothes, washed and ironed, were folded on the armchair near the bed. There was a new pair of stockings for her as well. Paul (or Rhonda) was certainly thorough.

Muriel dressed slowly, conscious of a great weariness of body while she marvelled at what she had done that weekend. She felt an entirely different person from the one who had been abducted and transported across three state lines on the previous Friday evening. Now it was time to go back to the routine, and for the first time in her working life Muriel was reluctant to return. Nevertheless, she knew that she must.

Paul was to drive her back to the city. Muriel wondered what he thought about what the others had done to her. Was he jealous because Ted and Chloe had pleasured her? And was she jealous because he had probably pleasured Rhonda? As she snapped the garters to the stocking tops, Muriel decided that she was not. There had been enough excitement for all.

The others came down to see them off. They all kissed her goodbye. 'Come back soon,' Rhonda said. She wore a bathrobe with, Muriel guessed, nothing much underneath. Rhonda gave no sign of resentment at her treatment. A mask? Muriel wondered. Well, there was nothing to be done about it. And she had enjoyed doing Rhonda for a change. Her reaction had made her seem more human. Muriel got into Paul's car and fastened the seat belt. But he had another surprise for her. He locked her wrists together with handcuffs. With another pair he fastened her ankles together, and joined the two with a short chain that obliged her to draw up her legs so that he could connect her wrists and ankles. Muriel was left strapped into the seat, unable to undo her seat belt or to get out and walk.

Only then did Paul enter the car. Muriel felt a surge of excitement, knowing that she was going to be transported helplessly back to New Orleans. The others smiled and waved goodbye. Muriel in her chains could only smile back at them.

It was a long drive back to New Orleans. Muriel tried several positions, none of them really comfortable, but she did not ask Paul to free her from the handcuffs and leg-irons. When it was dark he pulled into a rest stop which turned out to be deserted. Muriel was relieved, because by then she was in need of relief herself, both from the cramped position forced on her by the chains, but also from a full bladder. Paul parked the car and reached over to unlock her leg-irons. He dropped them to the floor of the car and unbuckled her seat belt. He got out and went around to open the door for his captive passenger. Muriel emerged awkwardly, showing a lot of leg and smooth nylon as she did so. She looked around nervously, but the place was deserted.

Paul led her into the nearby woods by the chain attached to her handcuffs. Muriel was overwhelmed by the delicious sensation of fear and anticipation which she by now attached to bondage and sex episodes. In the darkness under the trees he lifted her skirt and ordered her to squat. Muriel squatted awkwardly and relieved herself, some of the urine running down her stockings and into her shoes. Paul urinated against a tree while she envied yet again the arrangement that allowed men to pee without any of the awkwardness required of women, especially women wearing handcuffs in the woods. Her cautious nature told her she should not be here, but the darker side of her was trembling with anticipation and a strong sense of flouting public mores.

Paul tugged Muriel to her feet by the chain and lifted her skirt high above her waist. Since she was wearing nothing under it save the now damp stockings and suspenders, Muriel was effectively nude from the waist down. Paul pushed her against a tree and ordered her to put her arms around his neck. He put his hands under Muriel's bottom and lifted her from the ground, holding her against the tree while he guided his cock into her. 'Lift your legs and put them around my waist. Cross your ankles behind my back and hang on.'

Muriel had never experienced this particular position. She reflected that she had led a rather sheltered life until she had met Rhonda and Paul. With a sigh she settled herself against him and hung on. She had missed him during the episode in the barn, even though she had not been bored. Now, though, she was happy that he was boring into her. The darkness, the rough bark of the tree against her back, the handcuffs and the idea of fucking outdoors all combined to arouse her. She gasped and moaned as she felt him hard inside her and the cool air on her exposed body.

Muriel screamed when she came the first time, a ladylike scream but unmistakable. This was exciting stuff to her. And ever so much better than being had in a safe bed. Her next orgasm brought a louder groan, a sound that anyone would recognise at once. 'Kiss me,' she gasped. 'I don't want to scream again, but I can't stop myself.'

Paul bent his head and covered her mouth with his own, though Muriel's moan of pleasure still sounded loudly in her ears. When he came, she almost jerked her mouth away to scream, but he held her as they both recovered from the experience.

He lowered Muriel to her feet and pulled her back to the car by the chain. Muriel fought him, pleading with him to pull her skirt down. Paul paid her no heed, dragging her back to the car with her skirt above her waist and her nylon-sheathed legs in full view. Another car turned into the rest area and Muriel thought she would die of shame and embarrassment. Paul's car partially shielded her as she dived into the seat. She was shaking and sweating by the narrowness of her escape. 'Close the door!' she hissed at him. With maddening slowness he did so, hiding her nudity and the handcuffs from the occupants of the other car just in time. He got into the car himself and they drove away just as the other people were abreast of their car. They gave her a curious look but did nothing.

For the rest of the drive Muriel trembled at the thought that she had been seen and recognised. Public shame would be the next step, followed by loss of her job.

Paul did not seem concerned. At her apartment he unlocked Muriel's handcuffs. Hurriedly she pulled her skirt down, fearful now of discovery by her neighbours. Paul went in with her. Surely, she thought incredulously, he didn't plan to . . . He did. And, though she hadn't planned on it herself, so did she. She slept exhaustedly that night.

10

The Abduction

Muriel spent the next week half in fear that head office would call and half in fear that Paul would not call. 'I'm addicted,' she told herself, wonderingly.

Paul's call came on Thursday afternoon. Would she like to go sailing that weekend? Muriel guessed that the weekend would include a lot more than sailing. She agreed with a flutter of her pulse and a catch in her breathing. 'Yes. Oh, yes,' she said, not caring how much she betrayed her eagerness. They made the arrangements on the phone. He would call for her early on Saturday morning.

Friday passed in a haze of lust. Muriel scarcely knew what she was doing. There were strange looks from the rest of the staff. They had never seen the boss so flustered. Paul was going to come to her apartment for her. She could hardly wait for what would happen afterwards. At closing time she locked the bank with trembling hands and got into her car. She drove to the nearest supermarket to stock her refrigerator for the coming week, knowing there would be no opportunity for shopping once Paul came. She paid no attention to the black van that pulled into the space next to her car.

A woman got out and opened the sliding door. Muriel got out of her car as the woman turned to face her. In her hand she held a familiar-looking taser. Muriel recognised Valerie Sanderson at the same time as she heard the soft hiss of compressed air and felt the prick of the darts in her stomach and breasts.

'Keep quiet,' Valerie ordered. 'You know what this can do to you. If you open your mouth I'll pull the trigger.'

Muriel looked down in astonishment at the thin wires that led from the front of her blouse to the taser in Valerie's hand. She instinctively raised a hand to pluck the darts from her body, and Valerie pulled the trigger. Muriel felt a searing jolt of electricity flash through her. Her hand dropped nervelessly and she pitched forwards. Her knees buckled and the breath was driven from her lungs in an explosive gasp. The sudden pain was awful. She could not recover her breath to scream. Had Valerie not caught her, she would have fallen to the ground. The blonde woman pushed her collapsing victim into the van and climbed in herself, before sliding the door closed with her free hand. She must have pulled the trigger again, for Muriel felt another terrible wave of pain shoot through her, paralysing her muscles. She blacked out.

When she came to, she was bound and gagged. Her hands were tied behind her back. Looking down, Muriel saw that her ankles were fastened together with a black nylon strap such as electricians and plumbers use for wires and piping. She guessed that a similar one held her wrists. She recalled seeing the same kind of straps used by the police in subduing rioters. Muriel tugged at hers without effect. There was even less give in the nylon cable ties than in the rope Valerie had used to bind her on the last occasion. Wide strips of tape crossed her face from ear to ear and from nose to chin. The van turned a corner and she rolled helplessly to the outside of the turn. At the next turn she rolled back again. The drive through traffic seemed endless as Muriel struggled to free herself and tossed about helplessly as the van made its long journey to . . . where?

When the movement finally stopped, Muriel had time to take stock of her predicament. She knew by then that she would not be able to free herself. The gag prevented all speech and most sound. It was not going to come loose, either. She had tried to work her jaws and loosen the tape without success.

Outside Muriel heard the sound of a heavy door opening. Valerie came back and drove the van into a building. Even through the heavily tinted glass Muriel saw the light darken as they passed inside. The van stopped again. The outer doors closed, further darkening the scene. Valerie returned to the van and opened the sliding door. From a distance came the hoot of a horn, like that of a ship, Muriel guessed. In which case, the building was probably an old warehouse of the sort that lined the Mississippi River from Canal Street down to the Industrial Canal. Some had been disused for years. No one would find her here.

But why was she here? Had Paul ordered Valerie to abduct her and deliver her to him? She hoped that he had.

Valerie pulled the tape off. Muriel gasped with the pain.

'Believe it or not,' Valerie told her, 'it hurts less when it's done quickly. I'm going to untie your hands in a minute, but not your ankles. Don't even think of jumping me.' Valerie showed her captive a leather collar. 'Dog trainer,' she said tersely. 'If you make a sound, or attempt to escape, you'll get a shock like the taser's. Only this one can be repeated as often as necessary. Understand?'

Valerie buckled the collar around Muriel's throat. Then she pulled the taser's darts from Muriel's body.

She produced a set of side-cutting pliers and snipped the cable tie holding her wrists.

'I know you're supposed to meet him this weekend, and I want you to make a call to put him off.'

'Him' was clearly Paul, but how Valerie had known of it was not so clear.

'Why are you doing this to me?' Muriel asked.

'I'm applying for a loan, and thought that applying pressure to the loan officer might soften her up,' Valerie replied, taking the mobile phone from Muriel's purse. It did not sound as if she was joking.

'Call him. Say you're sick or something. I'll be listening in case you try to warn him.'

So it wasn't Paul who had ordered her abduction, Muriel thought, with the first stirrings of fear. Numbly she took the phone and dialled Paul's number. It rang and rang.

'No answer.'

'Send him a text,' Valerie ordered. 'Say you'll see him next Saturday. And you will, so long as you do what I say.'

Muriel asked Valerie to turn on the interior light so that she could see the screen as she composed the message. While Valerie reached for the switch, Muriel hurriedly tapped out, 'Help. Valer–'

Valerie turned back and saw the screen. Her face contorted with rage. She snatched the phone away from her captive, but not before Muriel had pressed the 'send' button. Valerie flung the phone down, shattering the case. She picked up a rectangular black plastic box and pressed a button on its top.

Once again Muriel was convulsed by the shock. It felt as if a steel band had tightened around her throat to stop her breath while her limbs jerked spasmodically. Valerie held the button down for what seemed like forever, while Muriel jerked and quivered in silent agony. When she finally released the button, Muriel lay gasping and shuddering in a soiled heap. Urine ran down her legs and soaked her skirt and stockings. As if from a great distance, she felt Valerie pull her arms behind her back and fasten them together again, jerking the cable tie so tight she feared it would cut her wrists. Valerie gave another tug to the strap binding her ankles, causing it to dig into the flesh beneath her stockings.

Valerie used more of the tape to gag her victim, winding it around her mouth and under her hair many times. Yet more tape, this time over Muriel's eyes. Valerie dragged Muriel to the side of the van and buckled her against something hard and unyielding, pulling a cargo strap tight under her victim's breasts. Another strap pulled her knees tightly together. Giving a last vicious tug to the strap, Valerie climbed out. 'Relax and enjoy the ride,' she snapped angrily. 'This is the sort of thing people like you do all the time.' She closed the door.

Muriel sat helplessly in silence and darkness while Valerie opened the warehouse door and drove the van out. There was another pause as the door clanged shut, and then Valerie set off with her captive into the great unknown.

As before, Muriel could not guess at her destination, but she imagined that it would be less pleasant than the last. This time she had no internal comforters to make the time pass agreeably, or to assure her that the abduction was designed to give her pleasure. She did not like to think about what lay in store.

This drive was much shorter. Muriel knew that she was not at Rhonda's place, but she had no idea where she was when the van stopped. Valerie released the strap that bound her upright and snipped the cable tie around Muriel's ankles. She did not remove the strap that bound her knees together. Muriel smelled herself and was dismayed. Aside from the unpleasant odour, she felt humiliated and . . . afraid. In the past, she had been allowed to use the toilet instead of soiling herself. This time Valerie showed no sign of allowing her captive that dignity.

Hobbled at the knees, Muriel was forced to get out of the van and stumble across a surface that felt like pine needles and twigs. She smelled pine resin and felt a cool breeze on her wet stockings. Valerie guided Muriel by the elbow for a few steps before turning and forcing her against a tree. The bark was rough on her hands and arms. Valerie tied Muriel to the tree. Rope passed several times around her waist and was pulled tight, pinning her against the trunk. More rope encircled her under the arms and around her chest. Valerie tied her ankles together and fastened them to the tree as well.

Muriel felt more afraid at the rough treatment. Neither Paul nor Rhonda was behind this. Valerie was acting on her own. 'Mnnngggg!' she gasped, shaking her head from side to side and working her jaws to try to get the tape loose. She also hoped that Valerie would speak to her, give her some clue about what was in store. And, though the idea shamed her, Muriel wanted to know that someone, even her captor, was near by. The prospect of being alone in her present situation was frightening.

There was no response. The wind stirred the trees and cooled her body. The silence that surrounded her was total. Muriel heard distant bird calls. There were occasional rustlings in the undergrowth that might have been squirrels . . . or something less innocuous. Muriel was a townie. The woods were all right for picnics, but being abandoned there was definitely no

fun. She had no real idea about the wildlife here-
abouts, and her helplessness allowed her imagination
to populate the forest with all sorts of ravening
beasts. And with snakes. She knew that there were
rattlesnakes in the woods. 'Nnnnggggg!' she cried.
There was no reply. She cried again, louder, and
began to struggle to free herself. She jerked and
pulled at the ropes that bound her to the tree. To no
avail. Muriel moaned in fear. Soon, she knew, it
would be night. The coming darkness would render
her more vulnerable to any nocturnal animal. She
would be easy prey for anything.

Muriel tried to force her fear down, knowing that
Valerie had deliberately left her here so that she
would imagine all sorts of dire consequences. It was
psychological torture, she told herself. If she died, or
was even seriously injured, she would be of no use to
Valerie if her objective was to rob the bank. But
suppose, whispered her overly active imagination,
suppose Valerie doesn't really care what happens to
you? Valerie had shown boundless contempt for 'her
kind of people' at the last abduction. Might she be a
psychopath who felt she had to do something about
them? To Muriel's fevered imagination all sorts of
possibilities became probabilities, and she could do
nothing to defend herself or to escape.

Muriel moaned and redoubled her efforts to free
herself. The ropes cut into her waist and chest. Her
arms and hands grew red and sore as she rubbed
against the rough bark, trying to saw through the
cable tie that bound her wrists behind her back. She
felt her hair falling over her forehead and cheeks,
damp with sweat, clinging to her face. Sweat ran
down her body, further wetting her clothing and
adding its own component to her odour. It occurred
to her that by making herself more obvious to the

wildlife by her scent she increased the chances of being discovered by some predator. But she could not simply stand there and make no effort to get free.

When she had exhausted herself, Muriel was still inescapably bound to the tree. She shivered as the cool of evening stole around her. Might it not already be night? This time, the shiver was not due to the cool breeze alone.

Hours passed. No one would find her. She would become a newspaper headline: local bank manager's body discovered bound to tree. Muriel moaned from time to time as waves of fear and despair swept over her. She would never again feel Paul's arms around her, never again be penetrated by his cock or driven to heights of ecstasy by Rhonda's whip. And she had to pee again. She held out for as long as she could, not wanting to wet herself anew, but in the end she had to let go. As the warm urine ran down her legs she felt further humiliation. She knew, from the anti-abduction classes she had taken at the bank, that kidnappers forced their captives to wet themselves to break their will. Often they were kept naked. Muriel supposed that she should be glad that she had been spared that indignity, but in her wet smelly clothes she knew that she was helpless and vulnerable enough. I'll not give in, she told herself. Unless you have to, whispered another part of her.

Muriel drowsed and woke from fearful dreams to an equally fearful reality. Although she was thirsty, she wet herself again. Where was Valerie? Had she driven away, back to the city? Was she even now sleeping comfortably in her bed, her captive forgotten? At some indeterminate point in that endless night, Muriel had an assurance that she was not alone. She jerked awake as the dog trainer collar came to life, the electricity shooting through her body. She groaned and shuddered, jerking in her bonds. The torture went on, and she surrendered to the agony of the electrical shocks that coursed through her. After an eternity of pain, she passed out.

Eventually she awoke, but to a new twist. At some point during that interminable torture she had lost control of her bowels too. She smelled herself and wrinkled her nose. She imagined the brown stains running down her legs, coating her stockings and filling her shoes. Muriel twisted weakly, wanting to move away from the scene of her awful humiliation, but could not. She felt the darkness close around her again, but at least she knew that she was not alone. That was some comfort, even if the proof was painful and humiliating. She almost wished that Valerie would shock her again, to prove that she was still there, still watching over her captive. Might still free her from her humiliation and fear. The night seemed endless, a long bad dream.

'You look awful.' Valerie's voice nearly undid Muriel. She was here! I'm not abandoned! She exulted inwardly. Had she not been gagged, she would have shouted for joy and relief. A groan was her only audible response. 'And you smell terrible.' Even these unkind words heartened her. Although she ought not to have welcomed the return of her captor, she could not resist the feeling that someone cared for her. Kidnap victims, she knew, often developed an irrational bond with their kidnappers. She had been warned against that by her instructors, but still could not suppress the feeling of relief at having even this sort of company.

Hands appeared out of the surrounding darkness, touching her, bringing inexpressible joy at her restoration to the human community. The ropes around her waist and chest loosened and fell away. Valerie unbound her ankles and snapped a lead to her collar. Muriel collapsed to the ground, and sensed the remains of her faeces smearing her legs and soiling her clothes. Valerie roughly helped her to stand and then led her captive away from the scene of her humiliation.

'Nocturnal emissions,' Valerie observed, 'are disgusting.'

Hobbled at the knees, Muriel staggered after her captor. Hope sprang anew. The nightly fears fled. Though still a prisoner, she felt irrationally relieved.

'Be careful now,' Valerie warned her. 'There's a step up.'

Awkwardly Muriel climbed the step. She felt and heard her shoes moving across a wooden floor. Shelter, she thought. A haven from the great outdoors, the woods and its animal inhabitants.

Valerie stopped abruptly, causing Muriel to bump into her. She dropped the lead and jerked the tape from Muriel's eyes. The sudden light dazzled her, so that the pain as Valerie pulled the tape from her mouth was not so bad. When she could see, Muriel discovered that she was in a rustic kitchen. The woods were visible outside the window.

There were four wooden chairs around a pine table. 'Sit,' Valerie commanded.

Muriel staggered to a chair, conscious of her soiled clothes clinging to her. Her stockings were covered in shit, and she felt the slimy mess against her thighs and bottom as she sat. Valerie had thoughtfully provided a large mirror on a stand across from Muriel's chair, and when she saw herself she felt the humiliation and fear wash back over her. She looked awful, as Valerie had said. Her hair was sticking to her face, all signs of grooming lost. Her soiled clothes were wet and sticky against her. There were brown stains on her silk blouse from the tree trunk, the buttons were mostly undone and the bow at the collar was hanging loose, revealing the new, more sinister collar she now wore. She looked away at once.

Valerie brought a warm cloth from the sink to wipe Muriel's face. She brushed the hair away from her face.

At the touch Muriel almost melted, forgetting that it was this same woman who had brought her to this state. 'Thank you,' she said before she could stop herself.

Valerie nodded and set about making coffee. 'You won't need to use the toilet,' she observed as she held the cup to Muriel's lips, 'but I do. I'll make some breakfast in a moment.' She set the cup down and left the room, presumably in the direction of the bathroom. Muriel was so relieved after her night's ordeal in the forest that she sat quietly for a moment. Then it occurred to her that this was her chance to escape. She struggled to her feet and staggered towards the door. Her hobbled knees slowed her considerably, and without her hands she would not be able to fend off branches or twigs. She made her way to the front porch. Valerie's black van stood in the front yard, but she knew that driving was out of the question unless she could free her hands. Common sense returned. Valerie could easily overtake her if she stayed on the road, so the woods were her only refuge. She took slow careful steps, wishing that she could run, fearful that Valerie would return and catch her before she could get away.

The trees clustered densely around the cabin and Muriel plunged into their shade, intending to put as much distance between her and Valerie as she could. Final escape was a problem for the future. She staggered on for several minutes, and when she looked back the cabin was out of sight. Hope rose at the thought that Valerie could not see her now, and was unlikely to be a good tracker. The forest now felt friendly, the dappled light and shade a refuge from her captor. As the minutes passed without the sound of pursuit, Muriel felt that she had a chance to get away. She would eventually come across a road, and hope that a passing motorist would free her and take her to safety. In her haste to escape, the matter of how others would see her was secondary. Surely her distress would be apparent to anyone. How many times did one find a bound and dishevelled woman beside the road?

A terrible pain suddenly shot through her body. Muriel screamed, staggered and fell. The collar! She had forgotten about that. Obviously Valerie was still close enough to shock her and bring her down. Even as she struggled to regain her feet, Muriel felt hope fade. Nevertheless she stood again, leaning against a tree with heaving breasts. As she gasped for air, she listened. There were no sounds from behind her. Muriel pushed herself away from the tree and staggered on. The low-hanging branches struck her face and body as she pushed blindly through the forest. Low bushes caught at her feet and ankles, tearing her stockings and her flesh and threatening to trip her. Nettles stung her exposed legs.

A second shock brought Muriel to her knees. She tottered, on the verge of falling. The pain stopped suddenly, and she drew in a great lung full of air. When the next shock came, she screamed it out again. Muriel lost her balance and fell to the ground, thrashing and jerking and gasping for air. The shock ended, and Muriel felt her hopes die. All Valerie had to do was track her by her screams. It would be impossible to remain silent against that kind of pain. Nevertheless she struggled to her knees, and then to her feet. She was sweating, her wet clothes clinging to her body. Dirt and pine needles stuck to her clothing and body.

The next shock felled her at once. She screamed. The current stopped. Muriel shook and gasped. The next shock brought another scream, and thereafter the shocks came at regular intervals. Muriel knew then that Valerie was coming for her, and she could not escape. Her screams would lead Valerie straight to her. Another shock. Another scream.

An eternity of pain later, Muriel heard approaching footsteps. Valerie appeared from the undergrowth. She shook her head in mock pity and jerked Muriel to her feet. She grasped the lead that dangled from her collar and dragged her back towards the cabin. 'I thought you'd at least wait for breakfast,' she said.

Muriel staggered along behind her. 'Why are you doing this to me?' she wailed, despite her resolve to be firm.

'I told you. I want to borrow all the money you've got in the bank, and you're going to help me.'

Muriel shook her head. 'I won't.' Her voice sounded firmer. Valerie did not press the button, as Muriel thought she would.

'Well, I didn't expect you to agree at once,' Valerie said, 'but you will in the end. There are still a few more softening-up exercises to go through before you're ready.' Valerie spoke casually over her shoulder as she led her bedraggled captive back the way she had come.

The woods that had seemed to offer her refuge seemed again hostile to Muriel. She knew that in the end she would have to help Valerie. She felt humiliated and filthy now. That would work against her the longer she was held. And she knew that there were other inducements Valerie could use against her. Nevertheless, she tried again to dissuade Valerie from her course. 'You know that there isn't that much money kept in banks any more. The security services take it all away at the end of each day to discourage raids on the bank.'

'Well, I expect there is enough to make this all worthwhile. A quarter of a million would make a nice nest-egg.'

Muriel shook her head. 'There isn't that much. I know that there is only about fifty thousand dollars, and a lot of that is in coins. You'd never be able to carry all that away. Let me go and I'll keep quiet about all this.'

Valerie looked scornfully at Muriel. 'You'd say that anyway. It's part of your training. Never reveal how much is in the vault, they tell their managers. And even if I believed you, I could never trust you to forget all this.'

'You have those photos of me. I don't want them made public. You could take . . . more if you wanted to. Of me. Like . . . this. It would be extra insurance.' Muriel felt shame as she begged her captor to release her unharmed, but she could not stop herself.

'True enough, but hardly the stuff to ensure perpetual silence. Photos of you in durance vile would only be used as evidence to convict me. And anyway, I don't believe you. There must be lots more money in the vault.'

They emerged into the small clearing where the cabin stood. Valerie led Muriel around the back of the cabin before she removed the dog collar. 'Wouldn't like to get this wet,' she remarked as she tethered Muriel by her ankle to a nearby tree. The only furniture was a picnic table with benches down either side. It was a Spartan cabin in the woods, nothing like Rhonda's place. Valerie left her there while she went indoors, before returning shortly with a pair of dressmaking shears. With these she proceeded to cut away Muriel's tattered clothing. Valerie slit her silk blouse up each sleeve and up the back. It fell to the ground. The straps to her slip and bra came next, then the waistband of her skirt. Muriel wore only the ruined stockings and garter belt.

'Still feeling sexy?' Valerie taunted her. She cut the garter belt away and stripped the remains of the stockings from Muriel's legs.

Muriel naked felt even more helpless than Muriel clothed. Valerie had not only stripped her but destroyed her clothing as well.

Valerie uncoiled a garden hose from the rack beside the door and opened the faucet. The water was icy cold as she sluiced Muriel down.

Muriel yelped at the cold water, but could do nothing about the discomfort. The sweat and urine and shit washed away as Valerie turned the hose over her, at one point directing the stream upwards between her legs and bottom. At length she was clean. Valerie turned off the water and dried her captive with a towel. 'Pneumonia would be a nuisance,' she remarked. She left Muriel standing naked in the sunlight amid the ruins of her clothing as she went back indoors.

Muriel felt small and vulnerable. She knew already that she could not free herself, but now lacked even the will to try once more. She thought of screaming for help, but remembered that her earlier screams had gone unheard. And Valerie was just a few yards away. Screams would bring her at the double, and might not bring comforting results.

Presently Valerie returned with food: a tin of tuna fish mixed with mayonnaise on a saucer and a can of Coca-Cola. 'Lunch,' she announced, setting the saucer on the picnic table. She untied Muriel's ankle from the tree and invited her to sit on the bench. She sat across from her captive and told her to eat.

Muriel knew that this was intended to humiliate her still further – break her spirit by forcing her to eat like an animal. But she was too hungry to care. She bent forwards and began to eat the tuna fish from the plate, getting the stuff smeared across her lower face and in her hair, which kept on falling forward. From time to time Valerie offered her sips of the soft drink. Muriel ate it all and wished there were more, but could not bring herself to ask.

When it was all gone, Valerie wiped her clean with paper towels. She replaced the dog collar. 'I've put in fresh batteries,' she announced, 'in case you thought of running away. You won't, will you?'

Muriel made no reply, but she knew that it would be easy for Valerie to catch her again, as she had the last time. She sat at the table while Valerie picked up the saucer and took it indoors. When she returned, she carried a ball-gag, a length of chain and a pair of handcuffs. With them she locked Muriel's wrists behind her back before cutting the cable tie that had bound her for so long. The relative freedom was a relief, but Muriel was still as helpless as before. She stretched her cramped arms as far as the steel bracelets allowed.

Valerie looped one end of the chain around Muriel's left ankle, then locked it in place with a padlock. The other end she attached to the tree. Only then did she remove the strap that bound Muriel's knees together.

'Open up,' she ordered Muriel.

Muriel opened her mouth and Valerie put the ball-gag in, pushed it behind her teeth and buckled the strap tightly behind her head. 'I've got to go back to New Orleans, but you'll be all right here. No one ever comes by. Only a few of the locals know there is a cabin here.'

'Nnnnggg!' Muriel objected, shaking her head violently to indicate how little she relished being abandoned in this fashion. Valerie intended to leave her here for heaven knew how long, exposed to what or whoever chanced by.

Valerie went back into the cabin, and presently Muriel heard the van start up. She listened to its diminishing sound until it was lost in the great silence of the woods. Only the soughing of the wind in the pine trees broke it. It was then that she came closest to panic of the sort that leaves its victims breathless with fear. She fought the handcuffs violently, jerking and twisting her wrists and attempting to slip the steel bands off over her hands. She yanked at the chain that tethered her to the tree. She persisted for a long time, driven by the fear of being left exposed in the woods, but in the end she was still a prisoner. Her breasts were heaving from her exertions and her breath rasped in her throat. Fear rose to choke her. She would have been screaming but for the gag. As it was, she could only make loud moaning sounds that even to her ears sounded feeble. And besides, there was no one to hear her.

Muriel stood on shaky legs beside the picnic table. Somehow it seemed better to stand than to sit passively, but she soon realised that she was as helpless in either posture. She paced as far as the chain allowed, but of course it was too short to allow her to reach the shelter of the cabin, or even that of the surrounding trees. She stood naked in the sunlight of the tiny clearing and felt despair rise like a tide to steal her strength and wits from her. She wept in fear, the tears running down her cheeks, her chest rising and falling spasmodically with the sobs.

Noon came and went. The shadows shortened, and then grew longer again as the sun slid away westwards. The clearing in which Muriel stood grew darker and cooler as the trees shaded her. Yet she felt no less conspicuous in shadow than she had felt in sunlight. In fact, the lengthening shadows reminded her of her last night in the woods. She did not know if she could face another night like that. Then, she had at least been clothed. Tonight would be vastly different and more frightening. And no one came.

Without clothes she felt even more vulnerable. Muriel tried to tell herself that this was nonsense, that it made no real difference. But her darker self was not convinced. Naked and without the use of her hands, she knew deep down that this night would be worse than the last.

Maybe Valerie will come back, she told herself, and indeed she knew that the woman who had abducted her had to return. But when? The uncertainty wore her courage away as surely as the approaching darkness. At twilight Valerie did not come. Nor did she return as the first stars appeared. There was a crescent moon, but it set soon after sunset. The woods grew dark and cool. The wind died away, and Muriel strained her ears for any sound that would betray the approach of wildlife. She drew closer to the tree to which she was chained, knowing that it offered no real shelter, but drawn to it anyway.

This is foolish. I'm becoming afraid of everything, reverting to the fears of primitive savages, she told herself. But she huddled close to the tree, watching the shadows for any sign of movement, any threat.

She tried to imagine that it was Paul, or Rhonda, who had taken her prisoner, and would come to her offering the peculiar delights to which she had become accustomed. Her fears told her better.

Muriel was close to hysteria when the sound of an approaching vehicle came to her, bringing relief and renewed terror. What if it were a stranger? She could not know if her fragmentary text message had got through and, even if it had, how was Paul, or anyone else, going to look for her? Valerie had said that no one knew of this cabin in the woods. The vehicle stopped in front of the cabin, out of Muriel's sight. She had no way of knowing who had arrived. She shrank against the tree.

When a light went on inside the cabin, Muriel was sure it was Valerie, but her captor did not come to her. The presence of someone near by made her lonelier and more fearful. Muriel made loud noises through her gag, hoping that Valerie would come and take her inside at least. But she did not. Muriel told herself that this was more psychological torture, designed to break her will to resist. And so it was. And it was working. She would have done anything then to be taken in out of the darkness and the silence of the woods. Muriel wanted to shout to Valerie that she would help her, do whatever she wanted, anything at all, only let her come inside.

Her throat grew raw with her attempts to speak, to scream. The gag frustrated her. Valerie, she knew, was deliberately ignoring her, but still she tried to attract the woman's attention.

The light went out. The cabin was silent in the silent woods, and Muriel was chained naked out under the distant stars, silent too at last. But not fearless. Never before had she appreciated how much four walls and a roof meant to her sense of security.

She longed to be inside some enclosed space. Every sound seemed menacing. Everything seemed hostile. She was defenceless, unable to fight or flee – not that flight into the dark woods seemed to offer her much. At least in the clearing she could see anything before it was upon her – not that that offered much solace either.

Muriel sat down at last with her back to the tree, her legs tired from pacing and standing. She even drowsed fitfully, waking suddenly as she imagined a sound near by. The long hours of darkness had left the normally resourceful bank manager worn out and demoralised. No doubt this was what Valerie had intended. Sleep deprivation combined with humiliation and helplessness to sap her resistance. Dawn found her heavy-headed and frightened. She got shakily to her feet and went as far as the chain allowed in order to pee. Squatting was a further humiliation. She was unable to clean or dry herself properly.

Valerie, when she at length appeared, seemed by contrast rested and fresh. She brought coffee and toast for breakfast. She removed Muriel's gag and fed her captive, holding the cup while she drank. Muriel nearly wept at this small touch, though she knew that the gratitude was induced by the previous night's abandonment. Valerie was admitting her again to the human race.

'Ready to a-robbing go?' she asked brightly.

Muriel found the courage to shake her head. The return of daylight had allayed some of her fears. She could not really believe that Valerie would seriously harm her.

'Well, then you need some more softening up. We have all day before us. And I have an idea. How would you like it if I brought Alison here? Then you

197

could watch while I tortured her. Maybe you'd be more willing to help me then.'

It did not sound like a real threat. Another witness would not be a good idea anyway, from Valerie's point of view. Muriel knew that in the end she would have to give in to Valerie's demands. No one knew where she was, and no one could help her.

'Well, maybe not. But I could always torture you some more. In the end you'll be begging to help me.' Valerie stood up and went into the cabin, leaving Muriel seated at the table in her handcuffs. When she returned, she held a short leather whip with a handle.

Muriel knew at once what was coming next, and she tried to brace herself. Valerie did not intend for this to be pleasurable. The fact that her captor did not bother with a gag suggested to Muriel that her screams (and she knew that she was going to scream) would attract no one. She was truly alone with this angry woman.

Nor did Valerie bother to tie her captive to the tree. She simply drew back her arm and let fly with the whip, striking Muriel across the back and upper arms. Muriel yelped in pain and surprise. Valerie struck her again. The next blow landed at her waist, the leather whip coiling about her. Muriel screamed at the pain this time. Valerie was not holding back. The scream trailed off into a sob in the silent woods.

When the whip landed on her breasts, Muriel screamed again and struggled to stand. She knew she could not escape, but she could not simply sit and let Valerie beat her. She fell back to the bench when the whip struck her across her chest, leaving an agonising red stripe across the upper slopes of her breasts. Before she could make a second attempt to stand, Valerie struck her full across the nipples. Muriel screamed in pain, but felt the first faint stirrings of excitement at the same time. She wondered briefly if there was anything to which her body would not respond.

Valerie struck her again. Muriel's scream rang through the woods but no one came to her rescue. She spread her legs to balance herself and tried to stand again. The whip landed on her cunt, whether by accident she could not say. But the next time it found the same place, Muriel had no doubt it was by design.

'Whore!' Valerie screamed as she struck her captive between the legs and across the breasts. 'I'll bet you won't like this very much! You'll never want to play your twisted games again when I get through with you! You won't want to let anyone near your tits and cunt again!'

Muriel stood, swaying, scourged by the whip. She took a few staggering steps, turning away from her tormentor. But the chain around her ankle stopped her, and Valerie was before her again, the whip rising and falling tirelessly. Muriel saw only a red haze of pain. Tears ran down her cheeks as she tried to shield herself from the fury of her captor. She hunched over, clamping her legs together to protect her cunt. Valerie lashed her exposed bottom and legs. She pushed Muriel to the ground and continued to lash her. Whenever she could, Valerie struck her captive across the breasts and nipples and between her legs.

And Muriel felt her body shift gears, felt the familiar excitement begin to flood her belly and breasts as the whip sought her out. She continued to scream, but the screams began to sound more like moans.

Valerie, perhaps mistaking the sounds for exhaustion, pursued her victim ruthlessly. At intervals she swore at Muriel, calling her a whore and a pervert, but she was beginning to sound breathless herself. In the respite Muriel came, moaning and shuddering. The first orgasm broke the dam, and she keened in pleasure as others shook her abused body.

Valerie stopped in wonderment. She did not understand the change in her captive's behaviour at first, but, when she did, she was enraged. She beat Muriel furiously, hissing with the effort, hoarsely calling her every name she could lay her tongue to. And Muriel shuddered in release. To her (and probably to Valerie) the pleasure seemed to go on for a long time. When eventually she lay quiet, Muriel seemed to slip into a trance. Valerie finally stopped lashing her, from exhaustion as much as anything, but she continued to regard her captive with disgust and rage.

'What kind of a pervert are you?' she asked the woman huddled on the ground at her feet. 'You came when I beat you! You're not normal!'

'Neither are you, Ms Sanderson, neither are you.'

Valerie jerked her attention from Muriel and looked wildly around at the surrounding woods. 'Who's there?' she said in a shaking voice. 'Who are you?'

'The voice of your conscience, Ms Sanderson. You have broken the Eleventh Commandment, and I am here to rub your nose in it.'

'What do you mean? Who are you? *Where* are you?' Valerie was looking wildly around at the forest, wondering at the same time if she were going mad, hearing voices, *responding* to them.

Rhonda stepped from her concealment and advanced on Valerie. She looked grim, and she too carried a whip. 'Retribution is at hand,' she said, brandishing it.

Valerie looked both relieved and contemptuous. 'You're just like her,' she said, nodding towards

Muriel. 'Just another whore. A lesbian too. A pervert! There's no place bad enough for your kind. You should be locked up forever.'

A faint smile relieved Rhonda's grimness. 'You, of course, are completely innocent? Even when we pay you to help us? And even when you accept the payment? Unless, of course, you have sent back my last cheque – or torn it up in righteous anger. And after this?' She gestured towards Muriel huddled on the ground.

Valerie opened her mouth to make an angry retort, but Rhonda silenced her with a gesture. 'Please. Spare me the righteous indignation. People like you are no better than people like me. A truth you are about to learn. I believe I am better with a whip than you are. Shall we find out?'

Valerie lowered her own whip and backed away. She did not fancy her chances against Rhonda, whom she knew at least by reputation. 'Leave me alone. This is none of your business.'

'Ah, but it is. You have taken one of my people against her will, and I can't allow that. What would the others think if word got around? I'm afraid you will have to answer to me. Ready? En garde!' Rhonda spoke mockingly.

Valerie dropped her whip and backed away further. Rhonda circled slowly. Valerie turned to face her, holding her hands up to ward off the blow.

Rhonda smiled. It was not a pretty smile. Carnivorous might best describe it.

Valerie turned and ran towards the forest. If nothing else, the trees would keep Rhonda from using the whip effectively. Paul stepped out from his concealment with a video camera, from where he had been filming Valerie's performance. She changed course to avoid him. Paul stuck out a foot and tripped her. Valerie went sprawling full length. It was not a light fall. She lay winded, making feeble motions to get up. Rhonda strode to her and jerked her to her feet by one arm – which she twisted behind Valerie's back.

The blonde woman whimpered with the pain, trying to stand on her toes to lessen the pressure on her shoulder and arm. Since Rhonda was the taller, it did not help much. Rhonda marched her captive back to the clearing. Paul put the video camera on the picnic table and went to help Muriel.

Muriel lay apparently in a faint, making soft moans but not moving much. Paul lifted her in his arms and laid her on the picnic table as well, turning her on to her side so that the handcuffs would not cut into her wrists. To Rhonda he said, 'Get the keys out of her.'

'You heard the man. Keys,' she demanded.

Valerie looked as if she would refuse. Another twist of her arm ended the resistance. 'Kitchen table,' she hissed through the pain.

'Wimp,' Rhonda said. '*I* would never have broken so easily.'

Paul got the keys and unlocked Muriel, who was showing signs of coming around. She also showed the signs of her beating. Red slashes covered her body. Valerie had intended to hurt her victim.

'Chain her to the tree,' Rhonda said with a nod at Valerie. 'I'll deal with her in a minute.'

Paul used the chain that had tethered Muriel to secure Valerie to the tree by her ankle. Only then did Rhonda let go of her arm. Valerie stood miserably rubbing her shoulder and trying to summon up some resistance.

'Take Muriel inside and ... well, comfort her.' Rhonda turned her attention to Valerie as Paul

202

carried Muriel into the cabin. 'Now, Valerie, what was all that about?'

Valerie said nothing.

Rhonda asked again, with visibly less patience. When Valerie again stayed silent, she fingered the whip. Valerie's eyes widened at the threat. She looked uneasily at the forest, perhaps hoping for rescue. When it didn't come, she looked again at Rhonda, but with a stubborn set to her body.

'I'm glad to see you have some backbone,' Rhonda told her, 'but it won't keep me from finding out why you took Muriel. Save yourself a lot of needless suffering and talk now.'

Paul came out into the clearing. Rhonda turned to him, noticing that he was still dressed. 'Did you do the job already? Why did you bother to get dressed again afterwards? We may need you again for her.' Rhonda indicated Valerie with a jerk of her head.

Valerie looked wildly at them both. Though still clothed, she instinctively covered her breasts and crotch with her arms. 'No!' she said loudly. 'Don't touch me! Don't come near me with that . . .!'

'Muriel is asleep,' he explained. 'You know, the stuff that knits up the ravelled sleeve of care and sexual torture. How are you getting on with Ms Sanderson?'

'She's being stubborn. It may take both of us to get the truth from her. But even if we don't succeed, we can always ask Muriel what went on. And we can still have some fun until Muriel feels able to talk.' Rhonda said this last with a meaningful glance at Valerie, who whitened but remained silent. 'Why don't we get Ms Sanderson out of her clothes. As we all know, being naked often weakens the will.' To Valerie, Rhonda went on, 'Would you mind just slipping out of your clothes? It's sunny and warm today. You won't be cold.'

Valerie flushed angrily. 'You're vile – all three of you, and all those others who play your wicked sex games! And you're crazy if you think I'll just take my clothes off and join you.'

'She can speak!' Rhonda exclaimed to the forest at large. To Paul she continued, 'Do you think we can persuade Valerie to join us? We might all benefit from her moral uprightness. She could be the voice of sanity at our revels, and we could have a contest to see who can change the most minds. I'll bet she will change her mind once she sees how much fun we have.'

Valerie looked incredulous. 'Do you actually think I'd do . . . what you do? Never in a thousand years. I'll report you to the police!'

'Didn't anybody ever teach you never to say "never"? And as to reporting us to the police, are you certain of your own position? I imagine someone in the District Attorney's office would be interested in the videos we made of you torturing poor Muriel.' Her voice hardened: 'Get undressed!'

Valerie hugged herself protectively and backed away as far as the chain allowed, shaking her head vigorously at the same time. There was real fear in her expression.

Rhonda pointed to the ruins of Muriel's clothes, still lying in a soiled heap where Valerie had cut them from her body the day before. 'I think you'll find some shears around the kitchen. Bring them out here so we can help Valerie undress.'

Paul went inside the cabin and returned with the shears. 'Muriel's still asleep. Too bad. She might have enjoyed this.'

The two of them advanced on Valerie, one to either side. She turned her head from side to side, trying to keep her eyes on them both. Her eyes were wide and her mouth formed a silent NO! She was shaking her head in denial and hugging her blouse to her body. Her legs were clamped together.

Paul suddenly grabbed both her hands and jerked them away from her body. At the same time Rhonda stepped behind Valerie and with one quick rip she cut the blouse from bottom to top, stepping aside as Valerie tried to kick her. The blouse slid down her arms.

Valerie tried vainly to jerk her hands free. Rhonda waited until her attention was directed at that before stepping in once again to cut through the bandeau of Valerie's brassiere. That too fell away, leaving her naked to the waist.

When her breasts were bare Valerie seemed to realise that this was really happening. 'Naaaooooh!' she screamed, jerking at her arms and kicking wildly at her two captors.

'Such a racket,' Rhonda said, smilingly holding her hands to her ears. 'I think we should gag her, don't you?' She picked up the ball-gag Muriel had worn the previous day and stuffed it into Valerie's mouth the next time she opened it to scream. Valerie fought wildly as Rhonda buckled the straps behind her head. Finally her screams were reduced to loud moans.

'That's better,' Rhonda said. She picked up the handcuffs as well, motioning for Paul to bring Valerie's hands together behind her back. Valerie continued to fight even as her wrists were locked behind her.

'That's even better. Now we have an unobstructed view of her tits. And very nice tits they are, don't you think so, Paul? I'll hold her if you'd like to give them a nuzzle,' Rhonda suggested helpfully.

Rhonda's mocking tone penetrated Valerie's hysterics. She fought the handcuffs wildly, looking down at her exposed breasts, doubtless wanting to cover herself. She flushed pink all over, the crimson tide painting her body suddenly from waist to ears. A look of horror came over her face.

'Wow,' said Paul. 'If she reacts like that when only her tits are on view, what will she do when we get the rest of her clothes off?'

'The University of Alabama could use her as an advertisement for the football team, with one of those sashes they use for beauty queens draped between her bare breasts.' Rhonda spoke with a straight face.

Valerie made loud protesting noises through the gag, shaking her head and trying to back away. Paul made as if to touch her breasts and Valerie tried to run away. She tripped when the chain on her ankle came taut. Rhonda was on her before she could recover, the shears cutting through the waistband of her trousers. Rhonda also slit the trousers legs up the back. The trousers fell away and Valerie flushed again.

'Nearly there,' Rhonda said. 'Just the panties to go.'

Valerie struggled but was no match for Rhonda. The shears snipped both leg bands to the waist, and Valerie Sanderson was naked. And red all over. She clamped her legs together and rolled on to her face, hiding the front of her body from them. Her hands jerked at the handcuffs.

'That's enough for now,' Rhonda decided. 'We'll leave her to get used to being naked while we see about Muriel. Who knows, she may even get to like it.'

Rhonda and Paul went into Valerie's cabin, leaving the owner helpless, naked and mortified in the clearing where Muriel had spent a night and a day.

Inside, Muriel still slept, though restlessly. Rhonda looked her over in a professional manner. 'Some of those cuts will leave scars, I'm afraid, even if we dared take her to a hospital in this state. They won't show in public, though. We'll have to ask her what she wants to do when she wakes up. Our backwoods Baptist delivery girl went too far.' Rhonda sounded grim as she beckoned him through to the kitchen.

Paul decided that he would not like to be in Valerie's shoes just now. Valerie herself was visible from the window, huddled miserably against the tree. 'What are we going to do with her?'

'Nothing very pleasant,' Rhonda replied. 'Our bonded courier needs to be taught a lesson. I think we'll get her tied to the table for a bit. Being spread-eagled usually suggests to the spread eagle what is going to happen next. I think you should take your clothes off and let her get a glimpse of what's in store for her – you know, put her into the proper frame of mind.' Rhonda smiled mischievously. 'Even if we don't get around to actually fitting the piston into the cylinder, it will still scare her witless. I think we will have to break her completely to our evil purposes. It's only economy. Where am I going to find another delivery girl? Better the devil you know than the one you don't.'

'Do you mean that I won't get to fuck her?' Paul asked with disappointment. 'She's got something coming for what she did to Muriel.'

'I agree, but fucking, rape if you will, has never appealed to me as a form of revenge. Rather, sex should be a reward for suffering.' If she was aware of the irony, Rhonda did not show it. 'Tell you what I'll do. I'll get naked too, and then you can have me, if you don't mind Muriel seeing the two of us at it. Valerie might like to watch as well.'

Paul did not reply, but his alarmed expression showed what he thought of having Muriel and Valerie witness him and Rhonda 'at it'.

'No sense of showmanship?' she teased him. 'You really like Muriel, don't you? Has she decided about joining our group? She'll have to get used to sharing if she does.'

'Not yet,' Paul replied. 'This may put her right off.'

'Or maybe turn her right on. I've seen it happen.' Rhonda smiled. 'Well, let's get Valerie into position and leave her to think a bit.' She led the way outdoors.

Valerie looked more frightened than defiant, though she tried not to show it as Rhonda and Paul approached. His nakedness alarmed her, and her eyes went automatically to his cock, which was beginning to show interest in the proceedings. Valerie went white at the sight.

Paul collected the rope Valerie had used to bind Muriel to the tree on the first night. He cut two short pieces off and handed one to Rhonda. They approached Valerie together. As before, she tried to look at both of them, her eyes darting from side to side as she shrank against the tree trunk. Taking her by both arms, Rhonda and Paul raised her to her feet.

'Turn around,' Rhonda commanded. Valerie refused with a shake of her head. Sounds of protest emerged from behind the gag.

Rhonda jerked her roughly, half turning her. She tied her piece of rope to Valerie's right wrist as Paul did the same to her left wrist. Together they dragged the protesting woman to the picnic table. Valerie tried to keep her legs clamped together rather than kicking at her captors. Eventually they got her in place. Paul lifted the struggling woman into a sitting position on the table. Rhonda pushed her around until she was sitting lengthwise on the table. She and Paul took the ropes while Valerie looked fearfully from one to the other, shaking her head and jerking at the handcuffs.

Rhonda nodded to Paul and they pulled the ropes tight in opposite directions. With one hand he unlocked Valerie's cuffs and pushed her down on the table top. He and Rhonda pulled her arms down and secured her wrists to the legs of the table. Valerie was panting and making distressed noises but they paid her no attention. Her ankles received the same treatment. Valerie tried to kick as they spread her legs, jerking at the ropes that held her wrists as well, but slowly, irresistibly, they spread her and secured her ankles to the table legs as well. Valerie was left lying on her back, spread like a starfish and struggling mightily to free herself.

Rhonda reached between their captive's thighs to probe her cunt. Valerie's body positively vibrated as she fought the rope and tried to shrink from the intimate inspection. 'Nnnggggg!' she said. Rhonda looked at Paul and shook her head. 'Dry as a bone. I don't think our courier girl is enjoying this at all. We may have to use petroleum jelly to assist entry,' she said threateningly.

At the word 'entry' Valerie froze. 'Nnnnngggggg!' she said again, shaking her head vigorously and trying to clamp her thighs together. She looked wildly at Paul's cock, which was nodding suggestively near her face.

'Right,' Rhonda said, 'let's go get the Vaseline and make the final preparations.' To Valerie she said, 'Think about the wisdom of Chinese proverbs while we're away.'

Valerie threw herself against the ropes in a frenzy, jerking and tugging, her body tense in fright. As they walked out of earshot Rhonda was saying, 'Do you think she's virgin?'

Paul replied, 'If she is, she must be the only one in captivity.'

Valerie renewed her struggles to escape.

Inside once again, Rhonda told Paul to check on Muriel. She looked through the window at Valerie struggling atop the picnic table.

Paul beckoned Rhonda to the bedroom. 'She's awake and wants to talk to us.'

They went in together. Rhonda sat on the bed beside Muriel. Paul took the chair across the room, conscious of being naked before someone who might not be ready for that just now.

'How are you feeling?'

'Sore and dirty,' Muriel responded. 'Where's Valerie?' she asked in sudden fear.

'Tied to the picnic table outside,' Rhonda answered matter-of-factly.

Her manner helped to calm Muriel.

'Do you feel like talking?' When Muriel nodded, Rhonda asked her what Valerie had been up to. Her expression hardened as the story unfolded. When Muriel wound down, Rhonda asked her if she wanted to give Valerie a lashing such as she had received. 'You have the right if anyone does. But whoever does it, she can't be allowed to get away with this. I believe some of those cuts will leave scars, even if we go to a hospital. Do you want to see a doctor?'

'No!' Muriel said definitely. 'He would call the police. He'd know how I got all this. Cops would ruin the show for all of us. Once you become known to the police they never forget you. Besides, I'd lose my job if any hint of what we do ever got out.'

'So do you want to pay Valerie back in her own coin?' Rhonda repeated.

Muriel shivered. 'No. I'm too sore and tired.'

'Well, what do you want to do with her?'

'I don't know. For now, I'd say leave her tied up so she can experience the same fear I felt when it was me out there. A night in the woods would be good for her.'

'You're entirely too soft-hearted, Muriel. I vote for a good beating and some real threats to keep her from trying anything like this again. And I believe we will need to involve her in the group games in order to keep her in our sight. Once she is a kettle, she won't be able to call the other pots black,' Rhonda said. 'I'm going out there while Paul helps you to clean up. I intend to put the fear of the whip and Rhonda Stuart into her.' She smiled as she left the room.

From the back yard Muriel and Paul heard a renewed protest from Valerie as she caught sight of Rhonda. 'I think we'd better get you cleaned up now. Rhonda is going to give Valerie a taste of the whip, whatever you think. In her book, Valerie has committed a grave offence and needs to learn how grave.'

Muriel suddenly clung to him, weeping and shaking. 'It was awful,' she wailed. 'She left me tied to a tree the first night. I had to soil myself. I couldn't help it! And then the torture began. I've never felt such pain and fear in my life. And in the middle of it all I *came*! I can't believe it. Valerie beat me harder for that than for anything else. She's crazy. I'm so glad you came when you did.'

Paul held her while she sobbed. 'Rhonda has many contacts. The most useful one was a man she knows in the Slidell land registry office. Once we knew it was Valerie who had taken you, Rhonda remembered that she lived somewhere around here. The friend in the registry office came in on Sunday morning and did the search for us. Rhonda got us here as soon as we knew where you might be. A lot of it was luck.'

From the back yard they heard a sharp cracking sound. Muriel broke away from Paul and ran to the window in time to see Rhonda strike Valerie a second time. Rhonda was being careful where she struck. No legs and stomach. She concentrated on Valerie's breasts and crotch, and her victim made strangled pain-noises as the lash landed on her vulnerable bits. Valerie jerked against her bonds, her whole body a naked protest against what was being done to her.

'That's what she did to me,' Muriel said as Paul came to stand beside her.

Valerie was weeping as Rhonda lashed her. The sobs stopped abruptly when Rhonda lowered her mouth between Valerie's wide-spread legs. The blonde head came up to stare in horror as Rhonda kissed her labia and nuzzled her cunt. 'NNNNNNNGGGGG!' she said, a howl of protest. Once again her whole body went taut as she pulled frenziedly against the ropes that held her open to her captor. Her wild struggles did not put Rhonda off. She used one hand to hold Valerie's torso against the table. The other hand was busy between her victim's thighs. Muriel knew what she was doing to Valerie, because Rhonda had done the same thing to her. Why wasn't Valerie experiencing the same pleasure, she wondered.

Valerie was struggling wildly to avoid Rhonda's mouth. Rhonda looked up and saw Paul and Muriel watching through the window. She stood up and spoke to them. 'I believe she would benefit from a few days' re-education in Florida. Help me get her into the van.' Between them, Paul and Rhonda stowed the naked, struggling woman in her own van. Leaving her bound and gagged, they all had something to eat before Rhonda directed Paul to take Muriel home and look after her. 'Drop around next weekend and see the change in our courier girl.' She drove off.

11

Transported

A month later, Muriel was expecting Valerie to collect her for another trip to Florida, and she was worried about the woman's reliability. Despite Rhonda's assurance that she had been 're-educated' (Rhonda made it sound like a scheme Mao Tse-tung might have conceived), the memory of her abduction and torture was strong. So Muriel waited nervously in the kitchen, drinking coffee and considering her options. She could have driven to Rhonda's house in Florida, or she could have gone with Paul, but Rhonda had discouraged that. 'I prefer to have my people transported to me,' she had said. Hence Valerie and her van. And Muriel's apprehension.

When the doorbell rang Muriel swallowed her heart and opened the door to Valerie Sanderson. Like Muriel, she was dressed formally in pin-striped business suit with knee-length skirt. Muriel wore stockings and a garter belt under her skirt, as she had done every day since her conversion. And no panties. She wondered if Rhonda had got Valerie to the same stage, but could not ask such a personal question. Valerie smiled apprehensively at her erstwhile captive.

'Hello, Miss Muriel,' she said, deferentially and a bit nervously. 'Miss Rhonda sent me to pick you up. Did she tell you?'

Muriel noticed that it was now 'Miss This' and 'Miss That'. More respectful and less contemptuous. She wondered if Rhonda's re-education had converted Valerie into one of 'those people' she had previously detested. Well, there was only one way to find out. 'Yes, she called yesterday with instructions. Come in,' she said. 'Would you like a coffee before we set out?' Muriel now found herself with a stomach full of butterflies, some of them as big as dinner plates.

Valerie smiled quickly. 'I will if you're having one, but I wouldn't drink too much if I were you. You know how Miss Rhonda wants you transported.'

Muriel knew. 'I'll make you a fresh cup and finish the one I started earlier.' The two women went into the kitchen.

Valerie stood nervously until Muriel told her to sit down and relax, a prescription she could have followed herself. It wasn't just Valerie, of course, that made her feel apprehensive. It was partly the impending trip, which she would make bound and gagged in the van that had taken her away before. And it was partly the reason for this particular trip. Following her abduction and torture (and perhaps because of it), she had agreed to become Paul's slave girl (strictly on a trial basis, she reassured herself). She felt somehow that she would be safer from unexpected abductors if she were under Paul's protection. When she thought logically about the arrangement, she knew that she would in fact be more likely to be abducted. Muriel expected that Paul would leave her helpless from time to time. She was looking forward to that, in fact. If Valerie (or anyone else of like mind) discovered her in bondage, it would be but the work of a moment to snatch her.

Muriel was ambivalent about Valerie, and about her own retrospective response to the abduction. Safe at home, she sometimes felt a shiver of excitement whenever she recalled Valerie's treatment of her. What would it feel like if something else like that happened to her? Suppose, for instance, Valerie was really here to snatch her again? No, that could not be, she told herself. Rhonda herself had arranged this gathering to mark the beginning of her slavery. Rhonda would know if Valerie failed to deliver Muriel as ordered. Still, Muriel felt as nervous as a bride on the big day. She was half inclined to back out, though she and Paul had agreed on a six-week trial – which was more than most brides got.

Valerie perched on the edge of the chair, her manner vastly different from that of her first arrival. Gone was the contempt and disdain and, yes, the underlying hatred of Muriel and 'her kind of people'. Rhonda's re-education programme must have been harsh indeed to work this change in the blonde courier in less than a month. Muriel had once asked Rhonda what she was doing to Valerie, but she had been told it was best she not know. 'You don't want bad dreams,' Rhonda had said menacingly.

They drank silently, both of them nervous and ill at ease. What do you say to a woman who is going to tie you up and take you away in a few moments? Muriel wondered. Presumably Valerie was trying to think of something to say to the woman whom she had recently tortured. Valerie broke the silence at last. 'Sorry. I'm sorry . . .' She made a vague, all-inclusive gesture.

Muriel nodded. 'Apology accepted.' She rose to put her cup in the sink, the butterflies fluttering in her stomach. Valerie rose as well.

'Are you ready, Miss Muriel?' She sounded diffident, less certain of her ground.

'Yes,' Muriel replied, nervous herself now that the moment had arrived. Her throat felt constricted. Speaking was an effort. Excitement and apprehension were rising as they always did at the outset of an adventure.

Valerie was taking the dildoes and chain from the bag she carried, not looking at Muriel. She made a vague gesture, the chain dangling from her hand. Muriel rose and went to the bathroom to pee and to collect the jar of petroleum jelly from the medicine cabinet. She took time to brush her teeth, knowing that she would probably be gagged for a long period. Returning to the kitchen, she saw that Valerie had laid out her equipment on the table. With a sigh she raised her skirt to her waist and bent over, grasping her ankles and feeling exposed. Which she was.

Muriel tried to relax as Valerie lubricated the anal dildo, but she felt her sphincter clamp down reflexively. Then it was pressing against her anus, sliding slowly in, meeting the closed sphincter. Relax, Muriel told herself.

'Could you relax a bit, Miss Muriel. I don't want to hurt you.'

Valerie had indeed changed. Muriel managed to let up a bit, and the greased dildo slid into her anus, filling her full and making her feel greasy too. She maintained the undignified pose while Valerie fastened the chain around her waist.

'You can stand up now, Miss.'

Muriel stood, and Valerie slid the thicker vaginal dildo into her. No need to lubricate that one. Muriel spread her legs, feeling stuffed in both places, while Valerie fitted the chain between her thighs, through the dildoes' rings, and locked it to the waist chain behind her back. With her two comforters now locked inside her, Muriel felt her excitement rising to choke her. Valerie helped her to lower and straighten her skirt. Muriel glanced down automatically to see if her seams were straight, thinking at the same time how bizarre it felt to worry about such minor matters when something much more important was happening to her. Valerie made a tentative move towards the front door. Muriel followed. She locked the door and put the keys into her purse. Valerie's black van stood at the kerb. Muriel went around to get into the back but Valerie stopped her. 'Not here, Miss Muriel. The neighbours . . .'

Muriel got into the passenger's seat, the dildoes reminding her at every movement of their disturbing presence. This felt like her first ride with Valerie, and she trembled with excitement as she remembered it. She concentrated on not coming as Valerie drove them both on to the Interstate highway at the Canal Boulevard junction. They turned east and drove in silence until they passed the Michoud Boulevard entrance. There, Valerie stopped and looked around for traffic. It was after the evening rush hour, and there was not much about. 'Ready, Miss?' she asked again.

Muriel nodded and got out. Valerie opened the sliding door and both women climbed into the rear of the van. Without being told, Muriel knelt upright and brought her hands behind her back. Valerie smiled gratefully. Apparently her altered personality made it difficult for her to order a woman she now called 'Miss' to assume the position for binding.

As she waited for Valerie to tie her hands, Muriel thought again of her last encounter with her. Painful and frightening as it had been, she shivered with excitement now at the memory. This occasion seemed tamer. The new model Valerie was gentler than she would have liked. Muriel missed the thrill of being ordered about and of being made to endure the random pain that both Valerie and Rhonda had inflicted upon her. She missed the thrill of being unable to resist her captor. She trembled as Valerie wound the thin cord around her wrists and pulled it tight. The tying of the knots and the cinching of the cord had a calming effect on her. Now she was committed, she told herself. No turning back.

With Muriel's hands now secured, Valerie moved on to her elbows. The cords pulled her arms together and her shoulders back. Muriel stared down at her breasts, jutting out suggestively in this enforced pose. Valerie pulled the cords tighter, and Muriel's elbows nearly met behind her back. She held still while Valerie tied the knots that would hold her captive for the next several hours. The buttons of her blouse were straining apart, the material between them pulled open, allowing her (and Valerie) to see the top slopes of her breasts.

'I hope ... I mean, there weren't any ... scars,' Valerie said softly, her mouth nearly touching Muriel's ear.

'Not there, at any rate,' Muriel replied.

'I'm sorry,' Valerie said again.

Muriel said briskly, 'It's done. Let's forget it.' She turned to look at Valerie.

Valerie looked relieved, and somehow softer. Rhonda's conditioning had gone deep, Muriel decided. A moment later Valerie kissed her on her lips, startling her nearly as much as if the vice president of her bank had pinched her bottom. Valerie held the kiss, at first tentatively, until she felt Muriel return it. She put her arms round her captive and held her tightly. They leaned together for long moments. Then Valerie tentatively moved her hand to the buttons of Muriel's silk blouse. She was silent as Valerie opened them all the way down. Muriel held still in astonishment as Valerie pulled the front of her blouse apart and slid her bra straps down her arms. When Muriel's full breasts were bare, Valerie moved around in front of the kneeling woman and kissed both of her nipples.

'They're beautiful,' she breathed, fondling Muriel's breasts as she kissed and sucked the nipples. Muriel felt an electric shock as Valerie manipulated her breasts. She bit back a moan. 'Did that hurt?' Valerie asked.

Muriel shook her head, not trusting herself to speak. Valerie resumed, breaking off occasionally to kiss Muriel's lips. Muriel was beginning to pant as the fondling went on. She clamped down on the twin dildoes that penetrated her, and knew that she was going to come if Valerie did not stop. Valerie did not, and Muriel did.

Muriel let out a long sigh of satisfaction, her breasts heaving beneath Valerie's hands and questing mouth. She shuddered and swayed, her knees threatening to let go and tumble her to the floor. Muriel fought to stay kneeling. Valerie broke off worriedly, holding her upright. Muriel tried to smile, fearing it was more of a grimace. 'That was ... wonderful,' she croaked.

'I'm glad you liked it, Miss,' Valerie said, 'but I guess I'd better stop. I don't want to deliver you all worn out. Miss Rhonda wouldn't like that.' The blonde courier-girl looked worried as she spoke of their mutual mistress. 'But I'd like you to know that I enjoyed it too.' She began to rearrange Muriel's bra prior to buttoning her blouse.

'Don't,' Muriel said. Valerie looked up quizzically. 'Don't ... do my clothes up again.' Her throat was still tight. Her words came out somewhere between a croak and a whisper.

219

Valerie looked worried again. 'I have to, Miss Muriel. If Miss Rhonda saw you with your ti– breasts like this, she'd know that we'd been . . . doing something. And she'd get out her whip.' Valerie shuddered as if at a painful memory. Recalling how she had been whipped by this same woman who now knelt before her trying to stuff her breasts back into her bra, she could understand the worry.

'All right, Valerie,' Muriel said. 'Here's what we'll do. Leave my clothes like this for now and finish tying me up. I guess you'll use a gag and blindfold.' Valerie nodded, and Muriel continued, 'So I'll ride half naked most of the way. Then, somewhere before you reach Rhonda's place, you can pull over at some dark spot and get me dressed again. All right?' Muriel saw some of the worry leave Valerie's expression. She appeared to be considering Muriel's suggestion with something like eagerness.

'Only . . .' Valerie began.

'Only what, Valerie?'

'Well, if I know you're lying back here with your ti– breasts exposed and all, I may not be able to keep myself from stopping somewhere dark, like you say, and . . .'

'Fondling me again?' Muriel finished the sentence for her captor. 'All right, go ahead. And you can call them tits if you're more comfortable with that word.'

Looking at Muriel's exposed 'tits', Valerie nodded agreement. 'But it will be hard, driving along knowing you're back here like this.'

'Then you'll just have to concentrate harder on the road. And stop more often. Do I need to be plainer than that? Remember that if you have an accident the cops will find me – as you put it – like this. And they would ask some seriously embarrassing questions of us both.'

'All right.' Valerie nodded. 'I'll be careful.' Suddenly she smiled. 'I'll enjoy knowing you're back here – like this. But still you're lucky. I have to be really careful about showing my tits now that I've been pierced.'

'Pierced?'

'Yes. Didn't you know? Miss Rhonda and Mr Ted did it to me as soon as she got me back to their place. I screamed and fought but they tied me down in that barn of theirs and did it anyway. I was terrified, afraid they were going to kill me. But they only put rings through my nipples.'

Muriel was fascinated. 'I've never seen a woman pierced there. Show me. Please?'

Valerie looked shyly at her captive. 'Are you sure, Miss?'

Muriel nodded and, as she knelt in the back of the van with her hands and arms tied tightly behind her back, she watched Valerie use her own to pull the blouse from the waistband of her skirt. She unbuttoned the front. The blouse fell to the floor, and Valerie unhooked her bra to reveal her breasts. Muriel noted that they were smaller than hers, and more pointed. But her eyes were drawn irresistibly to the stainless steel rings that pierced her captor's nipples. They looked both erotic and . . . penal.

Valerie cupped a breast for Muriel's inspection, turning the ring to show her where it was joined. 'I can't take them off, Miss, because they're welded.'

Muriel felt her anal and vaginal muscles tighten around the dildoes as she imagined the rings being welded. She bit back a moan of excitement. Her stomach felt suddenly hollow. She had to force herself to concentrate as Valerie continued her explanation.

'. . . has this wire-welding machine like jewellers use to make fine joins, and after Miss Rhonda pierced me

he put the rings through . . . and welded them shut.'
Valerie turned the ring to show Muriel a neat welded
where the ends met.

'Didn't that burn?'

'I thought it would. That's why I screamed and
jerked. But it only felt a bit warm. Mr Ted turned the
ring so the join would be furthest from my . . . tit, and
he covered the rest of my breast and nipple with a
little leather cover to keep the sparks from touching
me. Miss Rhonda said he had made the cover himself.
She said he had clever hands. She asked me if I'd like
a similar ring through my . . . spot, while I was having
the others done.'

Muriel translated 'spot' as 'clitoris', and she felt
hollow again as she imagined herself being ringed
there.

'No extra charge, she said. I screamed and struggled and shouted, and she said she guessed that all the
noise meant no. She told Mr Ted to get on with it, and
I screamed and struggled and shouted some more. But
I needn't have worried. One bright 'fzzzt!' and it was
done. I was a lot calmer when he did the other one.'

'Come closer,' Muriel said, and Valerie shuffled
forwards on her knees. Muriel looked closely at the
ring, noticing the clean hole where it passed through
the pink flesh of her nipple. 'Does it hurt now?'

Valerie shook her head. 'Oh, it took a little getting
used to,' she said, 'like when I put on a bra, but now
it feels normal. I like it. The effect, I mean, and
knowing that I have them there, out of sight. The first
time I went out in public after that I imagined I had
"nipple rings" tattooed across my forehead, but no
one noticed. Did you?'

Muriel shook her head. Balancing carefully, she
leaned closer and kissed the nipple Valerie was
showing. She felt an electric shock in her belly when

222

her lips met the warm flesh and the ring clicked against her teeth. Valerie sighed when Muriel closed her teeth on the steel and pulled back gently. Slowly, still balancing carefully, Muriel kissed the other nipple with its bright ring of steel.

Valerie looked happier than she had since her arrival. 'I guess that means I'm forgiven, doesn't it?'

Muriel nodded. Valerie came closer and embraced her captive, breasts pressed together, the hard steel rings rubbing Muriel's own nipples. 'Oh!' she gasped as they touched. She clenched herself around the dildoes inside her as she came. It was only a slight shock, but most welcome. Valerie held her tightly, moving slowly against her, and Muriel came again, stronger this time, as she imagined herself being ringed like Valerie and turned loose in public. She rested her chin on Valerie's shoulder and shook with her orgasm. She whimpered as she came, stifling the urge to scream. Muriel shook for a long time. Valerie held her upright.

Finally she said, 'Oh, I wish my hands weren't tied. Then I could do something nice for you.'

'You already have,' Valerie whispered as she pulled back and kissed Muriel on the lips. 'You already have.'

Muriel made an interrogative sound, and Valerie broke off the kiss to tell her that Muriel had made her feel human again, and forgiven, after what she had done to her. 'I wish I hadn't done it,' she said, leaking tears.

'It's over now, Valerie. Let it go. I have.'

Valerie held her again. Muriel wished she could return the gesture, but she could not ask Valerie to untie her. Her helplessness in fact enabled her to treat her captor gently. Helpless herself, the only response was gentleness. And she liked being tied.

'Miss Rhonda usually links them together,' she said, nodding at her rings, 'and uses a chain to lead me around. Mr Ted does the same. It's to teach me humility, they insist, but it just makes me horny. They usually notice sooner or later, and do something about it.'

Muriel felt faint as she imagined herself led about in such a manner – and what they would do about her condition.

Valerie at length drew back. 'Are you ready for the rest, Miss Muriel?' she asked diffidently.

'Nearly. There are a few other things for you to think of. You don't have to call me "Miss" unless Rhonda is around. And . . .'

'And what?'

'Well, when you handle me, be . . . rough.'

'Like the first time?' Valerie asked.

Muriel nodded. 'Yes. Like that.'

'All right. Kneel back on your heels so we can get you into this.' Already Valerie sounded more authoritative – rougher. 'This' turned out to be the leather helmet she had worn on her first ride with Valerie. It would cover her head and face completely. There were laces at the back to make it fit snugly. Valerie pointed out the eye-pads and the inflatable gag that went with it.

Muriel felt her throat tighten as she gazed at the preparations Rhonda and Valerie had made for her transportation. She forced herself to speak through her rising excitement. 'Put it on me, then,' she told Valerie, bowing her head so that the blonde courier-girl could finish doing up her live parcel. Muriel drew a deep shuddering breath as her captor fitted the helmet over her head and stuffed the gag into her mouth. Valerie arranged Muriel's hair so that it all went inside the helmet, and then began to pull the laces tight. Blind now, Muriel felt the leather tighten around her head. Valerie stopped at several points to tie the laces, and then resumed tightening elsewhere until Muriel felt as if her head were enclosed in a skin-tight mask. Satisfied at last, Valerie began to inflate the gag. It filled Muriel's mouth, trapping her tongue beneath it as it expanded. Her jaws were forced apart, further tightening the headgear.

Muriel shook her head but the helmet did not loosen. When she tried to speak, all she heard was a strangled 'Mmnnng'. She doubted if anyone outside the van would hear her, no matter how hard she tried to attract attention. Thinking of her helplessness excited her. Valerie kissed her roughly over the gag, holding Muriel's head with both hands, and then pushed her over. Blind and speechless, her hands and arms held immovably behind her back, Muriel toppled from her knees to land heavily on the floor of the van. Valerie grabbed her and roughly turned her over on to her stomach. The blonde girl was following her captive's own instructions, and Muriel felt a thrill of mixed excitement and fear as those hands roughly pulled her legs together and wound cords tightly around her ankles. Muriel felt Valerie cinching them tight, making them bite into her skin, and then tying the final knots. Valerie pulled up her skirt, and Muriel felt the cool air on her exposed legs from ankles to thighs. More cords went around her legs above and below the knees, pulled tightly and cinched between her legs. Then the hands went away, leaving Muriel helpless with her tits bare and her legs fully exposed to the view of anyone who found her. That no one would find her except Valerie did not lessen the thrill of being bound and gagged and taken away to the country.

Valerie was apparently unable to resist toying with her captive. She rolled Muriel on to her side and fondled her tits, kissing them hungrily and teasing her nipples until they rose into hard little peaks. Muriel gasped as she was fondled and teased. She thought she could hear Valerie's ragged breathing through the tight leather helmet that cut her off from the rest of the world. Or it might have been only her own ragged breath. It didn't matter to Muriel. Valerie bit one of her nipples. Muriel gasped and jerked in surprised pain. And then she came, shuddering and jerking like a landed fish as she fought her bonds and felt the pleasure wash over and through her. The dildoes inside her shifted as she struggled, and set her off again. Knowing that she was helpless and could not rid herself of her internal comforters drove Muriel wild. She heard herself making muffled noises of release, and hoped that at least Valerie could interpret what she was shouting through her gag.

So great was her release that Muriel hardly noticed when Valerie paused to hog-tie her. The courier-girl might have been changed profoundly by her re-education, but she still knew how to tie knots. When Muriel stopped shuddering and jerking, she was lying on her side, wrists and ankles bound tightly together, back arched and tits jutting from the front of her open blouse. Valerie stood up and opened the sliding door in the side of the van. Muriel felt a breeze on her exposed legs and sweating body, and there was a moment of panic as she imagined what would happen if someone drove by at that moment and saw her. Valerie prolonged the moment by leaving the door open. Muriel moaned through her gag, urging her captor to close the door and get her out of sight.

Valerie touched her again, stroking her thighs and her breasts. Muriel was helpless. She tried to move away, back into the darkness inside the van, but could not. And she felt her excitement growing again

226

even as she struggled to hide herself. The warmth in her crotch and belly spread as Valerie continued to arouse her. Oh, God, she thought, please stop. Don't leave me exposed like this. And then all thought was banished as she came, jerking wildly against the ropes that held her and moaning through the tight gag.

Some indefinable time (and several orgasms) later, Muriel realised that her captor was no longer arousing her. She felt drained, but still excited by her helplessness and exposure. She knew that the door was still open. The breeze cooled the sweat on her body. Panic gradually replaced the excitement. Where was Valerie? Did she intend to leave her captive here, to be found by any casual passer-by? Muriel moaned again, fearfully this time, and struggled wildly against her bonds.

Valerie, if she were still there, made no sound, spurring Muriel to even wilder but still fruitless struggles. Her breath grew short and loud as she jerked and pulled at the ropes that bound her. Soon she was panting loudly and there was a roaring in her ears. Unable to breathe through her mouth, Muriel was using up oxygen faster than she could take it in through her nostrils. Still she struggled, moaning as loudly as she could. And her body took charge again, even as she was frantically trying to escape. She felt the familiar warmth and pressure in her belly, and she came again, gasping for air. Then all was darkness and silence.

When Muriel regained consciousness, the van was moving, with her helpless inside it. As she rolled with the movement, Muriel felt her naked breasts and erect nipples rub over the rough carpet on the floor of the speeding van. She felt the dildoes shift inside her. As before, she was being taken over public roads, surrounded by countless others who knew nothing of her predicament. Muriel abandoned herself to the experience. No one heard her squeals of pleasure except Valerie.

Although Valerie stopped several times to climb into the back of the van and arouse her captive, the ride seemed endless. Muriel groaned with pleasure as her captor fondled her bare tits, slapping them and pinching her nipples. At one of the stops Valerie untied her legs and made her get out of the van. A cool breeze blew over her exposed legs and naked breasts. She led Muriel some distance away from the road to what the blindfolded and gagged woman fervently hoped was a private place. There Valerie made her squat and pee. Muriel groaned with relief as she emptied her full bladder on to the ground. Valerie left her for a moment and Muriel felt panic wash over her. Was the courier still resentful, or had the liberties Muriel had granted gone to her head? She imagined herself abandoned beside the road. Of course someone would find her, but maybe not until daybreak. And what would that lucky finder do?

Thus Muriel made herself fearful – and excited. She did not know whether to feel relief or disappointment when Valerie helped her to stand. She led her captive back to the van. As before, she was made to sit on the tailboard of the van while Valerie stooped to tie her legs again. As the cords bit into her flesh, Muriel came down on the side of pleasure. This time Valerie crossed her ankles and tied them tightly together. She felt herself trembling at the mental picture of herself that formed behind her blind eyes. Muriel felt the cords bite into her as Valerie bound her at knees and thighs. With her ankles crossed, Muriel knew that she would be unable to stand, and was not surprised when Valerie did not replace the hog-tie. With a grunt

Valerie lifted her bound legs and tipped Muriel back into the van.

But Valerie was not finished with her. Hands grasped her shoulders and pulled her further inside. Muriel felt rather than heard the door close, and then Valerie's hands were on her breasts. She was being rough, as Muriel had asked, and Muriel gasped with the pleasure of being handled. Valerie shifted her attention to Muriel's crotch, pushing the dildo into her and grinding it into her pubic bone – and her clitoris. Muriel would have screamed but for the gag. As it was, she made as much noise as possible. This went on for a long time, and then Muriel blacked out.

She came to in the moving van. Valerie had thoughtfully turned her on to her stomach before moving off. Muriel rubbed her breasts and nipples against the carpet, and shifted herself to make her twin plugs move inside her. All was well. She sighed with relief and rising excitement. This time, without the hog-tie, Muriel could roll easily on the floor of the speeding van. She used her relative freedom to arouse herself.

A long time later, it seemed, Valerie roused her from exhausted sleep to replace her brassiere and button her blouse. Muriel moaned as her captor made her presentable, and dropped back into exhausted sleep until she felt herself being lifted and carried. She made sleepy noises through the gag as she was laid on something soft. She didn't feel them untying her and removing her gag and blindfold.

Muriel woke in the morning as the sunlight grew strong enough to penetrate the drawn window-blinds. She was in the same room she had used on her last visit to Rhonda's place. She felt empty, drained. The empty feeling was due to the removal of the dildoes, the drained feeling to the long night of pleasure as she was transported here. She stretched her cramped limbs, discovering in the process that she was chained to the bed by her ankle. Muriel went back to sleep. A full bladder and an empty stomach woke her later. She discovered that her ankle chain allowed her to reach the bathroom. How civilised, she thought, as she squatted to relieve herself. She took a leisurely shower. Now if only someone would bring her some food.

Someone had done so while she was in the toilet. Muriel ate everything in a great hurry. She felt better now, clean, fed and securely fastened to her bed. What more could a slave girl ask? The last idea woke her fully. Tonight was the big night. The nervous-bride feeling would not let her drift back to sleep. She needed to be getting ready, she thought anxiously. But there was nothing she could do. Muriel nevertheless paced the room, dragging the chain behind her. Would somebody please come, she repeated silently. As on the last occasion, she felt it would be gauche to shout.

Around noon Chloe came in with a tray that smelled wonderful to the famished captive. As she ate, they talked of the coming evening. Muriel said she was very nervous, and asked if Paul had arrived yet. Chloe replied that Ted had finished her 'wedding dress', that she was not to worry, and that Valerie had been dispatched to ensure that Paul did not miss the big event. Muriel imagined Paul travelling as she had done the previous evening. Would Valerie be tempted to sample the goods before delivery?

Chloe giggled at the idea. 'Rhonda thinks of everything. You came with plugs to keep intruders away. He is coming in his little cage for the same reason. Even though none of us is worried about

virginity or violation, she likes to keep her symbols –
and her associates – in order. She'll be along herself
in a little while to pierce your nipples.'

Muriel felt her stomach go hollow at the thought.
'Like . . . Valerie?'

'Oh, then you saw hers? But yours won't be
welded, so don't worry. Ted will do that later if you
want him to, but tonight you just need some ordinary
nipple rings to hold things in place.'

Muriel wondered if there was any such thing as
'ordinary' nipple rings.

There were. The rings Rhonda showed Muriel were
nowhere as large nor as penal-looking as Valerie's.
She was relieved. Nevertheless the two women insisted that she be bound for the ceremony. Chloe tied
Muriel's hands behind her back. The two of them tied
her to a chair, securing her ankles to the legs and her
body to the chair back. Rhonda left to make the final
preparations. Muriel stared at herself in the mirror,
little stirrings of excitement coming and going.

The procedure itself was no worse, she concluded,
than having one's ears pierced. But considerably
more erotic – or symbolic, as Rhonda phrased it.
Muriel could see everything in the mirror, and she
grew excited as she sat helplessly while Chloe and
Rhonda made her nipples erect for the piercing. She
gasped as the metal passed through her sensitive flesh.
When they were done, they left her to gaze at her new
adornments. Muriel twisted in the chair, examining
her nipple rings. She decided that she liked them, as
she had liked Valerie's.

Nearly three hours later Rhonda and Chloe returned to dress her for the occasion. They left her
bound while they did her hair and her make-up. Ted
delivered the 'wedding dress', stopping to admire the
captive bride. When the two women were finished,

231

Muriel was spectacularly, indecently decent. And still nervous. Rhonda told Muriel to remain upstairs until someone came to fetch her. She helpfully locked Muriel's ankle to the bed before going to greet her guests.

12

Party

The party was in progress, people moving from bar to buffet to dancing area, groups forming and breaking up to re-form with different members. Except for the obvious fact that they were all into bondage, either as dominant or submissive – top or bottom in the jargon of bondage freaks – the gathering was no different from any other soirée. Roughly half of the fourteen or so attendees were in bondage of one sort or another, while the other half – the tops – were playing their chosen roles as masters or dominatrices.

Chloe had gone down earlier. She was now shackled into her bondage frame. At the end of the last dance Ted had left her there, in case anyone else wanted to dance with her, fondle or otherwise molest her. The frame was made of rigid steel in the form of a double-barred cross with two short arms. The upper bar was at shoulder level. Her wrists were shackled to either end of it so that her hands were separated while her elbows hung below her pinioned hands. A collar held her head back against the upright piece. A second band of steel held her waist against it as well. Her ankles were shackled to the lower crossbar so that she stood on her own feet but could not move her hands, feet, head or body. The frame was mounted on wheels (to enable her to 'dance') with whomever chose to take her on to the dance floor. In addition, she could simply be wheeled into a private place and fondled. To encourage would-be molesters, she was nude, every part of her body on display, helpless to stop anyone from doing whatever they wished with or to her. She was unable to eat or drink without someone feeding her or holding a glass to her lips. Nevertheless, her bizarre situation did not seem to bother her. She was in fact enjoying the attentions of those who engaged her in conversation, fed her or danced with her. Chloe liked her helpless immobility. This was the first trial of the frame Ted had made for her, and several of the guests stopped to admire it – and her.

The cage that had attracted Muriel's attention on her first visit stood empty near the wall. Next to it, likewise unoccupied, was the triangular whipping frame she had encountered on the same occasion. A short but painful-looking whip hung from the apex. The presence of these two devices suggested that they would be put to use later. Which of her guests Rhonda would introduce to her toys lent an air of mystery and excitement to the gathering. From time to time the guests glanced at frame and cage with a thrill of apprehension, wondering if they were going to be the lucky victims.

Ronan Wilkes was a submissive, so he almost always came to gatherings in the care of one or another of the group's domanitrices. Tonight he was with Tamara Davis, one of his favourite partners, though he had little say in the matter of who took him in charge. Like Chloe, he was nude, save for the steel ring that encircled his balls. It was locked in place. Tamara doubtless had the keys, but she might give them – and him – to anyone else if she chose.

Tamara held the chain attached to the ring, and so led him around whenever she moved from one group to another. A sharp jerk on the chain produced a surprising amount of docile obedience – Ronan's favourite activity.

Tamara, as befitted a dominatrix, wore a leather body suit that hugged her body while hiding it completely from view. Her long legs were sheathed in opaque black tights, and she wore extremely high-heeled, tightly laced knee boots. For added effect, she carried a cane, with which she switched Ronan or whomever else, male or female, she decided to favour with her attention. Some of the blows were playful, and some were not. She was a good judge of who wanted this sort of attention from her.

The male submissives mostly wore some sort of chastity device which rendered their penises inaccessible, either to themselves or to anyone else who did not happen to have the key to unlock them. That was to remind them and everyone else that they were someone's property, not their own masters, not free to mingle and choose partners of their own. There were a surprising number of them. Or maybe not so surprising if one considered the pressures and responsibilities of business and professional life. This was their way of opting out of responsibility in private. If they had given any hint of their inclination in public, they would have been permanently disgraced. Here they enjoyed a bizarre freedom for a few hours.

Many of the submissive women wore handcuffs, or had their hands bound with anything ranging from simple rope to the versatile nylon straps called cable ties in the electrical trade, and jiffy-cuffs by the police. Some were hobbled; some wore leg-irons.

Valerie Sanderson was present by royal command. Since her re-education she had become markedly

235

more tolerant of the members of Rhonda's circle. She was fast becoming one of the kind of people she had scorned. She knew that Rhonda would not hesitate to use the footage of her abusing Muriel to ruin her business if she did not comply with the dominatrice's commands. For this evening she had been commanded to play the role of single female at the mixed gathering, available to whomever wanted her. She wore a basque with stockings and suspenders, exposing her body to anyone who felt like fondling her. In order to encourage docility her hands were held behind her back in handcuffs, and she was hobbled by a pair of leg-irons with a very short chain joining her ankles. Valerie spent a good deal of the time blushing and trying to be invisible. From time to time Rhonda had to snap a leash to the chain that joined her nipples and lead her back to the centre of the room. The sight of Valerie being towed by her nipple rings caused heads to turn and her blush to deepen. 'Relax and enjoy the attention,' was Rhonda's advice to her reluctant recruit. Valerie could not take the advice. Her obvious reluctance made her all the more popular with the other attendees. She dared not flee the gathering altogether. Dressed as she was, and in chains, there was no place for her to go. And the prospect of being hunted down by her irate hostess was daunting. Rhonda would doubtless treat flight as an excuse for further re-education. Valerie had not yet grown to relish being whipped. Rhonda left her in the centre of a group of admirers. Valerie tried again to become invisible, retreating slowly from the group.

Rhonda noticed. She went to collect Paul and Ted. 'Come help me liven up the party,' she commanded. With them, she advanced on Valerie. The group of people around Valerie parted as Rhonda came through. Valerie shrank away, but there was no place for her to flee to. Rhonda struck a pose, her weight on one leg and her hands on her hips. Smiling ironically to her two helpers, she snapped, 'Seize her. Take her to the whipping frame and secure her there.' To the remainder of the group, she explained that, in her opinion, the party had gone dull. She proposed to remedy the situation. Valerie, she continued, had asked to be whipped, and she, Rhonda, was granting her wish.

Valerie went pale. 'N . . . no!' she stammered. 'I didn't! She's ly– mistaken!' She looked helplessly at the other guests as Paul and Ted took her by the elbows and pulled her towards the triangular frame standing against the wall. Rhonda followed, as did the other guests. Valerie's vocal opposition had by now attracted the attention of the entire group. They flocked to see the latest diversion. Valerie was screaming and trying to resist her captors. They dragged her the last few feet to the frame. There they had to pause while Rhonda removed Valerie's handcuffs and leg-irons. Paul and Ted held her arms while she struggled and protested. With the help of another man they lifted her on to the flat metal footplate and set about securing her hands with the rope that hung down from the pulley at the top of the frame. With her wrists bound in front of her, Valerie still tried to escape. Rhonda herself took hold of the other end of the rope and hauled Valerie's arms into the air. The struggling woman looked over her shoulder, screaming 'Naaoooh!' as the men tied her ankles to the bottom corners of the frame. Rhonda then pulled the rope taut and tied it off.

Valerie tugged at the ropes, but they held her inescapably. Her body quivered as she pulled and twisted. Rhonda, and the rest of the guests, watched with interest. Among the men who were not wearing cock restraints, the interest was immediately apparent. Even Paul felt his cock straining against the steel cage, and wished he could get it off.

Rhonda took the whip from its hook and offered it to her guests. 'Let him with the strongest arm strike the first blow.' Valerie twisted her neck as far as she could, trying to look behind her, pleading with her eyes to be spared a lashing. And she continued to jerk at the ropes holding her. It never occurred to her in her panic that escape was impossible. If she broke free, or if all the knots holding her should slip loose, it would take only a moment to re-secure her. She was surrounded by people who would prevent escape. It was more a matter of instinct than of reason. 'No! Please, no!' she screamed.

Rhonda made a face. 'Such a racket for such a small thing. I think maybe we would have more peace if she were gagged, don't you?' she asked of the assembled guests in general. Without waiting for a reply, she handed the whip to Ted. 'Keep her amused until I get back,' she ordered over her shoulder as she left the room. Behind her there was a sharp cracking sound and Valerie's pleadings were suddenly cut short by a loud scream of pain and fear. In the relative silence that followed the first lash Valerie's moans were clearly audible. Rhonda heard a second scream as Ted continued to 'amuse' their captive. Even in the kitchen, Valerie's screams were loud enough to alarm the neighbours, had there been any. The absence of neighbours had been one of the main reasons that had influenced Rhonda in her choice of this house over many others that might have served the purpose. The two gags she selected now would be more for local quiet than for any other reason. As an afterthought she took along a blindfold from her store. There were several more screams as she returned to the main party room.

Moaning, Valerie hung from her wrists, her knees sagging. There were half a dozen red stripes across her back. Ted and the rest of the guests surrounded the whipping frame. The lashing of Valerie kept them riveted. Only Chloe, helplessly fastened to her rigid steel frame on the dance floor, remained apart from the crowd. She strained to see the spectacle but the crowd prevented her from observing much of Valerie's ordeal. Rhonda could see that she was aroused. Her pinioned wrists twisted against the steel restraints, and her entire body seemed tense. Her breasts rose and fell rapidly with excitement.

Rhonda detoured to her side to whisper a promise that she could be the next occupant of the whipping frame if she were *very* good. 'I'm going to gag you now,' Rhonda continued. Chloe shuddered as the crack of the lash was followed by another Valerie scream. Then she opened her mouth to take in the gag. Rhonda pushed the rubber ball behind her teeth and buckled the leather straps tightly behind Chloe's head, under her long hair. Seeing her excitement, Rhonda caressed her between the legs. Chloe moaned and thrust her hips forwards against Rhonda's hand. Her breasts rose and fell rapidly as the arousal continued. Her attention was now firmly fixed on what was happening between her thighs. Valerie was forgotten.

Abruptly Rhonda stopped caressing Chloe. 'Can't have you coming too soon,' she told the panting, moaning captive. Chloe said something like 'eeese oooont oppp!' but Rhonda turned away. Over her shoulder she promised that she would do something nice for her as soon as she had finished gagging and blindfolding Valerie. Chloe flashed a brief grimace of frustration without in any way relaxing her taut muscles.

Rhonda made her way back to the main action. Valerie now stood erect, struggling against the ropes, her bottom too now striped with the marks of the whip. 'Please stop this and let me go,' she begged when she caught sight of Rhonda. By way of reply Rhonda forced a thumb and forefinger into the angle of Valerie's jaw, forcing her mouth open. She stuffed the rubber ball behind the captive's teeth and buckled the straps tightly behind her head. 'Nnnngg!' Valerie said as she tried to shake the gag free. Rhonda buckled the eyeless mask over her victim's face before stepping back and signalling to Ted that he was free to resume the lashing.

Ted took aim and struck Valerie across her bottom. The hapless victim jerked against the ropes and emitted a strangled scream from behind her gag. While Ted and the others were focused on Valerie's torment, Rhonda went back to Chloe. The blonde woman was twisting in her steel shackles, tense and panting. Valerie's screams, as well as the prospect of being beaten herself, had combined to arouse her. Chloe twisted in her shackles, her body covered with a light sheen of sweat. 'Eeeeese!' she said to Rhonda.

'Patience. Your turn will come. In the meantime I'll keep you on the boil myself.'

Ted was lashing Valerie and everyone was watching the show. What Rhonda was doing to Chloe went unnoticed by everyone except the blonde girl shackled to her iron frame. Chloe bucked and jerked as Rhonda alternately teased her breasts and shoved her finger into the prisoner's cunt. Despite her earlier resolve not to let Chloe come too soon, Rhonda was unable to prevent her. Perhaps it was the sight of Valerie's suffering that drove her over the top. It might have been the prospect of her own suffering that made her come. Whatever the reason, Chloe was out of control, moaning through her gag as she twisted under Rhonda's fingers. Ted brought the whip up between Valerie's legs, and she shrieked in pain despite being gagged herself. Valerie shuddered for long moments after that blow to her sensitive parts. It took the combined efforts of Paul and Ted to quieten her down. Ted let the whip trail on the floor as he inserted a finger into the place he had just lashed. Paul fondled Valerie's breasts and teased her nipples.

Between them they made her shudder with pleasure after the pain. Valerie threw back her head so that she stared sightlessly at the ceiling, her body quivering and jerking against the ropes that held her to the whipping frame. She seemed to have forgotten her earlier shyness as the two men worked over her helpless body. She was still some way from being able to transmute her pain into pleasure, as Muriel and Chloe did, but Rhonda planned still more re-education that would hopefully turn the courier-girl into a fully fledged masochist. Now she merely enjoyed the pleasure after the pain. And enjoy it she most certainly did, shuddering and moaning as they aroused her. The other guests watched with interest as Rhonda's newest initiate went into orgasm before them all. Coming along nicely, Rhonda thought.

Chloe was coming too as Rhonda continued to fondle and tease her. She was moaning steadily through her gag, perhaps anticipating her own encounter with the whip. Rhonda's streak of perversity showed itself as she brought Chloe to the brink of another orgasm, and then left her hanging. She walked away from Chloe, whose muffled cries spoke of her distress and desire. Ignoring the clear signals from the blonde shackled to her iron frame, Rhonda strode to the centre of the crowd gathered to watch

241

Valerie's performance and announced that it was time for the main event. Afterwards, she said, they were all free to make use of the bedrooms upstairs if they required more privacy for their collective sports. There were some signs of disappointment, but mostly they took the announcement with good grace, knowing that Rhonda had provided the means for their further entertainment.

Rhonda went to Paul and whispered in his ear, 'You're on in a minute.' He grinned nervously as she went to the CD player. The music stopped. In the silence Rhonda said, 'Please give your attention to the bride's entrance. I think you will be well rewarded by the sight.' She put another disc in the machine, and presently the familiar strains of Mendelssohn's Wedding March filled the room. They all turned to the stairs with expectation. Paul looked nervous in the cock-cage. Rhonda snapped a leash to the cage and led him across the room to await his slave girl's entrance.

To this group Muriel made her entrance from upstairs. On the top landing she paused to allow those below to see her clearly. The effect was stunning. A hush fell as she began to descend. Paul, too, was awed. He had never seen her wear this particular outfit before, and he guessed that it had been made especially for this occasion. His cock stirred within the steel cage. Rhonda noticed. 'Down, boy,' she whispered from the corner of her mouth, tugging on the leash to remind him who was in control.

It must have taken hours to prepare Muriel for this grand entrance, and she was probably feeling that she had achieved the desired impact. From a distance it looked as if she wore nothing but a harness of chain that hugged her body and outlined her figure most provocatively while covering the essential areas. The overall effect was more provocative – or more shocking, depending on one's point of view – than total nudity could ever be. Aware that she had the attention of virtually everyone in the ballroom, Muriel paced slowly down the stairs.

As she came closer Paul could see that her full breasts, jutting proudly forwards and upwards, jiggled ever so slightly to the rhythm of her footsteps, but that the rest of her firm body remained, well, firm. And as breathtaking as ever. He felt a tightness in his chest, a shortness of breath, as he gazed at his nearly nude mistress descending the staircase. Closer still, and he could see that she wore a sheer body stocking over the silvery chain harness. He was flattered, guessing that she had worn it because she knew of his liking for stockings and stocking-like garments. He wondered how much Rhonda had had to do with the choice of apparel. The sheer nylon clung to Muriel's every curve, moving as she did, moulding her breasts, belly and bottom, and her long full legs. She wore high stiletto-heeled shoes to complete the effect she knew he liked.

But it was the harness worn under the body stocking that captured everyone's attention. Around her neck Muriel wore a tight leather collar from which depended the rest of the harness, holding it up and in its place against the insistent tug of gravity and the movements of her flawless body. From the collar a series of thin chains spread over her upper torso, above her breasts, before branching over, under and around the mounds, making a particularly wicked brassiere effect that simultaneously offered her breasts up to view yet covered the nipples as if in deference to the prevailing custom.

Paul, and doubtless all the others, could see that the straps divided her breasts into three distinct areas.

Two straps ran down over the upper slopes, forming a vee that ended at her covered nipples, while a third strap ran down the lower slopes of each breast from the same area to the strap that encircled each one. This strap divided the lower halves of Muriel's breasts vertically. The total effect was to cause her flesh to bulge provocatively under the sheer nylon of her body stocking. Paul could see that all the straps were tight around and against her body. Her nipples were covered by tiny gold cups that allowed the dark brown flesh of her areolae to show enticingly around their outer circumferences but prevented a full view. The gold cups over the nipples themselves made them seem erect, as if she were sexually aroused (as she probably was), as well as being arousing.

At first Paul thought the cups merely for effect, but, as she crossed the floor towards him, through the crowds who parted as they stared at her, he saw that they truly contained her nipples. And if her nipples were not truly erect, they were nonetheless held captive inside those tiny gold cups by a pair of rings passing through the metal and obviously through her nipples as well, holding the whole arrangement in place through these anchor points. It was his first sight of Muriel's new rings. He approved, while wondering fleetingly how she had got all those holes to line up properly. It must have taken her some time, but the effort had been worth it. The effect was startling. He felt his cock stir in its confinement as he imagined her fastening these rings through her nipples and those gold cups. A sharp tug on the leash reminded him of Rhonda's control.

As Muriel passed the others in her progress up what had become in effect an aisle of people, Paul noticed that they were staring at her back view as well. He began to wonder what she looked like from that angle to make them point and stare and smile. I'll know soon enough, he thought. Just then there was still more to be seen from the front. A piece of chain encircled her below the breasts, like the bandeau of a conventional brassiere, anchoring everything in place.

Below her breasts she was as spectacularly covered yet uncovered as above. Between her breasts a chain ran down from her collar, dividing them and passing down to a tight waist belt. Two more chains led from there down over her stomach and abdomen. There they met a chromed steel plate that covered Muriel's mons veneris while leaving most of her pubic hair exposed. The plate tapered as it disappeared between her legs. It was in effect a chastity belt, Paul realised with a perceptible tightening in his own belly and cock. The look-but-don't-touch effect was terrifically erotic.

Knowing how Rhonda liked to dress her associates, Paul guessed that this was another of her designs. Rhonda relished the idea of keeping her charges from sexual intimacy by such means. That was why she had made him wear the cock-cage. 'Just for the party tonight,' she had told him. 'Though I plan to lend it to Muriel whenever I am away and you need a lesson in restraint,' she had warned.

Rhonda had summoned him to a private interview several hours before the evening's gathering. Paul had gone warily, thinking that their mistress might be feeling envious at the announcement of Muriel's impending slavery. Even though she herself would never accept such a position, she might still resent their becoming an item. Rhonda, however, had not seemed angry. She had merely told him that they both still 'belonged' to her, and that she would be visiting each of them, though not necessarily always together, to administer the usual discipline and dole out the usual pleasure. Then she had produced the cock-cage, ordering him to wear it for the evening. 'To make the heart grow fonder and the cock more eager,' she explained. 'The keys will be at your place, so that you can get unlocked when you get Muriel in private. But don't lose them, or have any copies made. Remember who they – and you – belong to.' That was as close as she got to a threat the whole evening.

As his slave girl approached, Paul felt both conspicuous wearing only the cock-cage (though he was not the only man so dressed and so restrained) and suspicious of Rhonda's apparent good-natured acceptance of the situation. Rhonda smiled ironically as she prepared to give away both the bride and the groom.

Muriel was smiling both for him and at the effect she was having on others. A bride, even one as unconventional as she, deserved to look her best on her big day. She enjoyed the attention and admiration from them and from him too. His glance returned to her costume. A few paces from Paul, Muriel looked directly at him with a smile. The sheer nylon of her body stocking was slightly reddish, giving her fine-grained flesh a slightly dusky look and gleaming softly as the lights struck the shiny material. She knew how much the look and the feel of the smooth material pleased him, and had dressed to give him pleasure. An altogether remarkable woman. Paul felt very lucky to have found her. In her left hand Muriel carried a leather bag with drawstrings.

Rhonda unclipped the lead from his cock-cage as Muriel approached, allowing Paul to meet her. She did not unlock the cage itself.

As they met, Muriel lifted her right hand and placed it behind his neck, drawing him to her for a kiss of greeting. Her delicate, subtle scent filled the air as they kissed, to applause from the gathered guests. As he embraced his slave, Paul's hands encountered the strap that ran up behind her back from between her legs to her collar. There were unexpected metallic bits all up and down the strap, he discovered as he caressed her back. When the kiss ended and Muriel drew back, he noticed that her collar had a ring fastened to its front.

Muriel turned to face the still applauding guests and made a slight bow, allowing Paul to see the back view that had attracted the notice of their friends. The chains that crossed and circled her body at breasts and waist were fastened behind her back with buckles that locked with tiny matching brass pad-locks. The central strap running from between her legs was fastened to the back of her collar with a similar lock that served to lock the collar as well. The effect of Muriel back-view was nearly as striking as Muriel front-view. Paul wondered idly where the keys to all these locks were. Muriel (or Rhonda) would tell him when it was time, he guessed. In the meantime the sight of his slave locked into the harness and so provocatively covered and uncovered was quite enough.

Waiters made their rounds with fresh glasses of champagne as the guests drew back to allow the couple space to be seen. Muriel was the cynosure of all eyes as she gave Paul her right hand.

'Friends,' Paul began, holding up his free hand for silence, 'you all know that Muriel and I have been together for a long time.'

He was interrupted by sporadic clapping and cries of 'It'll soon seem like a lot longer', and 'Don't do it' (mostly from their male guests), and 'Don't let him get away' (from their wives, lovers, mistresses and girlfriends). He waited smilingly until the clamour subsided. 'This party is intended to celebrate our relationship,' he continued. 'We're not going to prison.'

'That's what *you* think,' came the retort.

Paul motioned again for silence. 'Muriel and I are going away for a few weeks to get away from you all and get into some serious sex. Then we'll be back as usual to get into some more serious sex *with* you. It's a *holiday*. This is a going-away party we're giving for you all, and we expect you all to give us a coming-back party in a month or so. So don't anyone think of skipping town.' He leered at the women as he spoke this last.

More good-natured laughter and catcalls followed the last announcement.

Turning back to the gathering, he raised his glass. When they had all done the same, he gestured towards Muriel. 'To the loveliest lady of them all.' They drank the toast. Muriel smiled happily and blushed with embarrassment at the same time. Paul glanced at Rhonda once more, trying unsuccessfully to read her thoughts. She was in effect the woman scorned, even if only temporarily. Rhonda looked calm and unruffled. She wore her most enigmatic smile for the occasion. The waiters brought more champagne.

Muriel spoke to the crowd. Paul had not expected her to say anything, so he was as surprised as anyone else. 'Friends, there is just one more thing to do before we begin dancing again.'

There was an expectant hush. Muriel opened her bag. Paul had wondered why she carried it when all the other women had left theirs upstairs or on convenient coffee tables. Muriel first drew from it a dog lead, which she handed to Paul. The symbolism of the act, and of the item, was obvious to all. There was that tell-tale ring on the front of her collar. The next items were even more obvious. Muriel produced a pair of handcuffs and a set of leg-irons. They were of the Darby-type, familiar to their whole circle, though not universally used. Stooping, Muriel laid the bag on the floor and closed the leg-irons around her ankles, leaving them joined by some fourteen inches of chain. So there were to be no naked races for her that night, Paul thought in bemusement. Next she snapped the handcuffs around her left wrist and brought her hands together behind her back, where she locked the second cuff around her free wrist. Thus restrained, Muriel turned to Paul and lifted her chin, inviting him to snap the lead to the ring on her collar.

Still bemused, he did so. There was scattered applause, and a few remarks about just who was not aiming to make the arrangement permanent. 'Muriel is the prettiest ball and chain Paul has ever worn' was the best of all.

To Paul she murmured that the keys to her restraints were at home, and that he was to be in charge of her until they got there – and from then on. Paul leaned forwards and kissed Muriel on the mouth. This time there was more applause, and those who were able drank their champagne before helping those who were not.

'Let's dance,' Muriel commanded, to end the general pause and set the party into motion again.

Someone put on another CD, and the sound of ABBA sent the people towards the dance floor or the bar. The party resumed. Alone with his slave for a moment, Paul asked her, 'Did you intend to make this a permanent arrangement?'

'I had that in mind. Do you mind?' It was the kind of question that invited a positive answer, given without hesitation. Tears threatened if the reply was negative.

Paul gave the required answer, and found that he didn't really mind. The only question was whether they would continue their activities with their present group of friends. He hoped they might, since both of them had enjoyed the variety of experience the group offered its members.

He pulled her closer with the dog lead and bent to kiss her inviting mouth. Still holding the lead short, he pulled her face closer. His other arm went around her waist to pull her body close. Muriel smiled happily, turning up her face to be kissed with enthusiasm as she moulded herself to him. They danced, body moulded to body, while Paul wondered how the arrangement would turn out. She seemed determined to give herself away, and to make him responsible for her. It was just like getting married, without the tiresome ceremony and the raucous reception. Their fellow bondage devotees had seen her make the 'vow'. Now, it looked as if he would have to go along with her intention or risk looking like a cad. The archaic word fitted the situation. He wondered how many men had been trapped into a marriage (even if they insisted on calling it a 'relationship') in the same way. Men (he thought) talk about love in order to get sex. Women allow sex in order to find love. Both risk disappointment.

But there was nothing to be done just then. He held Muriel closely and they danced amid the other bizarrely matched couples at the party. Paul had to admit that she was exciting. He liked the feel of her flesh beneath the sheer nylon of the body stocking. She had certainly chosen the right costume to catch his interest. And the body harness was stunning. The contrast between the hard chain and Muriel's flesh was erotic. Her breasts were neatly divided into three zones by the chains, bulging slightly under the

250

smooth nylon. The nipple rings were most fetching too. The knowledge that she was effectively wearing a chastity belt made him want her all the more. The forbidden-fruit effect was giving him an erection – of which Muriel was well aware, and which the cock-cage contained. She smiled a small, secret smile as she rubbed her belly against his imprisoned cock.

'I'm going to ask Rhonda to lend me that cage sometime,' she told Paul.

'Not too often, I hope. You need to remember who is the top dog in this ménage.'

Rhonda regarded her protégés from the bar area. She smiled at their obvious state of arousal and frustration. The arrangement suited her penchant for controlling others. And as she watched them rubbing against one another Rhonda contemplated her plan for them, one that would make their 'wedding night' unforgettable.

During a pause in the music Paul led Muriel over to Chloe and tethered her to the metal frame. 'You two talk for a bit while I get us something to drink,' he told them both as he slipped away, giving them no opportunity to object. Despite Muriel's acceptance of the slave's role, Paul found himself excited by Chloe too. Her helpless immobility was a turn-on he found hard to resist. In fact, before Muriel had sprung her surprise on him, he had been planning to make an opportunity soon to get Chloe and her frame alone. He had often wondered how it would be to fuck a woman who was held rigidly in that position. Exciting, he suspected. Well, it would have to be another time. He left the two women chatting while he sought Rhonda.

There was the matter of the keys to his cock-cage and to Muriel's manacles and chastity belt. Rhonda, he knew, was sure to have them, or to know where they were. What he did not know was when she planned to hand them over. Sooner or later she had to. He feared that she might decide on later. Equally important was Rhonda's mood. She had acted calm and unruffled in a situation where most women would have been angry and jealous. Paul hoped to reassure himself that she did indeed accept the arrangement and would not sever her ties with him or Muriel.

As he moved towards Rhonda, Paul caught a glimpse of Tamara Davis dancing with Ted. They appeared to be enjoying the exercise. Chloe, shackled immovably to her iron frame, was an island in the sea of movement. She looked at Rhonda beseechingly whenever the dominatrix glanced in her direction. Ronan Wilkes was now with Rhonda. She was negligently holding the lead fastened to his balls while she surveyed the room. He gave the impression of striving for her attention. Paul felt a stab of jealousy. That was his usual place. Thoughts of having one's cake and eating it too forced him to smile wryly. The whole purpose of the evening was a celebration of his and Muriel's new pact.

Rhonda smiled at him when he reached her side. She looked, he admitted, stunning in her tight rubber suit. She also looked inaccessible. He wondered if her inaccessibility extended to the matter of the keys. He was suddenly afraid to ask for fear of seeming too eager to get Muriel (and not Rhonda) to a private place.

True, Rhonda had reassured him that evening that the new arrangement had her approval, but he thought it wise to touch base with her. After all, she still held the keys to the kingdom and gave no sign of handing them over any time soon. Unless she agreed to release him, both he and Muriel would have a solitary evening ahead. How does one ask one's

252

mistress for the keys that will allow him access to another woman without angering the mistress?

'Are you after the keys already?' she asked with an enigmatic smile. 'The evening is still young. Eat, drink, have fun. The wait will make the dénouement all the more enjoyable. Or would you prefer me to remove the protection from your projection so you could wheel Chloe off to some secluded place, tip her over on to her back and fuck her stupid?' Rhonda smiled archly as she noticed his cock swell within its steel prison. 'But it might disturb Muriel, mightn't it, if her new bridegroom left her for another woman so soon.'

'Rhonda,' Paul asked tensely, 'do you have the keys?'

'Of course I do, but I don't intend to let you escape from me so soon, just because of this evening's ceremony. There is another set waiting for you at your place, as I told you earlier. Surely you can wait that long. And Muriel will like travelling in her wedding dress, I know. She says that she enjoyed the trip here in Valerie's van immensely. I think you would both enjoy the homeward journey if you were kept from . . . enjoying one another for a while. If I know you, you'd just unlock Muriel and yourself and have your way with her. I intend to make you both wait a bit longer. In fact, I have an idea how you two should spend the remainder of the evening.'

Rhonda fastened Ronan's lead chain to the bar. 'You can be bartender for a while,' she told him. 'Paul, come with me,' she commanded. Rhonda went over to Chloe and Muriel, Paul following. She unfastened Muriel's lead and tugged her away towards the steel cage at the far end of the room. Muriel had no choice but to follow. Paul had more choice, and he chose to follow. Rhonda led Muriel into the cage and pushed her inside. 'You too,' she said to Paul. 'You can be the lovebirds in the gilded cage for the others to stare at.' Rhonda locked the door and walked away.

Paul and Muriel looked at one another in helpless amusement. Rhonda had commanded, and they had obeyed. Paul turned to the door and made a pro-forma attempt to open it. It didn't open. He returned to Muriel and put his arm around her shoulders, holding her tightly against him. 'I suppose the dragon lady has to let us know who's boss, even now,' he said.

'Especially now,' Muriel replied. 'Kiss me,' she commanded in her turn. 'It's the best we can manage until Rhonda unlocks us. Think you can wait that long?'

'Do we have a choice?' he asked as he kissed her upturned lips. The kiss was prolonged, and produced the expected pleasurable and painful results. Paul's cock stiffened in its prison, and Muriel moaned deeply as the kiss drew out.

Eventually they parted, and Paul caught his breath while trying to ease his cock. 'Rhonda intends us to travel back to New Orleans like this,' Paul told her. 'She believes we will both enjoy the experience, and that the delay will add to the pleasure. I also think she doesn't want to witness us going at one another with delight.'

They watched the remainder of their party from the isolation of the cage. From time to time the others brought food and drink. Paul fed Muriel and held her glass while she drank. The other guests began to leave gradually and, as the room emptied, the imprisoned lovers expected Rhonda to set them free soon. When finally the last guest had gone, or gone to the bedrooms for more private pleasure, Rhonda came to them. Smilingly she wished them good-night and switched off the lights.

nexus

The leading publisher of fetish and adult fiction

TELL US WHAT YOU THINK!

Readers' ideas and opinions matter to us so please take a few minutes to fill in the questionnaire below.

1. Sex: Are you male ☐   female ☐   a couple ☐?

2. Age: Under 21 ☐   21–30 ☐   31–40 ☐   41–50 ☐   51–60 ☐   over 60 ☐

3. Where do you buy your Nexus books from?
☐ A chain book shop. If so, which one(s)?

_____

☐ An independent book shop. If so, which one(s)?

_____

☐ A used book shop/charity shop
☐ Online book store. If so, which one(s)?

_____

4. How did you find out about Nexus books?
☐ Browsing in a book shop
☐ A review in a magazine
☐ Online
☐ Recommendation
☐ Other _____

5. In terms of settings, which do you prefer? (Tick as many as you like.)
☐ Down to earth and as realistic as possible
☐ Historical settings. If so, which period do you prefer?

_____

☐ Fantasy settings – barbarian worlds
☐ Completely escapist/surreal fantasy

☐ Institutional or secret academy
☐ Futuristic/sci fi
☐ Escapist but still believable
☐ Any settings you dislike?

_____

☐ Where would you like to see an adult novel set?

_____

6. In terms of storylines, would you prefer:

☐ Simple stories that concentrate on adult interests?
☐ More plot and character-driven stories with less explicit adult activity?
☐ We value your ideas, so give us your opinion of this book:

_____

_____

_____

7. In terms of your adult interests, what do you like to read about? (Tick as many as you like.)

☐ Traditional corporal punishment (CP)
☐ Modern corporal punishment
☐ Spanking
☐ Restraint/bondage
☐ Rope bondage
☐ Latex/rubber
☐ Leather
☐ Female domination and male submission
☐ Female domination and female submission
☐ Male domination and female submission
☐ Willing captivity
☐ Uniforms
☐ Lingerie/underwear/hosiery/footwear (boots and high heels)
☐ Sex rituals
☐ Vanilla sex
☐ Swinging
☐ Cross-dressing/TV

☐ Enforced feminisation
☐ Others – tell us what you don't see enough of in adult fiction:

_____

_____

_____

8. Would you prefer books with a more specialised approach to your interests, i.e. a novel specifically about uniforms? If so, which subject(s) would you like to read a Nexus novel about?

_____

_____

_____

9. Would you like to read true stories in Nexus books? For instance, the true story of a submissive woman, or a male slave? Tell us which true revelations you would most like to read about:

_____

_____

_____

10. What do you like best about Nexus books?

_____

_____

11. What do you like least about Nexus books?

_____

_____

12. Which are your favourite titles?

_____

_____

13. Who are your favourite authors?

_____

_____

14. **Which covers do you prefer? Those featuring:**
   (Tick as many as you like.)

☐ Fetish outfits
☐ More nudity
☐ Two models
☐ Unusual models or settings
☐ Classic erotic photography
☐ More contemporary images and poses
☐ A blank/non-erotic cover
☐ What would your ideal cover look like?

_____

15. **Describe your ideal Nexus novel in the space provided:**

_____

_____

_____

_____

16. **Which celebrity would feature in one of your Nexus-style fantasies?**
   We'll post the best suggestions on our website – anonymously!

_____

THANKS FOR YOUR TIME

Now simply write the title of this book in the space below and cut out the
questionnaire pages. Post to: Nexus, Marketing Dept., Thames Wharf Studios,
Rainville Rd, London W6 9HA

Book title: _____

NEXUS NEW BOOKS

To he published in February 2007

SLIPPERY WHEN WET
Penny Birch

Penny Birch assembles her famous cast of naughty girls for a slippery and messy week of fun. Gabrielle, the mischievous Poppy, and their nurse Sabina (from *Naughty, Naughty*) receive a gift from Monty Hartle of one week at an SM boot camp in Wales. Gabrielle is doubtful, but Poppy and Sabrina are keen, so they go. The camp turns out to be a converted home hired for the purpose, and is run by Mistress Kimiko, a poisonous individual with a serious uniform fetish. According to the rules Mistress Kimiko has absolute authority, save for the mysterious Master. The girls are assigned to the kitchens, which is asking for trouble . . .

£6.99   ISBN 978 0 352 34091 7

THE ROAD TO DEPRAVITY
Ray Gordon

Helen's husband, Alan, has walked out on her yet again. But this time she won't take him back. Thirty years old and extremely attractive with long black hair, Helen is enjoying her freedom and she has no shortage of men after her. But Alan won't leave her in peace. When she discovers that he's spying on her through the lounge window, watching her having sex with a male friend, she's initially shocked. But she soon realises that his voyeurism is a great turn-on.

Knowing that Alan is watching, she enjoys one sexual encounter after another. Taking things further in order to shock Alan, she experiments sexually with Mary, a young blonde lesbian. And Helen's sexual conquests plunge her deeper into the pit of depravity to the point where she enjoys group sex.

Alan takes his voyeurism to the extreme by hiding in the house and watching Helen with her sexual partners. Unsure what his long-term goal is, Helen again tries to shock him. Indulging in bondage and spanking, she's not sure whether she wants to be rid of Alan or continue to enjoy his spying. Until . . .

£6.99   ISBN 978 0 352 34092 4

NEXUS CONFESSIONS: VOLUME I
Various

Swinging, dogging, group sex, cross-dressing, spanking, female domination, corporal punishment, and extreme fetishes . . . *Nexus Confessions* explores the length and breadth of erotic obsession, real experience and sexual fantasy. An encyclopaedic collection of the bizarre, the extreme, the utterly inappropriate, the daring and the shocking experiences of ordinary men and women driven by their extraordinary desires. Collected by the world's leading publisher of fetish fiction, this is the first in a series of six volumes of true stories and shameful confessions, never-before-told or published.

£6.99   ISBN 978 0 352 34093 1

If you would like more information about Nexus titles, please visit our website at www.nexus-books.co.uk, or send a large stamped addressed envelope to:
  Nexus, Thames Wharf Studios,
  Rainville Road, London W6 9HA